To/

Mike

G000123131

L J MORRIS

Hunting Ground

(Ali Sinclair #2)

Best Wishes

L J Morris

For Ruth, my everything; and Luke and Daniel, who make me proud every day.

There is no hunting like the hunting of man, and those who have hunted armed men long enough and liked it, never care for anything else there-after.

- *ERNEST HEMINGWAY*

Prologue

The stained enamel bath in the derelict apartment was full of water that had been brought up from the river. The bottom of the bath was covered in a layer of rocks, and the sediment, moss and algae that floated on the water's surface was now mixed with blood and hair.

Justin Wyatt was strapped to a board that was balanced at the tap end. He'd lost count of the amount of times the board had been tipped up and his head had impacted on the bottom; how many times he had held his breath until his lungs were crying out for air. Breathing in water and falling into unconsciousness, only to be brought back up again.

He broke the surface, vomiting the filthy water back out of his body and gasping to breathe. His face was swollen and blood streamed from his nose. They had shouted at him time and time again, 'Tell us what you know and we'll let you live.' He doubted that.

Two hours ago, he was breaking into an office with a stolen key card, looking for some information, following up a tip. He needed some sort of evidence to back up the story he'd been told. He'd been naive, though. He knew there was a risk and he was prepared for that, but he thought if he was caught, he could talk his way out of it – pretend he was a burglar. The company was respectable, at least on the surface. He assumed they would just hand him to the police.

He couldn't have been more wrong. The story he had been told, everything he had found out was true. The conspiracy he'd uncovered was far too big to be derailed by someone like him. Now, he was sure he was going to die; his priority was to keep his mouth shut, to protect the ones he loved. He just hoped he'd left enough of a trail for them to follow, the ultimate treasure hunt. He would bring these people down, one way or another. That would be his greatest achievement, that would be his legacy.

He tipped back into the water again, his head smashed on the bottom of the bath and blood clouded in front of his eyes. He couldn't take much more of this; surely he'd be dead soon. His vision darkened, but again he was brought back up, coughing and spluttering.

There was no questioning this time. Instead, one of his captors was on the phone. 'Yes, sir ... No, sir. We don't think he knows anything ... He would've told us by now ... We'll do a background check on him and find out who he is, who he lives with. If he won't talk, maybe they will ... Yes, sir. We will. It'll look like suicide.'

Wyatt didn't want to die but he didn't want anyone else hurt because of him. The man put down the phone and walked into the bathroom. He looked at Wyatt then nodded to his accomplice. Wyatt, once again, plunged into the water, his head bleeding, his lungs screaming. He didn't have the strength or the will to fight any more. He stopped holding his breath and slipped into oblivion. This time, he wouldn't be lifted back up.

Chapter 1

Callum Porter walked along the rain-slicked pavement of Rue Saint-Joseph, from the tram stop on Rue du Pont-Neuf, towards his apartment in the Carouge district of Geneva. He'd moved into the Swiss city's 'Little Italy' shortly after he landed the job at the bank and was quickly accepted as part of the community. He'd always loved it here. It had a different atmosphere to the rest of the city: the shops, the architecture, the bars that came to life after dark. It was safe and clean compared to other cities he'd been in, and only a ten-minute ride to the city centre. Perfect, until now. The last few days had been a blur. Every sight and sound conjuring up memories that stabbed at his heart.

His apartment was on the top floor of a three-storey building, which was set back from a tree-lined side street, off the main road. He quickened his pace as the rain started to come down again, and soon turned into the apartment block and up the two stone steps into the entrance hall.

Inside the building's traditional architecture, was a modern design with clean, minimalist lines and glass and chrome trim. Water ran from Porter's raincoat as he unfastened it, and left small puddles on the faux marble floor. He walked to the mail boxes that ran along the left-hand side of the entrance, and checked for any deliveries. As usual, it was empty. He didn't receive much mail; he did most of his business online. The single lift in the foyer was on the opposite wall to the mail boxes but he preferred to use the stairs that were next to it. The only time he used the lift was when he had some heavy shopping to carry. He walked through the foyer and climbed the stairs.

On the third floor, the door to the stairs opened on to a single, long passageway with doors on both sides and a window at either end. His apartment, 317, was halfway down on the left. Simple glass and chrome wall lights came on to light his way as he approached. There was no one else around and it was quiet: his neighbours would still be making their way home. He pulled out his door key, slid it into the lock and opened the door.

The inside of his apartment carried on the minimalist decor of the rest of the building, but here and there were items of furniture that didn't quite fit in. Things that Porter had picked up in the antique shops and street markets in Carouge. An old wooden set of drawers jutted out into the hallway, spoiling the simple straight line that led from the front door to the kitchen. On the left-hand side of the corridor was the door to the single bedroom and, on the right, the entrance to the living room, where a well-used leather settee and two brightly-coloured, seventies chairs were arranged around a worn wooden coffee table.

Porter stepped into the living room and switched on the light. He let out an involuntary yell at the sight of a man standing next to the window. Porter's fight or flight response was screaming at him to turn and run. 'Who … who are you? What do you want? I don't have anything. Get out of my flat.'

Frank McGill held out his hands, palms up. 'Calm down, Callum, I'm not here to hurt you. I'm here to help.' He motioned towards the couch. 'Have a seat.'

Porter's mind, again, screamed at him to run, but his legs wouldn't move. He had the feeling this intruder would only chase him down, anyway. He looked at McGill. This man spoke with authority, he was obviously used to taking charge in situations like this and used to imposing his will – violently, if necessary. Porter took two steps to the right and sat down.

McGill was unkempt. He wore black leather boots, blue jeans and a faded green combat jacket. His hair was messy and he had a few days' growth on his chin. No one would pay him any attention, he wouldn't stand out in a crowd on the street; he looked homeless, the kind of man most people ignored as they rushed about their busy lives, unaware of the plight of people who lived on the street. If, later on, he was asked to describe him, Porter would say everything about him looked average: average height, average build, no striking features; not memorable at all.

McGill sat down on one of the seventies chairs, opposite the couch. He sat forward, his elbows resting on his knees. 'You don't know me, Callum, but I've been watching you for a few days. Whenever you left your office for lunch, when you were on your way home, I was there.'

'I never saw you, how is that possible?'

McGill smiled. 'It's what we do for a living, son.'

'Who is "we"? You're obviously British, MI5, MI6?'

McGill nodded. 'Something like that, but you don't need to know the details.'

'I don't suppose you've got any ID you can show me?'

McGill raised an eyebrow. 'You're gonna have to trust me.

The people I work for aren't big on ID.'

'What do you want from me? I haven't done anything, I just work in a bank.'

McGill pulled a black and white surveillance photo from his jacket and placed it on the table, in front of Porter. 'It's not you we are interested in, Callum. I came here to speak to this man.' McGill pointed to the photo. 'Can you tell me who he is?'

Porter picked up the photo and sat back on the couch, staring at it. After a few seconds of silence, he took a deep breath and let out a sigh. 'His name's Justin Wyatt.'

McGill could sense that the man in the picture meant something to Porter. 'We need to speak to him, Callum, it's for his own safety. Do you know where he is?'

Porter looked around the flat, as if he was checking for anyone who might overhear them – checking for more intruders. 'How did you find me? We weren't public about our relationship.'

'We tracked down Justin by identifying you. Do you know he contacted the British Consulate?'

'He told me he was planning to talk to the authorities, in case something bad happened, but I didn't know he had.'

'He made an anonymous phone call. He gave enough detail to get us interested and said he had more. He didn't want to give up too much, as he swore there was a mole in the British Government.'

Porter couldn't believe what he was hearing, he'd always assumed Justin was blowing his stories out of proportion; he'd thought the trouble he might get into would mean arrest, maybe imprisonment. 'But, if it was anonymous, how did you know it was him?'

'We traced the phone he used to make the call to the consulate and scanned through CCTV images of the area. We didn't know his name, but he was the only person to use the phone in that time frame. You showed up in other CCTV images with him and we put two and two together. You were easier to find. You weren't trying to hide in the way he obviously was.'

'And then you were sent to find me, to find Justin?'

McGill nodded. 'We were hoping to leave you out of it. I asked a few questions, hung around in the right areas. I followed you for a few days, hoping to see you together so I could follow him, but you never met up with him again.'

Porter looked down and ran his fingers around the image in the photo. He was struggling to speak, he would never get used to saying it. 'That's because he's dead.'

McGill let out a sigh of frustration. 'I'm sorry about that, Callum, I really am. What happened? Can you tell me about it?'

'They found his body in the river. He'd been washed downstream and dragged along the riverbed and rocks. They had difficulty identifying him but found his wallet nearby.'

'How did you find out about it?'

'They put a small report in the paper – a few sentences on page eight. They said he'd jumped. They said he killed himself.'

McGill could hear anger in Porter's voice. 'But you don't believe that, do you, Callum?'

Porter felt at ease with McGill. He was glad to be finally unburdening himself, telling someone else his secret. 'The night before his body was found he told me he was going to break into some guy's office. He was convinced he was

7

involved in something big: something that would change the world, he said. He was looking for evidence. I thought he was exaggerating.'

'Did you tell anyone that? Have you spoken to the police?'

Porter's face was ashen. 'No, I was too scared. They might have come after me next. Besides, like I said, we always kept our relationship secret. It's still frowned upon in some circles. I didn't want to attract attention.'

'It might already be too late for that. We found you; they will, too, sooner or later.'

'Who are "they"? What if they found him through me, too? What if he's dead because of me?'

McGill had to calm Porter down. It was obvious that the young man was afraid. His hands were trembling and he struggled to put a sentence together. McGill spoke to him, calmly and quietly, as he had to the young soldiers in Afghanistan – the ones who'd looked to him for guidance and reassurance. 'It's not your fault, Callum. If they knew about you, you'd be dead already.'

Porter was sweating and his heart was racing. He had hoped the authorities would realise someone had murdered Justin; he'd hoped he could go back home to the states and rebuild his life. He wasn't a naturally courageous man. He was quiet, timid, an introvert. The man sitting in front of him, on the other hand, looked the opposite. 'What do you ... they ... I mean ...'

McGill had to secure the information he was looking for and get out as soon as possible. 'The call to the consulate mentioned a notebook.'

Porter nodded. 'Justin gave me a book. He told me that, if anything happened to him, I had to keep the book safe and watch my back. I thought he was being overdramatic.'

'I'll need to see the book, is it here?'

'Yes, I'll get it.'

Porter went into his bedroom and slid the wardrobe away from the wall. Taped to the back of it was a small, brown paper parcel. He removed it and took it through to the living room. He held the parcel in both hands, reluctant to let it go. 'I promised to keep this safe.'

'You can trust me, son. It'll be safer with us.' McGill held out his hand.

Porter knew he couldn't protect the book and the information inside, he knew McGill was right. He handed him the parcel and stepped back, sitting down on the couch.

McGill tore off the brown paper and revealed a small notebook. The front cover was plain and a little dog-eared, with J Wyatt written in the top left corner. McGill opened it and flicked through it; page after page of handwritten notes and drawings, names, dates and places filled the book. McGill recognised some of the names but most of the information meant nothing to him, it would be something for the geeks back home to have a look at and decipher. He put the notebook into a plastic ziplock bag and tucked it into the inside pocket of his jacket. 'What were you planning to do with the book, Callum?'

Porter shrugged his shoulders. 'I don't know, maybe post it to the embassy in Berne, but I didn't know who to trust. There are some high-ranking officials mentioned in there.'

'You've read it?'

Porter shook his head. 'No. Justin told me about some of the people who are in it. I'm not sure I believed him, to be honest. What if he was right and they are involved? If his notes fell into their hands, no one would know about them. He would have died for nothing.'

McGill patted his pocket. 'You don't have to worry about it now, Callum. All you need to think about is staying safe.'

'I should call my dad. Tell him what's happened. He can help, he's a …'

'US senator. Yes, we know. I'll stay with you until you're out of harm's way. We don't want anything to happen to you because of this.'

The conspiratorial atmosphere in the apartment was shattered by a loud knock. Porter jumped to his feet and stared at the door. Within seconds McGill was standing next to him, whispering into his ear, 'Are you expecting anyone?'

Porter shook his head. McGill moved silently to the hallway and pulled a silenced Glock from under his jacket. He signalled for Porter to open the door. The young man was unable to move, scared out of his mind. Another loud knock made him jump and McGill, once again, signalled for him to open the door. Porter, hand trembling, reached for the lock and turned it slowly.

The door was violently kicked open and a large man, dressed all in black, pushed his way into the apartment, forcing Porter backwards. 'Where is the book?'

The man didn't shout but he spoke with quiet menace. He pulled out his own silenced semi-automatic and pointed it at Porter. 'I'm going to count to three. Tell me where the book is,' he lowered his weapon and pointed it at Porter's legs, 'or lose a kneecap.'

McGill had quickly weighed the guy up: if he was a real professional, he would have looked behind him by now to check for any threats; if he was the police or security services, he would have identified himself and he wouldn't have been alone. There was no backup following him into the room, he had left himself wide open.

Porter was terrified. McGill didn't blame him – it can be very disconcerting having a gun pointed at you for the first time.

Porter's attacker started his count. 'One ... two ...'

McGill raised his weapon and pointed it at the back of the big guy's head. 'Three.'

The man spun around but it was already too late. As the realisation that he had fucked-up showed in his eyes, McGill shot him in the forehead.

The big guy dropped to the floor, straight down. There was no resistance in his legs to stop the fall. He was dead as soon as the bullet hit him.

McGill quickly checked the corridor outside for any late-arriving backup but it was deserted. He stepped back inside the apartment and closed the door.

Porter was frozen to the spot. He hadn't moved at all. McGill grabbed his arm. 'Callum?' Porter didn't respond, he just stared at the dead body in front of him.

McGill grabbed Porter and shook him. 'Callum. Snap out of it or you'll end up the same way. We need to get away from here as quick as we can.'

Porter finally looked up at McGill. There was blood on his face and his skin was pasty white. 'Who ... who was he?'

'I don't know but he wasn't here to invite you to a party. At least it confirms that Justin was onto something big. If you'd given that guy the book, he would have killed you. There's no doubt about that.'

Porter slowly shook his head, still rooted to the spot. 'I feel sick.'

McGill dragged him across the living room and pushed him into the bathroom. 'Do what you need to do, Callum – throw up, splash water on your face, whatever, but get on with it. Get your shit together. I'm leaving, with or without you.'

Porter realised McGill had just saved his life, but he wasn't used to such extremes of violence. He'd never seen a dead body before, never mind a man shot right in front of him. He looked down at his T-shirt. There was a fine spray of blood covering the front of it. He closed his eyes. He could still picture the cloud of pink mist that had signalled the fatal shot. If he had been standing in the wrong place, the bullet could have hit him, too. He shook the thought from his head. McGill was a professional, he knew exactly what he was doing.

Porter took two deep breaths. The feeling of nausea began to leave him. He splashed some water on his face and pulled off his T-shirt.

McGill checked through the pockets of the body: no ID or cash, just a car key and a photo of Porter with the address written on the back. Whoever had sent this guy had access to the same information as McGill. When the bathroom door opened, he looked up at Porter. 'You okay?'

'Yeah, I think so.'

'Good man. Now, do you have some kind of backpack?'

Porter pointed towards the bedroom. 'Yeah, in there.'

'Right, pack some clothes. Nothing fancy, just something to change into. Throw in any cash you've got, passport, that kind of thing. And hurry up.'

Porter pulled some clothes from his drawers and threw them into the bag: T-shirts, socks, underwear, toothbrush.

Did he need to take shampoo? Christ, he felt like he was packing for a holiday. He grabbed his wallet and shoved it into his jacket, along with his passport. He pulled on a clean T-shirt and was ready to go.

McGill opened the door an inch and looked along the corridor, it was empty; he fully opened it and stepped out, looking both ways: nothing. He looked back at Porter, standing in the hallway. 'You ready?'

Porter nodded.

'Good. Follow me and stay close.'

Porter hurried after McGill, he knew his best hope of survival was in this man's company. He also knew the book was in McGill's pocket, so he didn't really need him – McGill could have just left him alone, in the apartment, with the corpse. He was helping him even though he didn't have to. That made him feel safer.

McGill led them along the corridor and through the door to the fire escape. After a quick check, they moved quickly down the stairs and out of the back door of the apartment block.

They stopped at the corner of the building as McGill retrieved his own small backpack, full of essentials, from behind a dumpster. He threw it on his back and winked at Porter. 'Always travel light, son, you never know what might happen.'

After one last check for any followers, they walked to the other side of the car park and out on to the street.

Porter kept his head down. He didn't want to make eye contact with any passers-by. He was sure they would know what had happened; like he had a mark on him somewhere that was telling everyone there was a dead man in his flat.

'Where do we go now? The consulate?'

McGill shook his head. 'We don't know who to trust, son. The guy in your flat had the same picture of you that I had. Someone had tipped him off, given him the information, probably blown my cover. Someone high up wants you dead and the notebook in their hands. We need to disappear.'

'How do we do that?'

'Just keep your head down and follow me.' McGill pulled up the hood on his jacket and Porter pulled on a baseball cap, thrusting his hands deep into his pockets; the rain started to fall again as they headed back along the Rue Saint-Joseph, away from the apartment.

Chapter 2

Ali Sinclair sat cross-legged in the dust, next to the prison block, and watched the comings and goings of the other inmates in the yard. It was how she spent most of her time. The corner she sat in was on the north side of the yard and in the shade all day, but that wasn't its only attraction. There were people out in the real world who wanted her dead. Rich, powerful people who had the connections and resources to put a high-value price on her head. The other prisoners – the gangs that ran the prison – wanted the money, and were more than willing to kill her to get it. She had to watch her back.

The corner she sat in was overlooked by a guard tower, although that was no guarantee of safety. Many of the guards in the prison came from the same background as the inmates. Some still had loyalty to gangs they used to be members of, others were corrupt and easily bought. Many simply feared for the safety of their families if they went against the cartels. Sinclair couldn't rely on any help from the guards.

The main reason she chose that corner was the razor-wire topped fence running along three sides. If anyone wanted to come at her, they couldn't approach from behind or climb down from above. Anyone who wanted the money would have to come at her head on.

It had been four months since the Mexican authorities returned her to the prison to finish the remaining five years of her original sentence. Despite behind-the-scenes efforts in London and Washington, the Mexicans had added another three years to her jail time and refused to let her serve the sentence back home. She knew she couldn't – she wouldn't – last that long.

Physically, for now, she was okay. Her broken bones had healed and she had managed to keep herself reasonably fit, but she knew from her previous two years here that the food wasn't good enough to maintain her health long-term. With no family to visit her and bring her extra supplies, she needed money to survive. Extra rations, like most things, could be bought – either on the black market or from the concession stands in the visitors' yard. Sinclair's problem was that the black market and the stands were controlled by the gangs, and they weren't likely to do her any favours. Any money that was smuggled in for her was much less than the bounty on her head. It was in the gangs' interests to keep her down, keep her weak. They just needed to bide their time, keep chipping away at her defences, until, sooner or later, they succeeded in killing her.

Mentally, Sinclair really was on the edge. The constant fear of attack meant she was unable to relax, unable to sleep for any length of time. At night, in her cell, she woke up at the slightest noise or sign of movement. Although she was sharing a crowded cell, with mainly European women, she couldn't let her guard down for a minute; the price on her head was substantial.

Frank McGill had visited her a few times in the beginning.

He'd told her not to worry, that everything would be alright, but she hadn't seen him now for more than a month. He had always been there for her and she believed him when he said he would never abandon her. She was convinced that something must have happened to him. He was the only one fighting her corner. The only one who would make sure that Carter and Lancaster, back in London, lived up to their promise to bring her home. Without McGill on her side, Sinclair had no hope.

She looked around at her surroundings. Visitors mingled with inmates amongst the concession stands, sitting under trees that the prisoners had planted to try and make the yard look more like a town centre park. They looked like ordinary people, on a normal day out, but the threat of violence was never far from the surface. Occasionally she would catch one of the other prisoners watching her; was it her paranoia or were they checking for a weakness, making plans for another attack?

She looked up at the birds that circled and swooped just outside the fence. These weren't the starlings she remembered being fascinated by as a little girl, these were large black vultures feeding on the rubbish discarded by the prison. Even they perched on the fence, watching her, happy to pick at her bones if given the chance. It seemed to Sinclair as if everything here would be happier with her dead. Maybe she should just give in, give them what they want, at least she wouldn't be afraid any more. The only thing stopping her was the voice in her head. It spoke to her constantly, telling her not to give up, to keep fighting, that she'd be okay. It was Frank McGill's voice and it was the only thing keeping her alive.

The sound of a bell ringing snapped Sinclair back to reality, it was chow time. The other inmates began to walk towards the canteen but she, as usual, hung around for a few minutes before tucking in at the back of the queue. By the time she reached the pile of trays at the end of the serving hatch, most of the other inmates had eaten and already left. No one hung around for too long, there were a lot of scores settled in the canteen.

Sinclair picked up a tray and looked at what was left on the food counter: lukewarm soup, mouldy bread and some chilli, very appetising. She decided the chilli would be the best option, the spice would have killed everything in it. As she picked up the ladle, she heard a commotion behind her. She instinctively stood with her back to the counter. Two women were going at each other in the middle of the canteen. One was lying on her back with her hands full of the other woman's hair; the other woman knelt on a bench, punching her adversary in the face. Guards ran in to break them up as the rest of the inmates cheered them on.

Sinclair was checking to her left and right – she didn't see the attack coming at all. A muscular forearm came from behind her and clamped around her throat, pulling her back against the counter. She twisted to break the hold but her assailant's other arm was now hooked across her chest. A young Mexican woman broke off from the canteen fight's baying crowd and ran towards the counter, the six-inch blade of a prison shank held out in front of her, ready to strike. Sinclair only had one option: she lifted her legs and pushed herself backwards over the counter. Her attacker lost her balance and her grip, and the two women landed in a heap on the kitchen floor.

The other kitchen workers scattered, they didn't want anything to do with a killing. Sinclair sprang to her feet and faced her unseen attacker for the first time. She was an older woman, with prison gang tattoos covering her muscular arms. Without hesitation, Sinclair kicked the her in the jaw before she could stand up. The woman went down, stunned, but she was tough. As she began to climb to her feet, Sinclair grabbed a heavy pan from one of the cookers and swung it hard. It hit the woman's head with a dull metallic ring, like a muffled church bell. Sinclair followed it up with another kick to the woman's ribs.

The younger woman clambered onto the counter and, screaming like a banshee, launched herself at Sinclair. The heavy pan crashed into the side of her head before she'd even landed, as Sinclair swung it like a baseball bat.

The two women lay on the floor, unconscious, blood seeping from head wounds. The other inmates had given up on the canteen fight and were now standing along the edge of the counter, watching, as guards ran into the kitchen and pepper sprayed Sinclair, leaving her coughing and heaving on her knees. Tears streamed down her face and mingled with the snot running from her nose onto the floor, as she curled into a ball to protect herself from the beating she knew was coming.

Chapter 3

The prison guard's keys rattled in the lock as she slid open the barred door of the cramped cell. Two three-high bunks ran along the walls on either side, with another three women sleeping on thin mattresses thrown on the floor. The leaking toilet in the corner dripped stinking water, which added to the smell of sweat and decay that permeated the prison. The stench was bad enough to trigger a gag reflex in anyone who wasn't used to it. Flies and cockroaches settled on every surface and the humidity was stifling.

Sinclair opened her eyes. She rarely slept for more than an hour at a time – unable to relax and often disturbed by the sound of women screaming as they were ripped from their nightmares. The guard was early; it wasn't morning yet and none of the other women in the cell were awake. The sky outside the cell's barred window was still dark, and the normal sounds of the prison coming to life weren't there. Something was wrong.

Sinclair turned and looked at the guard, who motioned towards her with her head. 'Sinclair, *vámanos*. Let's go.'

What the fuck did they want now? Sinclair was exhausted and her head throbbed. She was badly dehydrated and her whole body ached. She slid out of the middle bunk and tiptoed between the tangled limbs of the women occupying the floor, trying not to stand on anyone. She stepped through the cell door and stood in front of the guard, her arms outstretched. 'Okay, what? Am I due another kicking?' The side of her face was bruised and her ribs still hurt from the last talking to the guards had given her.

The guard grabbed her arm and propelled her down the corridor. 'You must clean up. You make visit.'

'Wait ... what? Visit? Visit who, where?' She'd never been taken out of the prison before. If anyone wanted to see her, they always came here. Something wasn't right.

The guard handed her a towel and a clean set of clothes in a plastic bag. The chance to have the showers to herself and her first set of clean clothes since she'd got there. Today was shaping up to be a good day, no matter what else happened. The guard opened the door and pushed her into the showers.

As Sinclair stood under the cool water of the shower, washing off the sweat and grime of several days, she tried to figure out what the hell was going on. If Frank was there it would be a normal visit, no need to clean up or go anywhere. The guy from the foreign office had only visited her once and that was to ask her to keep her mouth shut. After everything she'd done and the way they'd treated her for the last few years, she'd soon told him where to shove his request – after she had broken his nose. He'd scuttled away, holding a handkerchief to his face, and she didn't think he would be back. Maybe she was being transferred to another prison. But, the guard had said a visit, none of this made sense. She dried herself off and put on her new clothes.

Out in the corridor, the guard had been joined by the

prison's governor. She was a hard bitch who always dressed like she was going for an expensive meal with a rich boyfriend. She liked to remind the inmates of everything they didn't have. The rumours were that she was on the payroll of the drug cartels, but if that had been the case, Sinclair would be dead already. The governor knew the gang murder of a British woman in her prison would likely cause her problems she didn't need; she tried to keep the attempts to kill Sinclair to a minimum.

Sinclair pulled at the hem of her T-shirt. 'So, what's all this about? Where am I going?'

'You are going to meet with a lawyer, from your government. It's about your appeal.'

'Why don't they just come here?'

The governor shrugged. 'I'm thinkin' that the man from your embassy doesn't want his nose broken again, so won't bring them here. You are goin' to the British Consulate in Juarez. They will talk to you there.' The governor stepped closer to Sinclair, looking straight into her eyes. 'If you cause any trouble, we will take care of you when you get back.'

The guard laughed and nodded, she didn't need an excuse to give an inmate a beating. Sinclair smiled at the governor. 'I'm sure you will.'

The governor took a step back. 'Take her.'

The guard grabbed Sinclair's arm and frogmarched her along the corridor towards the exit.

The white prison van sat outside with the engine running. Sinclair, now in cuffs and leg chains, was bundled into the back by the guard, who slammed the door shut and climbed in the front beside the driver.

Sinclair checked the inside of the van – force of habit. The back was separated from the driver by a steel cage and all the windows were covered with steel mesh. The doors had no handles and couldn't be opened from the inside. There was no way she could escape from the van, even if she wasn't cuffed and chained. Maybe, once she got to the consulate, she could make a run for it.

The prison gates rolled open and they drove out into the Chihuahuan Desert. After twenty minutes the back of the van was like a greenhouse: the windows didn't open and there was little ventilation making it through from the front. Sweat ran down Sinclair's face and back as the temperature continued to rise. 'Any chance of some air back here?'

The guard glanced into the back but carried on talking to the driver. Sinclair shook her head. 'Bitch.' She lifted her T-shirt and wiped the sweat from her face. So much for cleaning up for her visit, she looked like she'd just run a marathon.

Suddenly, the van bounced as if it had hit something. Sinclair was thrown to the floor and the driver fought with the steering wheel as she brought the van to a halt in a cloud of dust.

Sinclair got up, a trickle of blood ran down her face from a small cut on her head. 'What the hell was that?'

After a furious exchange of Spanish, too quick for Sinclair to pick up much of, the guard and the driver got out of the van and went round to the back. This was all Sinclair needed. If someone had to come out from the prison to fix it, she would spend all that time in the back of the van. The guards wouldn't let her out. It would be like an oven within an hour.

As the dust cleared four men appeared, as if they had grown out of the ground in front of their eyes. All four wore desert fatigues and tactical vests. Goggles protected their eyes and they all carried M4 assault rifles and 9mm sidearms. They barked orders in Spanish at the two women outside the van, who decided not to fight and were soon face down on the road with their hands behind their heads.

Sinclair looked for anything she could use as a weapon, but there was nothing. She tested the security of her chains but there was no way of getting out of them either. If these four men were Vadim's, she would be dead in minutes – unless they had something worse in mind for her. If they were Cartel, they might hold her hostage – probably to try and sell her to Vadim. If that was the case, she would have to let herself be taken, and fight her way out when the opportunity presented itself.

The back door of the van was pulled open and two of the men gestured for her to get out. Sinclair got out as quickly as her restraints would let her. The other two men bound and blindfolded the guard and the driver and threw them in the van, slamming the doors shut. Sinclair was manhandled away from the road and dragged into the desert. She tried to struggle but the men just picked her up and forced her down into the sand. Shit, they were just going to kill her, right there. She closed her eyes. She was tired of fighting. She was ready for it.

In the distance was the sound of an approaching engine. Not a car, or a van, something bigger. As it grew closer and louder, Sinclair realised what it was. She'd travelled in helicopters often enough to recognise the telltale sound of the rotor blades cutting through the air.

Dust was thrown up in a cloud as the chopper came in to land and settled on the desert floor. The engines didn't ease off; the pilot wasn't planning to stay. Sinclair was, once again, picked up by the two men and carried to the black, unmarked aircraft. She was lifted into the back and joined by all four men. The chopper's engines revved and they lifted off.

Once they were in the air and clear, one of the men took off his goggles and helped Sinclair to sit up in her seat. He unlocked her cuffs and chains and offered her a bottle of water. 'Are you okay?'

Sinclair rubbed her wrists where the cuffs had been fastened too tight. 'Who the fuck are you guys?'

'Better you don't know, ma'am.'

Sinclair looked around at the four men. The soldier who had spoken to her had an American accent, but they wore no insignia and no flags. Their equipment was also American, but that could be bought – easily – on the open market. One thing was obvious, though, whoever these guys were, they were professionals. Special forces, private military contractors, they had had military training and were very good.

Sinclair shouted to be heard above the noise of the rotors. 'Who sent you? Where are you taking me?'

'You'll be filled in when we land, ma'am, we're just tasked with picking you up and dropping you on the US side of the border.'

Sinclair still didn't know who these guys were, but they didn't mean her harm. They weren't cartel or Vadim's men. For whatever reason, she was out of prison and would soon be out of Mexico. 'Thank you.'

The soldier nodded and sat in the seat opposite. Sinclair looked out of the helicopter's open door. They were flying low over the desert, towards the border, away from her nightmare.

Chapter 4

The unmarked helicopter touched down next to an anonymous hanger at the edge of Fort Stockton Airport, just off Interstate 10 in Texas. The pilot shut down the engine and two vehicles approached. One was a fuelling tanker and the other a white SUV.

The soldier opposite Sinclair leaned forward. 'This is where we part company, ma'am. The SUV is for you. We'll be taking on gas and moving on. Good luck.'

Sinclair looked at the four men. 'Thank you. Thanks to all of you.'

'Just a job, ma'am. Don't thank us, thank whoever hired us.'

'I don't suppose you can fill me in on that?'

The soldier shook his head. 'Sorry ma'am, above my pay grade.'

Sinclair smiled then climbed down out of the helicopter. The soldier closed the door behind her as she walked across the tarmac to the waiting SUV.

'Miss Sinclair.' The man who had got out of the SUV appeared to be in his early thirties. A short, stocky man with a receding hairline and pale skin. He was dressed in black trousers and a crisp white shirt, which had sweat patches under the arms. His sleeves were rolled up and he dabbed at his face and neck with a white handkerchief. He didn't look like someone who was used to working out in the field. In fact, he didn't look like he was used to being outside at all.

'Yes, that's me. And you are?'

'I've been instructed not to identify myself or who I work for, but you can call me Bob.'

'Okay, Bob. Can you tell me what's going on?'

'Sorry, miss. I was just told to pick you up here and take you to San Antonio. I've no idea where you've come from or what your destination is after that. It's better that way.'

Whoever had arranged all this was doing their utmost to keep it hidden. Private military contractors, drivers who don't know the full story, this had black ops written all over it. 'So, Bob. Where to now?'

'If you'd like to get in the back of the car, there's some water and a little food for you. It's three to four hours' drive from here. I imagine you could use a little sleep.'

'Thanks, Bob, and stop calling me miss; my name's Ali.'

'Okay, Ali. Let's go.'

They walked towards the SUV as the helicopter's engine fired up and prepared to leave. The fuel truck was driving back towards the hanger while the pilot completed his final pre-flight checks. Sinclair opened the rear door of the vehicle as the chopper lifted off the ground and hovered for a second. She stopped and waved at the men inside – the men who had got her away from hell. The soldier she had spoken to waved back as the helicopter tilted forwards and lifted into the air.

Sinclair got into the back of the car and closed the door. Bob started the engine and switched on the air conditioning. 'There's a cool box next to you, Ali. It's got water, sandwiches, fruit. Help yourself to whatever you need.'

'Thanks, Bob.' Sinclair lifted the lid on the cool box and pulled out a litre bottle of water, drinking half of it in one go. By the time Bob was pulling onto Interstate 10 and heading east, Sinclair was tucking into chicken sandwiches and oranges. The best food she had had in months.

* * *

When Sinclair opened her eyes they were on the outskirts of San Antonio heading east. On the right-hand side was what looked like a small town, maybe an airfield of some sort. After a few minutes, Bob indicated right and they turned off the main road onto a smaller access road. On the right was a wall, which carried the US Air Force insignia and the name Randolph Air Force Base. On the left was a small guardhouse with cream coloured walls and a terracotta tiled roof. A large canopy extended high above the guardhouse and covered the road.

Bob pulled up beneath the canopy, which was to keep off either the sun or the rain – or both. A combat-fatigue clad air force sergeant walked out of the guardhouse and across to the car. Bob rolled down his window and handed the sergeant some papers. He scrutinised the documents and looked through the window at Sinclair before returning to the guardhouse. Sinclair watched as he picked up the phone and seemed to listen carefully, before nodding, as he confirmed instructions, and putting down the phone. Back at the car he handed Bob his documents and waved them through.

Sinclair was surprised at how easily they had been allowed in. One phone call and no need for them to show any ID. It took someone from the upper echelons to organise that kind of access; did Carter have that pull? Lancaster might, but how would he get the Americans involved? She was too tired to think about it, she was sure she would be told what she needed to know soon enough.

As they drove into the base it reminded Sinclair of Catterick Garrison, back in England. It was a military base but had everything a small town had: housing, shops, schools, sports facilities – everything to support the military families who called it home.

After a few minutes Bob stopped the car outside a small bungalow, which Sinclair assumed was officer's accommodation, at least it would be in England. Outside was a young woman wearing the uniform of an air force lieutenant. Bob turned around in his seat. 'This is as far as I go, Ali. Good luck, whatever it is you're doing.'

Sinclair patted Bob's shoulder. 'Thanks for your help, Bob. I won't forget it.' She got out, closing the door behind her.

Bob pulled away and Sinclair watched as he did a three-point turn and headed back towards the gate. Waving to people as they left was becoming a habit.

Sinclair looked at the young lieutenant. She knew there would be no point asking her what was going on. She was just another small part of Sinclair's journey and wouldn't know the full story. Sinclair wasn't going to find out what was happening until she got to her final stop, wherever that was. Right now, she just wanted to relax, have a shower and get some sleep. She walked up the pathway and the two women entered the bungalow.

The young lieutenant switched on the lights and showed Sinclair into the bungalow. 'My name is Lieutenant Steele and I've been informed to address you as ma'am. There is plenty of food in the kitchen and there are clothes for you in the bedroom. Help yourself to the toiletries in the bathroom and there is a small suitcase for you to pack things for your journey.' She passed Sinclair a plastic wallet. 'This contains your identity and travel documents. I'll be back tomorrow afternoon to pick you up. Please don't leave the bungalow before then. Is there anything else I can get for you, ma'am?'

'You could stop calling me ma'am, my names Ali. It's been a long day and I'd like it if you used my name. It'll make me feel more relaxed.'

Lieutenant Steel nodded. 'Okay, ma'am, I mean, Ali. My names Chelsea, Chelsea Steel.'

'It's good to meet you, Chelsea. I don't suppose you can fill me in on any details, can you?'

'Sorry, Ali. I was just given orders to make sure you were comfortable and then come back and get you tomorrow. Don't you know what's going on?'

Sinclair smiled. 'It's a long story, Chelsea. One that you'd be better off not knowing.'

Steel looked at the bruise on Sinclair's face. 'I put some make-up in a bag in the bedroom. You should probably cover that up before you leave.'

Sinclair put her hand up to her face. She'd forgotten how bad she must look. 'I'll look much better after a shower and some sleep.'

'Of course. I'll go, and leave you to get cleaned up and relax.'

'Okay, Chelsea, and thanks for all your help.'

'It was a pleasure, ma'am, I mean, Ali. See you tomorrow.'

Lieutenant Steel left the bungalow and closed the door behind her.

Sinclair didn't know what to do first, her head was spinning.

Twenty-four hours ago, she was lying in a stinking cell in a Mexican prison, and now she was in a plush, officer's bungalow on a US airbase. She fully expected to be woken up by one of the guards and find herself back there. If this was a dream, she was going to make the best of it. First, she was going to stand in the shower for at least half an hour.

Chapter 5

Sinclair looked out of the window of the Gulfstream C-37A as it came in to land. She still didn't know who was organising all of this, but they had pulled some pretty big strings. She was being passed off as a military liaison and was using a false name. She had been provided with the uniform and ID of a captain in military intelligence – her old rank – before she boarded the T-1 Jayhawk from Randolph to Andrews Field in Washington. The Gulfstream she transferred to at Andrews was usually used by government and defence department top brass, and was definitely more comfortable than the Chinooks and Hercules transports she was used to bouncing around in the back of.

The Gulfstream taxied to a halt close to the passenger terminal and one of the air crew opened the door, extending the steps to the ground. Sinclair had been told to leave the plane last, so waited until the other passengers had grabbed their bags before she picked up her small suitcase and joined the back of the line. Everyone else had now filed out and were making their way to the terminal. Sinclair stood at the top of the steps and looked around to confirm what she had suspected when she looked out of the window. She recognised her surroundings, she'd been here many times before. This was Ramstein. She was back in Europe.

Ramstein air base in southwestern Germany is the headquarters of the US Air Force in Europe, but it also serves as a base for NATO Allied Air Command. That's why they had flown her here, there would be other British personnel on the base and she wouldn't stand out. It also explained why they had put her in uniform for the flight. She descended the remaining steps and followed the other passengers, who seemed to know where they should be going.

Ahead of her, and off to the left, between the plane and the passenger terminal, Sinclair could make out a driver in a British Army uniform, standing next to a Land Rover Defender. Sinclair checked the other passengers, there were no other Brits on the flight. The Land Rover must be waiting for her. She veered away from the other passengers and headed towards the vehicle, the plastic wheels on her suitcase clattering against the tarmac as she went. As she approached the vehicle, the driver, a corporal, came to attention and saluted her. Sinclair almost forgot to return the gesture, she hadn't been in uniform for a long time and it all still felt a little surreal. She transferred her suitcase to her left hand and quickly saluted. 'Carry on, Corporal.'

'Ma'am.'

The corporal took her suitcase and put it in the back of the Land Rover before joining Sinclair in the front. 'Welcome to Ramstein, ma'am.'

'Thank you. Feels good to be back.'

The driver put the vehicle into gear and set off. Sinclair took off her cap, it wasn't the right size and was digging into her head. 'Where are we going, Corporal?'

'I'm taking you to a hanger on the other side of the base, ma'am. I'll leave you there and be on my way.'

'I don't suppose you know who I'm supposed to meet there?'

The driver shook her head. 'That wasn't included in my brief.'

'Seems to have been a theme during the last couple of days.'

'Ma'am?'

'It's okay, Corporal. I'm just trying to make sense of the things that have happened in the last couple of days. It's all been a bit of a whirlwind.'

'We were given the orders at short notice. I don't think our sergeant knew any more than I do.'

Sinclair smiled. 'I think a lot of the detail is above all of our pay grades.'

The driver turned onto a smaller road, on the other side of the base from the passenger terminal. Along the road was a row of hangers that seemed to be empty, all bar one. Sinclair could see lights and movement inside the hanger at the end of the row. The corporal stopped the Land Rover outside it and Sinclair got out. The corporal, like all the others had, drove off and left her standing alone, wondering what was coming next.

She looked inside and saw a figure walking towards the open hanger door. She could only see the person in silhouette but, as they approached, she thought she recognised them.

Simeon Carter stepped out of the hanger. He was, as always, well-dressed and wearing a look of calm and composure. Sinclair was never sure if that was genuine or part of the cover Carter used to reassure his agents.

'Hello, Captain Sinclair. It's good to see you again.'

Sinclair wasn't sure if she was glad to see the old cold war spook or not. Forty-eight hours earlier she had been in a Mexican prison cell, concentrating on staying alive. Now she was in uniform again and on a US airbase in Germany. She was grateful for that much, at least, but what was expected of her in return? 'I take it I have you to thank for my change in surroundings, Simeon.'

'I did promise to bring you home after your last job for me. I'm just sorry it took so long.'

Sinclair looked passed Carter to the inside of the hanger. 'Where's Frank?' She knew that if Frank McGill was here, he would have been the first person to greet her.

Carter gestured towards the open door. 'Come inside, Ali. I can tell you all about it.'

The inside of the hanger had been set up as a staging post for deploying troops. At one end, a long cabin had been built as accommodation. In there would be beds, showers and a kitchen – all mod cons. It gave troops a little privacy and was easier to keep warm in the winter. Opposite the cabin there were rows of plastic chairs arranged around a whiteboard: a meeting area for briefings and planning. There was another, smaller cabin next to the chairs, beside a pile of storage crates that had stencilled lettering to indicate the various equipment that was contained within them. The hanger's facilities were completed with comfortable chairs and a small television in one of the corners.

Carter led Sinclair to the meeting area. The only other people in the hanger were two men watching a German sitcom on the TV and two who were now closing and securing the hanger doors.

'Have a seat, Ali. I'll try and give you as much information as I can, as quick as I can. I'm sure you've got a lot of questions.'

'Where's Frank?' Sinclair was beginning to worry. McGill hadn't been in touch with her in the prison for a few weeks now and he was nowhere to be seen here. Carter seemed a little cagey, like he was keeping something from her.

'To be honest, Ali. We don't actually know exactly where he is.'

'What? Is he alright?'

Carter held up a hand to calm Sinclair. He knew she would be worried. 'He's dropped out of sight. We can't contact him and no one has seen him for some time.'

'Why would he do that?'

'We think someone has blown his cover. We think he is in hiding.'

Sinclair stood, her chair fell backwards. 'What do you mean, "you think"? How do you know he hasn't been taken? What if he's hurt, or worse?'

Carter pulled out a piece of paper and held it out to her. 'This was the last message we received from him.'

Sinclair took the paper and unfolded it. Printed on it was a single line of text:

Position compromised. Send Sinclair.

'When was this?'

'He's been missing for two weeks now. We tried to find him but there's no sign.'

Sinclair knew she was the only person McGill really trusted. A message like this meant he had no confidence in the integrity of the people he was working for. She would have to be careful, it could be a warning. 'How was he compromised?'

Carter looked at his feet, aware that Sinclair wasn't going to like what he was about to tell her. 'It looks like there was a breach of security. McGill was working for us, picking up intel, tracking someone down. No one was supposed to know about it but us.'

'But someone did know about it, didn't they?'

'The hierarchy always know something, even if it's not the details. We can't keep everything secret.'

'There's more, though, isn't there, Simeon? What else are you afraid to tell me?'

Carter was slowly shaking his head. 'We can't be 100 per cent certain, but it looks like Vadim may have found out what was going on. He might have sent some of his men after Frank.'

Sinclair's fists clenched. Vadim had put a price on her head and now he was trying to take out Frank. She wasn't going to stand by and let that happen. She had dreamt about coming face-to-face with the mole again, they had unfinished business. Carter wanted her to work with a police artist, to identify Vadim so he could be taken down but, in her heart, she wanted the chance to face him herself. He had caused a lot of people a great deal of pain. She wanted to see his face when he realised what was coming, that it was all over, that she was the one who'd come to get him. Sinclair realised that she had clenched her teeth just thinking about it. She looked at Carter. 'Where was Frank when he disappeared and how do you plan to get me there?'

Carter had already put everything in place to send Sinclair after McGill. This was exactly what he'd wanted. 'I was hoping you'd be ready to help out, Ali.'

'Why wouldn't I? Frank is like family to me, I'd die for him. Besides, if I didn't help you, I'm sure I'd find myself on a plane, winging my way back to the Mexican Desert.'

Carter knew that there were people who would prefer to

abandon Sinclair to her fate in Mexico, but he wasn't one of them. 'I would never do that to you, Ali. If you didn't want to be involved, I would make sure you got away – anywhere you wanted. I have enough contacts to set you up with a new identity, I owe you that much, at least.'

Sinclair knew Carter wouldn't deliberately hurt her, she was just venting her frustration. Carter wasn't part of the establishment and Sinclair had begun to think of him as someone she could rely on. 'I know, Simeon. It'll just take me a while to feel safe again; to stop feeling like everyone is out to get me.'

'I understand, Ali. I hope you can trust me fully, in time.'

Sinclair nodded and smiled. 'Okay, Simeon. Enough bonding, what's our plan?'

'Well, we need you to find Frank and the information he has. Bearing in mind he doesn't want to be found, we can't really plan anything other than getting you to Geneva.'

'Geneva?'

'That's where he disappeared.'

The two of them sat down and Carter took a folder from a briefcase that was on one of the seats next to them. Inside the folder was the transcript of Wyatt's phone call to the British Consulate, and some CCTV photographs that showed him with Porter. Carter pointed him out to Sinclair. 'This guy's name is Callum Porter. We found Wyatt by tracking him. Danny Kinsella, back in London, was able to find out who he was and where he lived. Frank went to Geneva to speak with Wyatt but, by the time Frank got there, he was dead.'

'You think he had evidence on Vadim?'

'We think he has evidence on the whole organisation. Big names in the upper echelons of government. People who would do anything to stay in power.'

Sinclair pointed at the photograph. 'This guy, Porter, who is he?'

'Wyatt's partner. He was easier to track as he wasn't trying to hide. Wyatt was doing everything he could to stay anonymous. Porter also happens to be the son of a high-profile senator in the US.'

Sinclair smiled. 'Now it all makes sense. The break out, the secret military flights. He pulled some strings to arrange all this.'

'We had to get you here without the authorities finding out what we were up to – without Vadim finding out. The senator is ex-military and his family are in the oil business. He has a considerable amount of resources and he wants his son home. Any of us would have done the same thing, if it was in our power.'

'I don't suppose his help extends to providing us with backup?'

'Unfortunately, no. Once you go in, you're on your own, as usual. I'll go back to London and keep an eye on things there. Danny Kinsella will provide you with any intel you need and he'll carry on trying to locate Frank.'

'What are my terms of engagement?'

'Just like last time: you don't officially work for MI6. Do what you have to.'

Chapter 6

As the sun came up, Sinclair showered and dressed in the civilian clothes that had been provided for her. The uniform she had travelled in had done its job and now she was back to being ex-military. She'd slept in the small cabin in the hanger, where her new kit had been left. A selection of jeans, cargo pants, T-shirts, underwear, a hat and gloves; she was dressed like a typical backpacker making her way around Europe.

She rolled up the spare clothes and packed them into the rucksack that had also been left for her. She filled two water bottles and slid them into the bag's elastic side netting, and placed the simple first-aid kit into the front pocket. Her fake passport and driving licence were in a ziplock plastic bag in the leg pocket of her cargo pants, along with five hundred euros and five hundred US dollars for emergencies. She had no idea where she would end up and some countries more readily accepted dollars.

Along with her passport, Danny Kinsella had set up a credit card in her false name, which was linked to one of his accounts. She slid it into a nylon wallet, with another five hundred euros, and closed the Velcro fastening. She put on a dark green waterproof jacket and slung the rucksack onto her back. She tied her hair into a ponytail and picked up the mobile phone Carter had given her; the charger was already in her bag. Looking in the mirror, she looked every inch the tourist she was trying to pass for. All she needed now, was a weapon.

She stepped out of the cabin, into the hanger. Carter had left early in the morning for London, but the four men she had seen the night before were still there. Three of them were arranging equipment from the packing cases into several sets of identical kit. They were preparing for more soldiers to arrive. These men were obviously Regiment, on standby for some operation she wouldn't be asking them about.

Sinclair walked over to the fourth soldier, a man in his mid-thirties with hair too long for regular army. He had weathered skin that suggested he'd spent some time working in the desert, and the lean, athletic physique of someone who worked hard on their fitness.

As Sinclair approached, Sergeant Mick Butler nodded to her. 'Good morning. Sleep well?'

Sinclair put down her bag. 'Better than I have for a long time.'

'That's good. Me and the boys,' he gestured towards the other three, 'know some of what's gone on. Mr Carter told us what happened on your last job and how you ended up in prison. Sounds like you've had some serious shit.'

'Enough to last me a lifetime. I'm never going back there, to Mexico, no matter what happens. I'd die first.'

Butler held out his hand. 'I hope it doesn't come to that. I'm Mick.'

Sinclair shook his hand. 'I'm Ali. Good to meet you, Mick.'

Butler took Sinclair to a trestle that had been put up next

to the briefing area. Laid out in front of them were a nine millimetre semi-automatic and two magazines. 'These are for you, Ali. I assume you're familiar with them?'

Sinclair picked up the weapon, it was a Glock 19. Smaller than the Glock 17 and ideal for use as a concealed weapon. She picked up one of the magazines and loaded it into the grip. 'Yeah, I've used these before.' She put the pistol into her jacket.

Butler handed her the spare magazine. 'That's thirty rounds between the two mags. If you need more than that, you're in more shit than a single weapon will get you out of.'

'Thanks, Mick. With any luck, I won't need it at all.'

'Here's hoping.' They shook hands again. 'Good luck, Ali. It looks like your transport is here. Hope to catch up with you again, when all this is over.'

Sinclair looked to where Butler had nodded. A young woman in civilian clothes was standing in the entrance to the hanger. 'Thanks again, Mick. Hopefully I'll see you again.'

Sinclair walked out of the hanger, climbing into the Range Rover that the young woman had arrived in. Butler watched the car drive off then slid the hanger door shut.

Chapter 7

Ali Sinclair walked out of Geneva's Cornavin train station. Standing under the steel and glass canopy, beneath the large clock hanging above the station's main entrance, she looked up and down the Place de Cornavin. Rows of bicycles were parked next to the glass shelters of the tram and bus stops opposite the entrance; electrical cables, which powered the trams, hung above her head, tracing the tramlines route.

The buildings she could see along the street were all of a similar size and architecture. All symmetrical and between six and eight storeys high, nothing too overstated. Each floor was a row of individual, rectangular windows with no gaps between the buildings. To her right, she could see the parasols and outside tables of a coffee shop. That would be a good place to start. She'd bought a street map from a shop in the railway station, she needed to study it and unwind a little. Her journey from Ramstein had taken four different trains and eight hours. She needed a coffee and some fresh air.

Sinclair picked one of the outside tables and placed her bag on the chair next to her. She ordered a large latte and spread out the map in front of her. She was looking for a cheap hotel and an Internet café. The waiter arrived with her coffee and Sinclair did her best 'lost tourist' impression. 'Could you show me where I can get some Internet access, please. Need to mail my mum.'

The waiter pointed out a couple of cafés that were close by, and suggested some hotels she might want to check out. By the time he walked away, flashing a smile, he had also left his phone number and an invitation to go for a drink. Sinclair smiled back and, once he was out of sight, threw the phone number in the bin. The last thing she needed was some loved-up lothario following her around like a lost puppy.

Sinclair finished her coffee and headed along the road in the direction of one of the cafés. She had to try and contact McGill – she needed to know he was still alive, for her own peace of mind. The last message they had received from McGill was through an anonymous email account. McGill had logged in to the account and written the message, before saving it as a draft rather than sending it. It was a way of keeping messages a little more secure, as it couldn't be intercepted or traced unless it was sent. To read the message, someone would need to know the account name and password. Of course, the account could be hacked but, short term, it was a simple way to communicate.

The café was on a side street next to an organic food shop. The café itself was vegan, and quite popular with the more health conscious locals and tourists who frequented the area. In one corner there were four computers that could be used free of charge by customers. Sinclair walked up to the counter and ordered an orange and apple smoothie and took a seat in front of one of the screens. She logged into the email account and checked for anything from McGill. Danny Kinsella had been posting regular cryptic messages, but McGill wasn't going to break radio silence and give away his position. Sinclair had to send a message that McGill would know was from her, something that couldn't be from anyone else. She looked at her map and thought for a moment before typing a message:

Plainpalais Skatepark. 16:00. Tomorrow.

She signed it, GI Barbie. It was a name the US Marines had used for her when she worked with them in Afghanistan. A comment on the mixture of her good looks, blonde hair, and skills as a soldier. She hated it, but only someone who'd served with her would know anyone called her it. Frank would know. She saved the message and logged off.

The map that the smiling waiter had marked up for her showed there were a handful of small hotels in the area. Sinclair was looking for one that was big enough to allow her some anonymity but small enough to be cheap; large enough to have some security but not be bristling with CCTV and security guards. She circled one a few streets away. Grabbing her bag and slinging it over her back, she thanked the man behind the counter and set off to look for a room.

* * *

The hotel that Sinclair chose was low-cost, compared to the rest of Geneva, but not the cheapest. It was part of a chain – the kind where the rooms look identical no matter which part of the world you're in. The room she was in was quite basic – bed, shower, TV, kettle – but it was more than she needed. The years she'd spent in the squalor of the prison had taught her to get by without any of life's luxuries. Maybe, when this was over, she would treat herself to a five-star holiday or a

45

spa weekend.

She positioned a chair next to the window so she could watch the goings-on in the street below. She took photographs of any cars and their passengers that stayed for more than a few minutes. The cheaper hotel opposite was the one the waiter had suggested; if anyone had seen them talking and gone to him for information, he would send them there.

Most of the vehicles that stopped outside the two hotels were taxis, but now and again a plain car would pull up and she would photograph it. She doubted it would tell her anything, but she would rather be safe than sorry.

She looked at her watch, it was midnight. She needed to lie down, tomorrow was going to be a long day. She dragged the chair to the other side of the room and jammed it under the door handle. If anyone came in, she would at least get a warning. She kicked off her boots, placed her gun beside her on the bedside table and lay down.

It was already daylight when Sinclair opened her eyes, she hadn't slept that late for years. It had taken her a long time to fall asleep. Although she was exhausted, her body was still on Mexican time. She would adjust in a few days but, right now, it suited her. She preferred to be awake late, that was when most of the shit happened.

She showered and dressed before packing her bag and getting ready to leave. She wanted to check on the meeting location before she met with McGill. The earlier she got there, the harder it would be for someone to watch her and stay unnoticed. Anyone arriving after her and hanging around would be easy for her to spot.

Before she left her room she looked out of the window and checked the street in front of the hotel. A car pulled up opposite and parked for a few minutes, it looked familiar. She picked up her phone and scrolled through the photographs: it was the third vehicle she'd taken a picture of the previous night. It didn't necessarily mean the car was looking for her, maybe she was being paranoid, but it wasn't a chance she wanted to take. Her paranoia had kept her alive in situations like this before.

Sinclair grabbed her bag and, after pausing to listen at the door, left her room. The hotel's fire escape ran down the back of the building, with doors on each floor. Unlike a lot of bigger hotels, the fire doors weren't alarmed – one of the reasons she had gone for the cheaper end of the market. She pushed the door open and descended the metal fire escape, down to the hotel car park.

At the back of the hotel there was a small garden, between the building she had come from and another hotel that backed on to it. Sinclair made her way through the trees and climbed the low wall that separated the two buildings. She entered the back of the other hotel, made her way through reception, and exited from the front entrance as if she were a guest there. She hailed a taxi and headed for the meeting.

Chapter 8

Mc Gill had been checking the email account every day for the last two weeks, looking for contact from Sinclair. He didn't trust anyone else and didn't reply to any messages, even when someone had masqueraded as Sinclair. McGill was confident he would know it was Ali's actual message when it arrived.

Each morning he would visit a different Internet café and log on to the mail server through a VPN, so his location couldn't be tracked. Every day a new message appeared in the draft mail folder from someone claiming to be in his team, and every day he ignored it. He had no way of knowing who it was really from. Someone high up had leaked information and blown his cover, he was taking no chances. If he had to cut all ties and disappear, he would. That morning when he'd logged on yet another email had been drafted, but this one was different. Only one person would sign a message, GI Barbie.

McGill logged off and checked his watch, he had a little longer than five hours before the time Sinclair wanted to meet. He had to make plans. If things went wrong, if this was a set up, he needed to be able to drop everything and run.

He and Porter were staying in a one-bedroom basement

flat they had rented, away from the city centre. The police weren't actively looking for Porter, but McGill was sure that Vadim's organisation had connections that would keep them informed if Porter was found. McGill hadn't allowed Porter to go outside since they'd got there. The young man was going stir crazy. It was good that Sinclair had arrived; they needed to get Porter away from Geneva, something McGill couldn't do on his own.

McGill entered the flat; Porter was lying on the couch in the dimly lit room. The curtains were constantly closed and the naked bulb in the ceiling had begun to give Porter headaches. The only light came from a small lamp they had moved from the bedroom and placed on the floor near the kitchen.

Porter sat up when McGill entered. 'Any news, Frank?'

'My backup is here.'

'It's about time. Where have they been?'

'It's a long story, son. Maybe I'll tell you it one day, but now, we need a plan for tonight.'

* * *

Sinclair arrived at the Plainpalais a little after one o'clock – three hours before her meeting with McGill. The Plainpalais was a huge, open area in the heart of the city. It hosted flea markets, circuses and rollercoasters, depending what day and time of year it was. It was also in the centre of the city's nightlife. The university was close by and many students met up there before a night out. Today it was full of people shopping at the mid-week flea market. The skate park, where she would meet McGill, was always busy, and it attracted a lot of skaters and teenagers to the area. There were enough people to keep her anonymous, but not too many to obscure her view and allow someone to sneak up on her.

Sinclair chose a bench from where she could see the skate park and as much of the surrounding area as possible. She waited until the seat was vacant and sat down, placing her bag next to her to discourage anyone else from sitting there.

She checked the photographs in her phone to remind herself of the cars she had seen the previous night, and checked the area. There was no sign of them and no sign of anyone paying her too much interest. She got comfortable on the bench and waited for McGill.

* * *

McGill and Porter packed up all their kit and put it into the back of an old VW Camper that McGill had paid cash for. McGill told Porter to stay in the flat. He didn't want the extra hassle of trying to watch out for him, as well as looking for Sinclair. 'I'll go to the meeting and make sure everything's okay. If it is, we'll come back here and get you, okay?'

Porter nodded. 'I'm ready to go home now, Frank.'

McGill could tell that Porter was a nervous wreck. He'd never experienced anything like this before and had had no training on how to cope with it. The reason McGill hadn't left Geneva was that he couldn't look after Porter and watch his own back without putting them both at risk. Now Sinclair was there, they had a chance of getting through it. 'I promise I'll do everything I can to get you to a safe place, Callum. If I'm not back here by midnight, get in the van and head for France, try and get to a US embassy. It's your best bet.'

'Whatever happens tonight, thank you, Frank. I know

you've done everything you can. I really appreciate it.'

'Don't worry, Callum. We'll be okay. You'll be on your way home before you know it.'

McGill left the flat and closed the door behind him. He'd made sure that anything to link him with the flat had been left in the campervan. If he was taken out, at least they couldn't use him to find out where Callum was. If anything happened to McGill, the chances of Porter surviving on his own were slim. McGill couldn't afford not to go to the meeting, though; he was exhausted. Checking the email and buying food during the day and keeping watch through the night had sapped his energy. He only snatched a couple of hours sleep at a time and felt like he was walking around in a daze. He couldn't keep it up much longer.

McGill climbed the stone steps outside the flat until his eyes were at the same level as the pavement and he could just see along the road. He stood there for several minutes, checking for anyone watching, loitering, or walking past more than once. There was nothing suspicious, just the normal, everyday traffic of people going about their business. He climbed the last few steps, checked left and right once more, and set off for Plainpalais.

* * *

Sinclair had been on the bench for nearly two hours. She had already been approached by two men who thought she was looking for business, and given money by an old woman who thought she was homeless. She'd kept a good watch in all directions and, until now, hadn't spotted anything untoward. In the last ten minutes, however, she'd spotted the same car

51

that had rung an alarm bell outside her hotel. She pulled out her mobile and checked the photograph she had taken the previous night. It was definitely the same car and driver.

The car had three people inside: driver and passenger in the front, and another passenger in the back. It was an old, dark blue saloon. There was nothing remarkable about it, it was a perfect surveillance vehicle. Nothing about it made it stand out, other than the fact that Sinclair had now seen it three times, that was too much of a coincidence. Most people wouldn't have noticed whether they'd seen the same car, briefly, more than once. Even if they had, most people wouldn't perceive it as a threat, but Ali Sinclair wasn't most people.

Sinclair knew, once he had heard she had escaped from prison again, Vadim would probably start to look for her there. He wouldn't do it officially, that would mean explaining the reasons why and how an escaped convict was in Geneva, four days after being broken out of a prison van in the Chihuahuan desert. Whoever was following her must have been watching the railway stations, it was the obvious way for her to arrive. She knew they wouldn't make a move on her yet. Although Vadim wanted her dead, his bosses wanted Porter and the book first. Sinclair checked her watch, it was still one hour before Frank was due to arrive.

* * *

McGill had spotted Sinclair sitting on the bench. He had taken an hour to work his way around Plainpalais and close in on her position. He mingled with people shopping in the flea market and checked for anyone out of the ordinary, anyone who might be watching Sinclair. The only thing that stood out was a blue saloon car. Three men sitting in a car in the afternoon didn't look right. He watched as one of the passengers got out, walked around the market and returned to the car. He didn't buy anything. He didn't even look at anything. The whole time his attention was focussed in Sinclair's direction. Whoever they were, they weren't trained in surveillance.

McGill walked through the market crowd and stood less than fifty feet from Sinclair. Even if she spotted him, it was unlikely she would recognise him. With his hood up and his head down, he could be anyone. He had to contact Sinclair and get her to follow him without the watchers realising who he was.

Sinclair checked her watch again, it was four o'clock. Frank should be there anytime, if he'd got the message, if he wasn't dead already. Then she heard a voice she instantly recognised, a voice she was relieved to hear again.

McGill was standing directly behind the bench, pretending to take a picture with his phone. 'Dark blue saloon, two o'clock, three up. Follow me.'

Sinclair watched as McGill walked away and mingled with the flea-market shoppers. She stood, picked up her bag, and followed him.

When Sinclair moved off, two of the three watchers got out of the car and walked towards the market. As they closed in, they separated. One covering the southern edge and the other heading north. Sinclair sped up and was just behind McGill as they came out of the market, on to Avenue du Mail. They ran across the road and into the grid of streets opposite, turning regularly to put distance and angles between them and their pursuers: left, right, left right; they came out on a street with a low wall on the other side. They both ran between the parked cars and cleared the wall into a cemetery.

When they reached the other side, McGill moved to the left and tucked in the shadows at the base of the wall. Sinclair went right and hid behind a large tree. The first chaser to clear the wall followed the same route as Sinclair had, turning to the right. When the second chaser landed inside the cemetery McGill shot him.

Although McGill had screwed the suppressor on his nine-millimetre, the scream, as the shot man fell, alerted his partner to the threat. The first chaser stopped dead and spun around, but before he could run back towards the wall and help his buddy, Sinclair stepped out from behind the tree and dropped him with two solid kidney punches. She grabbed the man's collar and drove him face first into the tree trunk. He lay at her feet, unconscious, blood pouring from a large wound on his forehead.

McGill unscrewed his suppressor and put the weapon back in his pocket. He ran to Sinclair, wrapped his arms around her and lifted her off her feet. 'It's great to see you, Ali.'

'Thank god you're alive, Frank. I thought I'd lost you.'

McGill put Sinclair down, still holding on to her arms. 'What took you so long?'

Sinclair punched his arm. 'I was in prison, in Mexico, you tosser.'

McGill smiled. 'Let's get the fuck out of here.'

They jogged through the cemetery and exited through the gate on the opposite side.

Chapter 9

Sinclair and McGill arrived back at the basement flat at six o'clock, after taking a roundabout route and doubling back a few times to throw off any followers. They approached the steps to the flat but waited until the road was deserted before stepping down. When McGill opened the door, Porter wasn't in his usual place on the couch. The small lamp and the bedroom light were both switched off, the flat was in darkness. They closed the door and McGill switched on the main light. 'It's okay, Callum. It's us. You can come out now.'

The kitchen door creaked open and Porter peered into the room. He was carrying a large carving knife, from the kitchen drawer, out in front of him.

McGill pointed at the knife. 'What were you planning to do with that?'

Porter felt a little foolish. He knew he would probably have hurt himself rather than any intruder. 'Oh, I don't know. I just thought … well … never mind.' He turned and dropped the knife back into the drawer.

Porter looked at Sinclair. 'Is this your backup?'

'Yeah, this is Ali. Don't let her looks fool you, she's saved my arse more times than I can remember. Ali, this is Callum

Porter.'

Sinclair smiled. 'Hello, Callum. It's good to meet you. I owe your dad a big favour.'

'You know my dad?'

'We've never met, but a few days ago I was in a Mexican prison and now I'm here. That, in part, is down to your dad.'

Porter didn't understand this at all. 'A Mexican prison? What …?'

'Don't worry, Callum. It's a long story for another time. All you need to know is you can trust me, and I'll keep you safe.'

McGill butted in. 'Right. Before we all get misty-eyed, let's get on with this shit, shall we? We leave in an hour. We can't hang around and wait for anyone else to come after us.'

Porter looked quizzical. 'Anyone else? Has something happened?'

'We were followed when we were at the skate park. Two guys came after us.'

'What? What if they followed you here?'

McGill shook his head. 'Not happening, Callum. I shot one of them and Ali smashed the other one's face in with a tree.'

Porters mouth hung open, searching for words but none would come out. They were talking about this stuff as if it were an everyday occurrence. He was glad they were on his side.

It was Sinclair who broke the silence. 'Okay, enough of the small talk. Callum, grab anything you need to take with you. Frank, I could murder something to eat.'

Porter pointed towards the street. 'All of our kit is in the van, we're ready to go.'

McGill headed for the kitchen. 'I'll knock us up some train smash before we go. It's my speciality.'

* * *

They sat at the tiny table and tucked into bowls of McGill's speciality: corned beef, baked beans and tinned tomatoes, all thrown in the same pan and heated up – train smash.

Porter was surprised how much he had come to like McGill's cooking in the last two weeks. 'You'll have to give me the recipe for this, Frank.'

'You don't need a recipe, mate. Just throw everything in a pan, turn up the heat, and Bob's your uncle.'

Porter looked confused. 'Who's Bob?'

McGill laughed. 'It's just a saying where we come from. Just means, "and there you go".'

Sinclair finished her bowl. 'That was lovely, Frank. I haven't had it since we were in Helmand.'

McGill sat back in his chair. 'Chef McGill, that's me.'

Porter dropped his spoon into his empty bowl. 'You served in Afghanistan, too, Ali?'

Sinclair pointed towards McGill with her thumb. 'That's where I met the green machine here.'

'Yeah, I was always digging her out of the shit.'

'In your dreams.'

Porter felt safe and relaxed for the first time in weeks. The way Sinclair and McGill joked with each other as they ate, made him feel like they were about to go on a camping trip, not running for their lives.

McGill collected the bowls and threw them into the sink. 'I won't bother washing them. Okay, boys and girls, toilet time before we go. We're not stopping till we get there.'

Porter went into the bathroom and closed the door. McGill stood close to Sinclair, suddenly serious. 'He's close to cracking, Ali. I couldn't run with him on my own. If we'd had a contact he wouldn't have been able to back me up. He'd be more likely to give us away and get us killed. If it hits the fan, one of us needs to grab him and keep him down.'

Sinclair nodded. 'Are you planning to offload him? Leave him somewhere safe, like the US Embassy?'

'No. Too risky. Until we know who's involved, we can't trust anyone. Besides, some of the notebook is in code. We need him and the book to get all of the info.'

'Couldn't we get him to write the code down?'

McGill shook his head. 'Not that kind of code. There are references to memories between the two of them. Words that have no significance to us, mean something different to Callum. He's the key to deciphering it. It could take months to go through it all.'

'You think Vadim is in there?'

'Whoever is involved, this is wide-ranging. Powerful people are involved. People who now want the three of us dead and the book in their hands.'

Sinclair let out a short laugh. 'Lucky us.'

Porter came out of the bathroom drying his hands. 'Okay, I'm ready to go, if you guys are?'

Sinclair picked up her bag. 'You lead the way, Frank. Callum, you follow Frank, and I'll pick up the rear. If anything happens, keep your head down until one of us tells you otherwise. Okay?'

'Okay.'

McGill switched off the light and opened the door, checking up and down the street. He crept up the steps with Porter close behind him. Sinclair closed the door and followed them up.

The van was a hundred metres down the street. McGill didn't want the position of the van to give away which flat they were in. The three of them moved quickly and quietly. They reached the van and jumped in: McGill in the driver's seat and Porter and Sinclair in the back with their heads down. Anyone looking for them would be watching for two or three people in a vehicle, not a lone driver. McGill fired up the engine, switched on the lights and pulled away.

* * *

The border between Switzerland and France is open, there are no passport checks and customs posts are not always manned. McGill headed for a crossing that was unlikely to have any customs officers and they sailed through without even having to stop. 'Welcome to France, boys and girls. The first stop on our scheduled service will be to take on coffee and have a piss. All those in favour, say aye.'

Porter and Sinclair both raised their hands. 'Aye!' The school camping trip atmosphere persisted as they all cracked up.

Two hours later they were parked at the side of the road while McGill made them all a coffee. McGill placed the mugs on the table in the cramped interior of the van then squeezed on the bench seat next to Sinclair. 'I don't think these vans were designed for three adults.'

Sinclair picked up her mug. 'I've slept in worse places.'

McGill smiled. 'Did you manage to send the photos of the book to Kinsella, back in London?'

'Yeah. It took a while, but I managed to get a decent phone signal just as we were crossing the border. I sent him the few pages you and Callum had worked on and a few of the other pages we haven't looked at yet, so he can go through them. I'll have to send him the rest, bit by bit, whenever I can.'

'That'll make the actual book less important, but they would've expected us to do that anyway. They'll still be coming after us. They'll want to know what's in the book, and, don't forget, Callum's the key to it all.'

Porter took a sip of his coffee. 'Thanks for that. I was just starting to feel like we'd escaped.'

'It's okay, Callum. Me and Frank won't let anything happen to you.' She looked at McGill. 'Will we?'

McGill reached over the table and clamped a hand on Porter's forearm. 'Stick with us, kid. We'll get you home safely.'

Chapter 10

Simeon Carter placed a steaming mug of fresh coffee on the desk then stood back and took a sip from his own. 'How's it looking, Danny?'

Danny Kinsella tapped at his keyboard and scanned the three computer screens in front of him. 'I've downloaded the pictures from Sinclair and converted the images to text files. It took a while making sense of some of the handwriting, but it makes it easier to analyse. It'll save us time in the long run.'

'And have they revealed anything so far?'

Kinsella had been up all night, running the data through algorithms and scripts. He was looking for patterns and repeated numbers, words and phrases. Checking for any connections with places, people and events. 'It's starting to come together, I've found a few things.' He picked up his coffee. 'Have a look for yourself.'

Carter sat next to his young protégé and stared at the screens. None of it made sense to the old Cold War spook, he didn't even know which screen he was supposed to be looking at. To him it was all just a jumble of words and numbers. 'You know I can't make any sense of all this, Danny. The digital revolution has passed me by.'

Kinsella smiled and patted the older man's knee. Their

relationship was as close as any father and son and he sometimes had a little fun at the older man's expense. 'You're definitely a relic of the Cold War, Simeon. I need to teach you some basics, so you can join the rest of us in the twenty-first century.'

'I don't need to learn it, Danny. That's why I have you. Humour me and translate it into English.'

Kinsella turned back to his keyboard and tapped his way through the images from Sinclair. 'If you look at the pages from the book, you'll see that Wyatt has created a code to encrypt his writing. All codes require a key to read the content. In most simple codes, that key can be cracked by brute force, by crunching the data through a powerful enough computer, it's just a matter of time. This is different. This code can't be cracked because it uses information only Callum knows, as a basis for the crypto.' He switched to another screen that showed seemingly random letters and numbers. 'On each page I've found a word that doesn't seem to fit with the others. That is the keyword that needs to be deciphered by Callum. From the sound of it, he isn't aware that he knows the code. Frank had to drag the information out of him.'

'So, we need the boy to decipher it all?'

'Absolutely. Without him, we can't get through the code.' Kinsella pointed at the screen. 'I used the info Callum has given Frank so far and ran the first pages through some scripts. It turned into this …' He clicked his mouse. Among the jumble of letters and numbers were lists of recognisable words, names and numbers.

Carter sat forward. 'I recognise some of these names, they've been in the press in the last couple of years. If I remember correctly, they were mainly featured in the obituaries.'

'That's right, the first list is a mixture of CEOs, bankers and politicians who have died in the last two years, alongside the dates they died.'

'Are they linked?'

'Other than the fact that they moved in the same circles, nothing obvious. Some had attended G7 or UN summits, some were invitees of the Bilderberg Group. One thing they do have in common, is that they all died in what could be described as "questionable circumstances".'

'Questionable in what way?'

Kinsella consulted his notes. 'Well, we have three suicides, four car crashes, two drownings, a plane crash that accounted for three of them, and a mugging.'

Carter looked at Kinsella's notes. 'So, it could just be a list of prominent people who have died unexpectedly.'

'That's a possibility, but if you look at the names at the bottom of the list ...'

'The ones without dates?'

Kinsella nodded. 'Two of them have died since Frank got hold of the book.'

'How?'

'One car crash and one mountaineering accident.'

Carter wrote down the remaining three names on the list. 'I think we need to let these people know they might be in danger. What's the second list?'

'That's a list of the people who moved into the positions of the deceased.'

'And are they linked?'

Kinsella shook his head. 'Not that I can find, but I'm working on it.'

'Okay, what else is in there?'

Kinsella scrolled through the data. 'There are details of a safe-deposit box in Paris, in Callum's name. Without him, we'll need court orders to get access. I'm assuming we don't want to go down that route?'

'Not unless we can help it, Danny. Is that it?'

'There's also a third list of names but I've only tracked one person down, so far.' Kinsella highlighted a name on the screen. 'Dr Henry Shawford, retired Cambridge English professor. Nothing remarkable about him outside his academic career. He's widowed and currently lives in Paris.'

'That's a good place to start. I'll get local police to check on the first list members who are still alive, you get in touch with Sinclair and McGill and get them up to Paris. I want to know what's in that deposit box and I want them to speak with Dr Shawford and find out what he knows.'

'Will do, Simeon.'

Carter stood and put on his coat; he paused before leaving. 'We need to know what else is in those pages, Danny. Quick as you can.'

Kinsella nodded. 'It could take a long time to get through all of this, Simeon.'

'We'd better make sure the boy stays safe then.' Carter opened the door and left the flat.

Chapter 11

The campervan was old and it rattled as they made their way north. After they had received the message from Kinsella, they stocked up with some food and water for the trip and set off.

Sinclair tipped the remaining crumbs from a bag of crisps into her mouth and washed them down with a long drink of water, wiping her mouth with the back of her hand. 'That's better. I was bloody starvin'.'

McGill was finishing off a sandwich as he drove. 'How's our passenger?'

Sinclair looked in the back. 'Fast asleep. You know, for a young man, he does sleep a lot.'

'Yeah, stress of the situation taking its toll I think. He's exhausted. If we weren't both so messed up, we'd probably sleep more, too.'

Sinclair took another drink of water and replaced the cap. 'When did you become a psychiatrist?'

'Well, I've had to see a few in my time, maybe it's rubbed off.'

Sinclair looked down at her hands, fidgeting, clenching her fists. 'I want you to promise me something, Frank.'

'Anything, you know that. You don't need to ask.'

Sinclair rubbed her hand across her face. 'If everything goes wrong. If they come for me and try to take me back … there. I want you to kill me.'

McGill slammed on the brakes. He looked at Sinclair and grabbed her hands. 'No way, Ali. I can't promise you that. I couldn't do that.'

'I can't do it again, Frank, I can't go back, you don't know what it's like. I'd rather be dead.'

'Listen to me, Ali. You won't go back. I won't allow it. If anyone comes for you, I'll kill them all and we'll disappear. If it comes down to it, we'll go out fighting. We'll go together.'

Sinclair looked up at McGill, tears running down her face. 'You're all I've got, Frank. Promise you'll stay with me, wherever we end up.'

'That much I can promise.' He reached out and pulled Sinclair towards him, holding her. 'You're my family.'

In the back, Porter woke up. 'Are we there yet?'

Sinclair sat back and wiped the tears from her face, blowing her nose on a tissue. 'Jesus, it's like having kids.'

McGill started to laugh. 'Just a quick stop, Callum. We'll get going again in a minute.'

'Okay, cool. How much longer do you think it'll be?'

'A few hours yet. Help yourself to some of the food before Ali eats it all.'

Sinclair slapped McGill's knee. 'You've got through a lot of it yourself, fat boy.'

McGill smiled as he put the van into gear and pulled away.

Chapter 12

Sinclair sat at the window of the small apartment, overlooking La Défense – the business district situated to the west of Paris. The apartment belonged to Danny Kinsella. It was nothing too fancy, just somewhere to crash when he was working for his French clients. The others were still asleep, but Sinclair's body clock was messed up and she was still having nightmares. The sleep she'd had on the sofa was restless, waking suddenly at the slightest sound, fully expecting to be back in her cell. She sipped her coffee and watched the raindrops run down the window. She liked watching the rain, liked the fresh smell in the air when it stopped. It was something she had missed. Her body had become accustomed to the heat and she was feeling cold, but she didn't mind that. She was looking forward to seeing snow again, getting some snowboarding in when this was all over. If they were still alive.

The bedroom door opened and McGill stepped out, looking a little dishevelled and worse for wear. 'Is that coffee fresh?'

Sinclair snapped out of her thoughts. 'Yeah, kettle's just boiled.'

'Great, I could do with a bucket full. I think the last few weeks have caught up with me.'

'That's just your age, Frank.'

McGill waved his finger at Sinclair. 'I knew there was something I missed about you.' He plodded into the kitchen and made himself a cup of strong black coffee. He took a drink and nodded at the bedroom door. 'We need to decide what we are going to do with Callum.'

Sinclair lowered her voice. 'He's in danger, Frank. Even though he doesn't know anything, he's the key. They'll never stop coming after him. We need to make sure he's safe.'

'I don't have a problem with that. It'll make things a little bit more difficult for us, though.'

'It's thanks to his dad that I'm sitting here and not still rotting away in that stinking prison cell. I want to repay what he did for me. I want to make sure Callum gets home safely.'

'Okay. He stays with us until it's safer for him not to. We have to admit, there's a strong possibility we're gonna end up in some pretty deep shit in the next few weeks. He can't deal with that. When it gets too bad, we must leave him somewhere. Agreed?'

Sinclair nodded. 'Agreed.'

The bedroom door opened again and Porter appeared. Sinclair and McGill exchanged a glance. Porter looked better than both of them. He looked fresh, obviously hadn't slept in his clothes, and even had a smile on his face. He looked like he was on holiday.

Sinclair pointed towards him with her mug. 'See, I told you it was your age, Frank.'

McGill shook his head and muttered under his breath, 'The shit I have to put up with.'

They both laughed. Porter looked puzzled. 'Did I miss something?'

Sinclair smiled. 'Nothing important. Just catching up. Help yourself to a coffee and we'll go through the plan for the next couple of days.'

The three of them stood around the small dining table, in one corner of the apartment, opposite the kitchen. Sinclair spread a tourist map out and drew a cross on it. 'This is where we are now.' She drew two more crosses and pointed to them in turn. 'This is the CPT Bank. There is a safe-deposit box in there that we need to access. This, is where a guy called Dr Henry Shawford lives. He's on one of the lists in the book. We'll go to the bank first and leave the doctor until later this afternoon.'

McGill turned the map around to take a better look. 'What do we know about the safe-deposit box?'

'Danny sent us the account details, but we have no idea what is in it. It's in Callum's name but there should be a key for it.'

Porter removed a pair of keys from a leather cord around his neck and placed them on the map. 'Justin told me to keep these safe and tell no one about them. I never knew what they were for.'

Sinclair picked them up and examined them. 'You certainly kept these quiet. This is the one we need – the box number is engraved on it.' She handed them both back to Porter. 'You keep hold of the keys till we need them. You've done a good job with them so far.'

McGill would have preferred to keep the keys himself. They weren't exactly secure around Porter's neck, but he knew Sinclair was trying to make Callum feel like he was part of a team, that he had a contribution to make to the mission. It was a small gesture but working as one team would have a massive effect on their chances of survival if the shit hit the fan. McGill pointed at the map. 'You and Callum go in and take care of the box; I'll cover you from this coffee shop on the other side of the road. If it goes pear-shaped, we meet back here.'

Sinclair looked at Porter. 'You okay with all this, Callum?'

Porter nodded. 'I'll do whatever you need me to.'

Sinclair wasn't sure the young man appreciated what might be involved. 'You're sure? We have no way of knowing what information Vadim's thugs got out of Justin before he died. They could be waiting for us.'

Porter nodded. 'I can do this. I want to do it. For Justin.'

McGill patted him on the back. 'Everything will be fine. Just do whatever Ali tells you. Okay?'

'Okay.'

'Good man.'

Chapter 13

Outside a coffee shop on the Avenue de l'Opéra, McGill picked a seat that had a clear line of sight to the front door of the CPT Bank. He'd been there long enough to be on his second cup of coffee and nothing, so far, had looked suspicious. The traffic was light and he hadn't seen any vehicles doing multiple passes or parking up to watch the bank. He watched as Sinclair and Porter walked along the pavement on the other side of the road and approached the door.

Sinclair nodded to McGill then she and Porter entered the foyer of CPT. There were banks in Paris that dated back to the Napoleonic era, with large ornate interiors and lists of high-profile, ultra-rich clients. CPT had none of that, at least, not officially. Most of their clients banked online and shuffled money between international accounts in the world's various tax havens. CPT was a bank that specialised in anonymity, and some of its clients were hiding vast amounts of money from the tax authorities.

The interior was small and modern, almost minimalist. The foyer had plain white walls and a black and white tiled floor that made it look like a bathroom. Chrome spotlights were recessed into the low ceiling and in the wall opposite the door

71

was an ATM and a cashier's window. A young woman smiled at them from behind the bulletproof glass. *'Bonjour, puis-je vous aider?'*

Porter stepped up to the glass and asked to see someone about his safe-deposit box. At least, that's what it sounded like to Sinclair. She spoke a couple of languages fluently, but French wasn't one of them. She remembered a little from her school French lessons, but this conversation was going much too quickly for her.

After a few minutes, a second, slightly older woman, opened a door into the foyer and beckoned them to follow her. Sinclair quickly checked behind them for anyone watching, then followed Porter and the second woman through the door.

The back office of CPT wasn't as minimalist as the foyer, but it was no less modern. Through the glass wall on the right-hand side of the corridor, they could see bank employees sitting in cubicles, staring at numbers that flashed up on their screens. They were watching the markets. This bank did more than just store people's money, they were also an investment broker.

At the other end of the corridor there was a separate computer in a recess in the wall. Porter was asked to provide his details and proof of ID for the woman to check. A few keystrokes later and they were led through a steel cage into the vault. The walls were lined with hundreds of boxes. Each one had a dull grey front and two locks. Between the locks were the boxes' numbers. Porter was led to box number 696, his box. He removed the key from around his neck and turned it in the lock.

* * *

McGill got up from his table and took out the tourist map. He'd spotted a man shortly after Sinclair and Porter had gone into the bank. The man had now been past the coffee shop several times and seemed to be paying particular attention to the windows of the bank. McGill held the map in front of his face as the man walked past him and into the shop, heading for the toilets. McGill wondered where Vadim found these amateurs. Nobody with any professional training would leave a solo surveillance operation to go for a piss. McGill looked around, there was no obvious backup or anyone else who looked like they had taken over the op. He followed the man into the shop.

McGill opened the door to the gents and put on his best, and only, American accent – the one he'd learned watching old US cowboy movies and cartoons at the cinema on a Saturday morning as a kid. 'Hey, buddy. D'ya speak English?'

The man froze. He wanted to pretend to be a local and just shake his head, but this guy had the worst American accent he'd ever heard, a cross between John Wayne and Goofy. It couldn't be real, surely? His hesitation cost him. Before he could do anything to protect himself, McGill punched him hard in the solar plexus. His knees started to buckle and he gasped for breath. McGill followed up by smashing the man's face into the porcelain sink and dragging him, unconscious, into one of the toilet cubicles.

* * *

Sinclair and Porter emptied the contents of the safe-deposit

73

box onto the table in the private room they'd been shown into. Wyatt had planned for things going wrong. He was obviously expecting to be on the run at some point. The box contained five thousand euros in small denomination notes and two thousand pounds. There were fake UK passports for both Wyatt and Porter, with matching driving licences and bank cards, and a USB memory stick.

Porter couldn't believe any of this. 'What was Justin involved in? It's like something out of a spy novel.'

'He knew what he was doing might be dangerous. He was putting things in place for both of you to escape.'

Porter shook his head. 'He never told me any of this.'

Sinclair put her arm around Porter. 'He was trying to keep you out of it. To keep you safe.'

Porter picked up Wyatt's passport and stared at the photo page. He ran his finger across the image. 'Why didn't he keep himself safe?'

Sinclair lifted Porter's chin and looked him in the eye. 'I promise you, they won't get away with this. I'll do whatever it takes to bring them down. Trust me. Okay?'

Porter nodded. 'What do we do now?'

'We take all this stuff and get out of here.'

They put the contents into their pockets and closed the box's lid. When they opened the privacy curtain, the woman who had shown them into the vault reappeared and took the box from them. 'Is there anything else we can help you with today, *monsieur*?'

'No, thank you, that's everything we need.'

'*Bon*. I will show you back to the front. Follow me, please.'

They followed the woman back along the glass corridor and through to the foyer. They said goodbye to her and exited the bank.

* * *

McGill stood on the same side of the road as the bank, looking back at the coffee shop. His handiwork had obviously been discovered; one of the waitresses was speaking to a policeman who took notes then spoke into his radio.

Sinclair and Porter walked out of the bank and made their way back along the road. McGill jogged to catch them up and guided them down a narrow alley, away from the traffic of the main road. He looked back to the coffee shop, where two men in a black 4x4 were now paying a lot of attention to the man being lifted into the back of an ambulance.

'What is it, Frank?'

'The guy going in the ambulance, I had to take him out. He was following us.'

'Are you sure? You've been on the run a while now. It could be your mind playing tricks.'

McGill handed Sinclair a wallet. 'He was definitely watching you two. I searched him and found his wallet. Just money in it. No ID, no cards. That's not normal.'

'It doesn't mean he was following us, though.'

McGill held up a phone. 'He also had this.'

Sinclair looked at the screen. It showed a detailed street map of the area they were in. 'The red dot is where we are.'

McGill nodded. 'It's tracking your phone.'

'Shit! Are you sure?'

'Yeah. I watched it show you in the bank then along the road. They know where we are.'

'Right, we need to get rid of all electronics. Give me your

phone, Frank.' She took out all the sim cards and smashed the phones on the ground. From her phone, she also took the memory card. 'Need to keep hold of the photos on this.'

Porter was scared. 'Who *are* these people? How did they even know we had those phones? How can they track us like that, Ali?'

'It's not as bad as it looks, Callum. If they were tracking us from the start, they would have picked us up by now. The fact they were watching us at the bank, and didn't see Frank coming, probably means they weren't sure the phone they were tracking was mine. They wanted to check before they made a move. It's just a good job Frank spotted them first.'

McGill held out his arms to the side and bowed his head. 'I aim to please.'

'Well. Let's get out of here before we stop to pat ourselves on the back.'

They took one last look at the commotion at the coffee shop then ran down the alley, away from the *Avenue de l'Opéra*.

Chapter 14

The 16th arrondissement is a mainly residential area of Paris, not far from the centre of the city. It's quiet, leafy streets and broad avenues are lined with typically Parisienne stone buildings mixed with the more modern architecture of offices and apartment blocks. It houses Paris's major sporting locations: Parc des Princes, Roland Garros, Stade Français. It also hosts some world-class museums, all within walking distance of the Eiffel Tower and Arc de Triomphe. All of this makes it an expensive area to live in, on a par with Chelsea or Kensington, and not where you would expect a retired academic to call home.

Sinclair, McGill and Porter took the Metro to the Rue de la Pompe and walked to Dr Henry Shawford's apartment. McGill looked up at the building's ornate, nineteenth century architecture, the large rectangular windows and wrought-iron balconies that made up the front of the apartment block. 'How much do you think it costs to live here?'

Sinclair puffed out her cheeks. 'More than we could ever afford. What do you think, Callum? Do you think a retired university professor could afford to live here?'

Porter shook his head. 'No way. Not unless he comes from a rich family. Do we know if he comes from money?'

'Danny never said. He just sent us the address and some basic background. He's one of the names mentioned in the notebook. You do know what else is in this area, though?'

McGill and Porter remained silent. Sinclair looked at them both in turn. 'The Russian Embassy.'

McGill let out a short laugh. 'You think he's a Russian agent?'

Sinclair smiled. 'He wouldn't be the first Cambridge scholar to be on their payroll.'

'How come no one ever offered me bags full of money to be a double agent?'

'You don't know anything, Frank.'

'Oh, yeah. There is that, I suppose.' They both smiled; Porter looked at them, puzzled. He still hadn't got to grips with their sense of humour.

'You stay here with Callum, Ali. I'll get the door open.' McGill walked across the street to the apartment block's front entrance. The external doors were solid wood, stained dark green and varnished. McGill tried the handle: the door opened and he went in. So far, so good. The small entrance lobby he was standing in was no bigger than a standard garden shed. Both sides were covered in highly polished brass post boxes, with a secure, wrought-iron gate guarding the entrance to the rest of the building. He retrieved a lock-picking set from the inside of his jacket and got to work on the gate's lock. Within a minute, the gate was open. He signalled to Sinclair, and she and Porter jogged to the entrance to join him.

Inside, the staircase was in keeping with the rest of the building. An ornate, wrought-iron bannister, topped with a polished mahogany handrail, followed the marble steps up the outside of the entrance hall. At the top of each flight of stairs were the entrances to two apartments. Shawford lived at number eight, the top floor.

There was no noise within the building. None of the apartments they had passed sounded like they were occupied. The people who lived there were unlikely to have nine to five jobs and it was too early in the evening for them to be at one of the swanky restaurants that littered the area. They were more likely to be away on business or holiday; the idle rich.

The three of them crept up the stairs, not talking and keeping noise to a minimum. As they reached the landing outside Shawford's door, McGill and Sinclair drew their weapons. They had no idea what they could be walking into. After being followed at the bank, this could all turn out to be a trap. McGill shuffled up to the door then reached out and rang the bell. He took a step back and levelled his weapon.

After a couple of minutes they heard slow footsteps approaching on the other side. The door opened only as far as the chain would allow and the thin voice of an old man spoke in French, but with a very heavy English accent. *'Oui?'*

Sinclair answered in fluent Russian. 'We need to talk to you, Dr Shawford. It is a matter of life and death.'

Shawford closed the door and removed the chain. As soon as the door reopened, McGill pushed his way into the apartment. Sinclair followed and pushed Shawford into the lounge. She held her finger to her lips to instruct both the old man and Porter to be quiet.

McGill joined them in the lounge and re-holstered his weapon. 'All clear, the guy is on his own.'

Sinclair guided Shawford to a couch beside the large marble fireplace, opposite the room's huge window. 'Okay, Henry.

Can I call you Henry? You and I are going to have a little chat.'

The old man was scared and visibly trembling. He stared at McGill, the man who had pushed his way into the apartment. 'Who are you people? I don't have any money.'

McGill looked around the room at the decor and various artwork and ornaments. 'Well, I would say that's debateable.'

Sinclair put her hand on Shawford's knee. 'We aren't here to hurt you, Henry. We may be about to save your life. Your name appears on what looks like a kill list, belonging to an organisation that looks hell bent on triggering World War Three.' She showed Shawford the notebook. 'The list is in here, Henry. Who are they? Why would they want you dead?'

Shawford sagged and shook his head. 'I knew they wouldn't leave me in peace.'

'Who, Henry? Who wouldn't leave you in peace?'

'The people I've been working for all these years. First it was the KGB, then, when the Soviet Union collapsed, it was FSB. Now? Now they don't have a name, but they are very rich and very powerful.'

McGill sat at the opposite side of the fireplace. 'So, you've been selling secrets to them? Is that what paid for all this?'

'I don't have any secrets to sell. I've been much more important to them than simply selling secrets.'

Sinclair sat beside Shawford. 'Tell us about it, Henry. The more we know, the more we can do to stop them.'

Shawford sat back and crossed his legs. 'I got involved back in the sixties. I was at Cambridge and Kim Philby had just defected. He was an ex-Trinity College alumnus and there were a few of us who were inspired by him. Gathering information from MI6 and passing it to the Soviets. It all seemed so glamorous, so James Bond.'

McGill sat forward. 'People died because of him. He was nothing more than a traitor.'

'But in the Soviet Union he was a great hero. He received the Order of Lenin.'

McGill started to speak again but Sinclair silenced him with a look. 'Go on, Henry. What happened? I assume you were recruited?'

'I offered my services at the Soviet Embassy. I thought I would become a secret agent, but I'm not that type. I'm an academic. They had something else in mind for me.'

'And that was?'

'During the Cold War, Directorate S ran sleeper agents in the UK, US and Canada. Long-term undercover operatives who could pass for locals. They had back stories, family trees and every piece of documentation they needed. I helped them integrate into our society. I found them accommodation and work. I introduced them to my friends, created a whole network, it was beautiful.'

Sinclair had heard this story before. 'That's not new info, Henry. We all know about sleeper agents and how they would be activated when the Russians needed them. We've all read the books and seen the films, but the Cold War is over. The Soviets lost. These agents either went home or were captured. I'm sure a lot of them are dead.'

'That's right, but a large group of them stayed exactly where they were. With the KGB gone, they went into business for themselves. They married and had children, built business empires and large fortunes. They became pillars of the very society they had been sent to infiltrate. Now, their children, the second generation, are taking control.'

Porter clicked his fingers. 'That's what the list in Justin's book was about. He worked out that powerful people were being killed, and replaced by this second generation. They're taking over the world, one CEO at a time.'

Shawford uncrossed his legs and shifted in his seat. 'Justin was the name of the young man who came to see me a couple of months ago. He asked about the same things you have.'

Porter stood up. 'What? You met Justin?'

'Yes. He had worked out a lot of things, but he didn't have all the details.'

'What did you tell him? Did you tell this organisation about him?' Porter took a step towards Shawford, pointing at him angrily. 'Are you the reason Justin is dead?'

'I didn't tell anyone.' Shawford looked at Sinclair and McGill. 'I didn't.'

McGill grabbed Porter's arm and pulled him to the other side of the room. 'Calm down, Callum.'

Sinclair glared at Porter. 'It's okay, Henry, we believe you. Don't we, Callum?'

Porter sat down, lowering his eyes. 'I'm sorry.'

Sinclair smiled and turned back to Shawford. 'Now, Henry, tell us what happened when Justin came to see you. What did you tell him?'

'I'm not a young man, Miss Sinclair. I know I don't have long left, and if they decide to kill me then … so be it, but I won't let my life's work be forgotten. It's too important.'

'What did you tell him, Henry?'

'I told him I was trying to write my memoir but that I was struggling, I'm not a natural writer, I struggled when I tried to make things sound dramatic, entertaining. He offered to ghost write it for me.'

'So, you gave him the information.'

'I gave him all the notes I'd written about my life story; from Cambridge to now. He said it would be a best seller.'

Sinclair could sense there was more. 'What else, Henry?'

'I gave him the file I'd kept – details of the agents we put in.'

Sinclair thought of the USB stick they had found in the safe-deposit box, could that have the information on it? 'What sort of file? Is it on a USB stick?'

'No. I don't get on well with new technology. All of the information is in a brown cardboard folder, held together with a red ribbon.'

They hadn't found it yet. 'Did Justin tell you what he was planning to do with the file?'

Shawford shook his head. 'Just that he would take it to London and keep it safe, until the time was right to use it.'

'How much information is in there, Henry?'

'All of it. All the UK sleeper agents I dealt with: their real names, fake identities and occupations, addresses, the whole shooting match. He said he wouldn't use it until after I was dead.'

'Is there any information on this second generation, Henry?'

'Yes, I kept track of all the members of my network. Their successes, their children, everything.'

McGill let out a long whistle. 'No wonder they killed Wyatt. He could've taken the whole organisation down.'

Sinclair held up the notebook. 'He still could, if we get to the file first.' She looked back at Shawford. 'Henry. Do you remember any of the details in the file?'

'Of course. I remember all of my creations.'

'Do you know the name Vadim?'

A smile appeared on the old man's face. 'Ah, yes. He is my masterpiece. We put two generations of the family, Vadim's father and grandfather, in as sleepers at the start. I created a backstory that went back another century; linked them with the aristocracy. That got them places the other sleepers couldn't go. Now, Vadim is on the verge of real power.'

'What do you mean? Who is he?' Sinclair saw the red dot on Shawford's head a fraction of a second before the window behind her shattered. She dropped to the ground and dragged the old man with her, but it was too late. The bullet had struck his left temple.

McGill dived to the floor and crawled to the window. 'Looks like a sniper from the opposite roof. Stay low and get to the door. Time to leave.'

Sinclair and Porter stayed on their stomachs and dragged themselves to the door. McGill checked the sniper was no longer there then crawled over to join them. 'That guy had a clear shot at you, Ali, and he didn't take it. That must mean he was only after Shawford. He didn't know we were here, or who we are. He must be on his own.'

'He knows we're here now.'

'He's probably calling for backup right now. Okay, Callum. Out the door and down the stairs as quick as you can. No point being quiet now.'

All three of them ran down the stairs to the entrance. McGill took the lead. 'Stay back. I'll check the street.' He opened the solid front door just enough to see out into the street. It was quiet: two joggers and a dog walker on the opposite side; a cyclist passing the door. No sign of a sniper or a backup team. It was as if nothing had happened. He raised his hand to beckon the other two forward, just as a black 4x4 screeched up to the entrance. McGill slammed the door shut and locked it. 'Move. NOW.'

Sinclair and Porter bolted for the staircase as the first silenced rounds splintered the wooden door and it smashed onto the marble floor.

McGill jumped up the first three steps as bullets pinged around his feet. 'Get back up to the apartment. There has to be a fire escape.'

The three of them sprinted up the stairs as the sound of smashing wood came up from the entrance hall. Sinclair kicked open Shawford's front door without even breaking her stride. Porter followed her through as McGill stood at the top of the staircase and fired shots into the stairwell to keep their pursuers' heads down.

Sinclair ran through the apartment and into the bedroom at the back. The steel fire escape had been retro fitted to the back of the old stone building. She pushed up the sash window and looked down the four storeys to the back alley. Two men were rounding the corner and heading for the bottom of the steel steps. Sinclair looked back along the apartment's hallway to where Porter stood, not sure what he should be doing. 'Callum. In here. Now.'

The young man did as he was told – he was terrified. Sinclair pointed out of the window. 'Out on to the fire escape and up to the roof. Don't look back.' She watched as Porter disappeared through the window then she shouted back at McGill, 'Frank. Time to go.'

McGill ran through Shawford's door, into the bedroom, and followed the other two out of the window. He checked below him. The two men were now on the first flight of steel steps, their boots clanging on the metal and making the whole thing vibrate. He fired a shot at them then holstered his pistol and climbed up to the roof.

Sinclair and Porter were just ahead of McGill and were now running across the roof of the adjoining building. At the edge of that roof was a gap of around ten feet s to the next, slightly lower, building. Porter jumped the gap and fell awkwardly but was quickly back up and running again.

Sinclair cleared the gap easily and soon caught up with Porter. She ushered him towards another fire escape at the far end. 'Start climbing down, Callum. I'll wait for Frank and we'll catch you up.'

Porter nodded. He was out of breath and bleeding from the scrapes he had picked up when he fell. 'Okay.'

As Porter started his descent, Sinclair looked back at the other roof. McGill was sprinting for the edge, arms and legs pumping. The first bullet hit him in the left calf but the adrenaline coursing through his blood stream was enough to keep him going. The second round hit his right thigh as he was taking off and threw him off balance. As soon as he was airborne, he knew he wasn't going to make it. The third bullet hit him in the small of the back.

'FRANK.' Sinclair ran back towards McGill, firing shots as she went. She hit one of the men in the centre of his chest and he went down, no longer a threat. The second man took cover behind an air conditioning vent as Sinclair's shots ricocheted off its metal surface.

McGill landed chest first on the building's parapet and slid backwards. He grasped the brickwork and was now hanging with the brick edge under his arms. His strength was dwindling and his vision was blurred, he wasn't going to be hanging there for long.

Sinclair dropped her gun and dived towards the parapet. She grabbed McGill's arms and braced her feet against the bricks. 'Hold on, Frank.' She pulled as hard as she could, but McGill was almost dead weight.

Fighting to stay conscious, and with three gunshot wounds, he couldn't help much. 'Get out of here, Ali. There's nothing you can do.'

'I'm not letting you go, Frank. Come on, work with me here.' She pulled with every ounce of strength she had left. Her muscles burned with the effort. It was starting to work, McGill was moving, inch by inch, but it wasn't happening fast enough.

The man who had hidden behind the air conditioning vent came out of his cover and approached them. He swapped out his magazine and re-cocked his weapon. 'Game over. You lose.' The two men from the 4x4 were now at the top of the first fire escape and were making their way towards them. 'Let go of him and stand up.'

Sinclair looked into McGill's eyes, pleading with him not to give up. McGill smiled at her. 'Let me go, Ali. It's okay.'

'NO.' She looked up at the man who now stood above them. 'If you're going to shoot us then get on with it.'

He levelled his gun and took aim at a point between McGill's shoulder blades.

Porter pulled his trigger first. It was a perfect shot and struck the man between the eyes. Death was instant. No chance to retaliate, just a sickening thud as he hit the concrete four storeys below. Porter fired again, killing one of the other two men and wounding the other. He dropped Sinclair's weapon and grabbed hold of McGill's arm. Together they pulled and heaved until the three of them collapsed, onto the roof, panting for breath.

Sinclair immediately started checking McGill's wounds. 'I

think you've been lucky, Frank.'

'Lucky I'm not a stain on the concrete like our friend down there.'

'You're lucky the wounds aren't worse.'

'I don't know, they don't feel lucky. The one in my thigh spun me round a bit. I think it moved me out the way of the last one.'

Sinclair rolled McGill towards her and checked his back. 'This one's gone in and come straight back out again, left a hole in one of your love handles. The one in your thigh is a flesh wound but there's no exit for your calf. Bullet's still in there. Do you think you can walk? We need to get out of here.'

'Give me a minute.'

Sinclair looked at Porter. He was as white as a sheet. All of this was way outside his comfort zone. 'You okay, Callum?'

'I will be, might need to throw up first, though.'

'Where did you learn to shoot like that?'

'I'm from Texas. Grew up with a gun in my hand. Never had to kill anyone before.'

Sinclair gave him a reassuring smile. 'Well, we both owe you a big one.'

McGill held up his arms. 'Enough of the soppy shit. Help me up.'

Sinclair and Porter grabbed an arm each and lifted McGill to his feet. They draped his arms around their shoulders and McGill hobbled along, hanging between them.

* * *

When they got back to the campervan, Sinclair and Porter

lifted McGill into the back and Sinclair got out the van's first-aid kit. McGill's three wounds were still bleeding, but not as badly as they had been. She treated them with antiseptic, packed them with gauze and taped them up. That was as far as her medical knowledge went.

The van was parked on a quiet side street and was screened from the surrounding properties by trees, but they had to move on. Vadim's men now knew they were here. Sinclair looked at Porter. 'We can't go back to Danny's apartment, we don't know how compromised we are. Did you leave anything there? Anything they could use to find us?'

Porter shook his head. 'No, Frank told me to pack everything in here in case we had to run.'

'Good thinkin', Frank.' She patted McGill on the arm. She could tell he was in pain but trying not to show it. 'You need proper medical treatment and a place to hide.' She popped two painkillers out of a foil strip and handed them to McGill. 'Take these, get some rest.'

McGill half sat up and swallowed the pills as Sinclair poured water into his mouth. 'Thanks, Ali.'

'We need to re-group and figure out what to do next – I don't know what to do, where to go. Any ideas?'

McGill laid back down. 'Old friend of mine … retired out here … the south. Isolated farmhouse near a place called Pau. He'll help us … we can trust him … take all night to get there …'

Sinclair covered McGill with a blanket and brushed some dirt from his face. 'It's okay, Frank. You rest now. I'll look after you.'

Chapter 15

Data scrolled up one of the computer screens in Danny Kinsella's apartment as he tapped at the keyboard. The other screens showed a combination of documents, photographs and live news video. The glow from the screens reflected off Simeon Carter's glasses as he scanned them, trying to follow the information. 'What does it look like, Danny?'

'We've been hacked.'

'Can you tell who by?'

'No. Whoever they are, they're good. This was done by someone with a lot of resources and manpower. Possibly state backed.'

'The Russians? GCHQ?'

'Could be the North Koreans, for all I know.'

Carter took off his glasses and rubbed the bridge of his nose. 'How bad is it?'

'It could've been worse. Most of the information is secure. I keep it on a separate part of the network that isn't connected to the outside world. What they got was mainly protocol info. They tracked some of my messages and calls to the phone we gave to Sinclair. They couldn't see the content of the messages, I encrypted them, but they can see the number of the phone any messages went to.'

Carter's heart sank. 'And they used it to find Ali and Frank.'

Kinsella nodded. 'It's looking that way. The phones we gave them have been switched off, probably destroyed.'

'What makes you think that?'

'Modern phones are never really switched off. They just go into standby. You have to take the battery out or smash the whole thing.'

They hadn't heard anything from Sinclair for more than twenty-four hours. They had no idea where she and McGill were, or if they were still alive. Carter was worried. He had confidence in his team's abilities, but it didn't make not knowing any easier. 'Can you find them at all, Danny?'

'I can't track them if they don't want me to, they're too good for that, but it's almost impossible to completely disappear in the modern world.'

'What do you mean?'

'I can cross-reference news and police reports, check webcams and CCTV, we can find them by the effect they have on the world around them, like ripples in a pond. It won't allow us to follow them but I think we can assume they are still alive.'

'I hope so, Danny, I really do. What have you found so far?'

Kinsella tapped a few keys and pointed to two of the displays. One showed a series of news reports about the incident at Shawford's flat. The other showed a police report that Kinsella had hacked into. 'These reports show a gunfight took place at Henry Shawford's flat. From the police report, it looks like Shawford was shot in the head from the roof a building opposite. They found three more bodies and a lot of blood on the roof. All the dead were male, none matched

91

McGill or Porter's description.'

'It sounds like the sort of chaos they would cause. They got away then?'

'Yeah, but at least one of them is wounded.' Kinsella tapped another key and brought up a blurred CCTV image of a campervan. 'One thing that only we know, is the type of vehicle they are in; Sinclair told us when she sent her last message. If you look closely at this picture, the driver is Porter and the passenger is Sinclair.'

'McGill is the one that's wounded.'

'He could be dead.'

Carter took off his glasses and cleaned them. 'I don't think so. If McGill was dead, Sinclair would have left his body somewhere. We would have picked up a report.'

Carter knew Sinclair would be looking for somewhere to hole up; a place for McGill to heal and time to formulate a plan. All he and Kinsella could do was keep gathering evidence to out Vadim. That had to be their priority.

Kinsella scrolled through the police report. 'There is something that this tells us.'

'What's that?'

'They've stopped trying to make these deaths look like accidents. Shawford was hit by a sniper, there's no hiding that. Whatever they're planning it must be big, and it must be happening soon. They aren't worried about the police investigating the assassination of a retired academic.'

Carter hated not knowing where Sinclair and McGill were. He couldn't protect or support them if he had no idea what was going on. He really needed Kinsella to find something – and fast. 'Keep at it, Danny. We need to know what we're up against.'

Chapter 16

Maison des Fleurs was a typical southern French farmhouse. The main house was two storeys of local stone topped with a red tiled roof. The walls had been whitewashed in the past but, after years of neglect, were now faded and weathered. Flaking pale blue paint clung to the wooden shutters that were mounted to the wall at either side of the four front windows. One of the shutters leaned at an angle, its bottom hinge finally giving in to the rust. The matching pale blue door had black wrought-iron fittings that were speckled with rust but looked like they'd had more care than the shutters. Two empty hanging baskets framed the front entrance and added to the image of abandonment.

To the left, were two slightly smaller buildings, built in the same style as the house, but with no windows, and recently painted. The right-hand side of the farmyard was dominated by a large wooden barn, which looked newer than the rest of the buildings and was well maintained. Two acres of land stretched out, away from the house, and at the other end of the plot was a group of long-derelict greenhouses, the glass in their frames broken and the wood rotten. The whole property had the look of being in the middle of a renovation project.

Sinclair slowed and stopped the van in front of the stone

gateposts at the end of *Maison des Fleurs'* sweeping driveway. 'There's no movement up there, no vehicles.'

Porter peered through the windscreen. 'Are you sure *this* is it?'

Sinclair pointed to the lopsided sign that hung from one of the gateposts. *'Maison des Fleurs*. It's the right place.'

'Do you think it's safe? It couldn't be a trap, could it?'

'I wouldn't be surprised by anything Vadim did, but Frank wouldn't lead us into an ambush.'

'So, what do we do?'

'We'll go up there, put on the lost tourist act, see how it goes.'

'Couldn't that be a bit risky?'

'Yeah, but Frank needs help. It's a risk we're going to take.' Sinclair put the van into gear and swung on to the driveway.

The tyres crunched on the gravel as Sinclair parked the van in front of the house. She looked in the mirror and checked on McGill. He'd been asleep for most of the ten-hour journey. Only waking long enough to drink some water every couple of hours. 'How is he?'

Porter sat next to him and checked his pulse and his breathing. 'He's not too bad, Ali. A bit of a temperature and his pulse is a little fast, but the bleeding has more or less stopped.'

Sinclair smiled. 'He is pretty indestructible. You stay with him for now, Callum, out of sight. I need to check things out.' She pointed at the house. 'We don't know this guy at all.'

Porter nodded. 'Okay. Be careful.'

Sinclair opened her door and stepped out into the early morning sun. She rubbed her eyes, they were tired and felt gritty. She and Porter had driven for two hours at a time while the other one watched McGill. It had been a long night. She shielded her eyes with her hand and squinted in the bright sunlight – she couldn't see anyone. There was no sign of a car and the gravel on the driveway had weeds and moss growing across its surface. Maybe Frank's friend had moved on.

She walked up to the door and knocked. 'Hello?' The door wasn't locked and it creaked open. She probably should have said something in French, but all she knew was: my name is Ali, and, which way to the library? 'Anyone there?'

'You looking for something?'

Sinclair spun to her left. Standing at the corner of the building was a man carrying an old shotgun. He looked to be in his sixties, but it was hard to tell. He was tall and tanned with grey stubble covering his face and head. He didn't look threatening, but Sinclair had to be ready. She tightened her grip on the Glock 19, nestled in the small of her back, and gave the man a wide smile. 'I'm sorry. We were just looking for somewhere to camp. Thought you might let us set up on your land?'

The man shook his head. 'There's no camping here. This is private property.'

Sinclair could tell the guy didn't want any visitors, she didn't even know if he was Frank's friend. She didn't want a shoot-out in broad daylight, so she decided to leave and come back on her own to take the things she needed. 'Okay, thanks. We'll move along, leave you alone.'

'You've got blood on your clothes. Everything okay?'

Sinclair looked at her jeans. She hadn't really noticed the state she was in: too tired, too worried. 'Just a nosebleed.'

'You can't fool me, I used to be a medic. I know major blood loss when I see it.' He edged up to the van and looked through the back window. 'Who's hurt?'

'My friend, Frank. Frank McGill. He said you might …'

'Frank?' The man slid open the van's door and climbed in. He slapped McGill's face and tried to bring him round. 'Frank? Frank?'

McGill came to and tried to focus. 'Holy shit, Gabriel Vance. How're you doin', you old fucker?' He passed out again.

Vance sat McGill up and looked at Porter. 'Help me get him into the house, now.'

They carried McGill into the house and up the stairs, sitting him on a bed in a back room.

Vance issued orders to Sinclair and Porter. 'There are towels in the bathroom, cover the bed then lie him on it. I'll get my medical kit, one of you go down to the kitchen, get a bowl and fill it with hot water.'

Sinclair and Porter did everything Vance told them to, without question. In this situation, he was in charge.

Vance got to work, cutting off McGill's clothes and examining his wounds. It was obvious he had a lot of experience in this kind of thing – Sinclair recognised a battlefield medic when she saw one. She chewed the inside of her lip; her panic replaced by frustration at not being able to do anything. The stress and adrenaline rush of the last few days was catching up with her. She needed to relax, needed to sleep, but she wasn't leaving until she knew Frank was okay.

After two hours, McGill's wounds had been cleaned and dressed. Vance checked the drip he had set up and administered some antibiotics and morphine. 'He's going to be fine, looks like he had a lucky escape. He'll sleep for a few hours, I'll check on him later. Now, we all need a cup of tea and something to eat, and I think you owe me an explanation.'

'Okay, doc. Put the kettle on and I'll follow you down.'

Vance and Porter left the room and went downstairs to the kitchen. Sinclair sat on the edge of the bed and held McGill's hand. 'Don't scare me like that, Frank. I'd be lost without you.' She kissed his forehead. 'I'll speak to you when you wake up.'

The kettle was boiling as Sinclair joined the others in the kitchen. Porter was sitting at the table as Vance made three large mugs of tea. 'It's the only thing I miss about England, a nice, hot mug of builder's tea.' He placed the mugs on the table and took a seat. 'Milk and sugar there if you need it; there's plenty of food in the fridge when you're ready.'

Sinclair stirred her tea and sat down opposite Porter. She took a sip and stared at her mug, trying to decide how much detail to give Vance. She decided to tell him everything. They didn't have many people on their side and she sensed this guy could be a big help. If Frank trusted him, that was good enough for her.

Vance listened in silence as Sinclair told him all about the last year: the events on the island and the subsequent cover up; her being sent back to prison because no one was supposed to know anything; the second prison break and the conspiracy they had uncovered. She didn't miss out anything. When she had finished, she took a drink of her tea and let out a long breath. If someone had told her that story, she wouldn't have believed them.

Vance emptied his mug. 'You sound like you've been through the wringer a little.'

'You could say that. We've had a few close calls.'

Porter nodded. 'I can confirm that.'

'Callum has helped us more than he knows. If it wasn't for him, I wouldn't have got Frank off that roof.'

Vance patted Porter's forearm. 'I'm grateful for that, son. Anything you need, just ask.' He turned back to Sinclair. 'So, this guy, Vadim, wants you dead because you can identify him?'

'Mainly, and because we've wrecked his plans more than once. I think it's starting to become personal, he just doesn't like us very much.'

'But you have no idea who he actually is?'

'No. Only that he must be high up and he has access to intelligence. Whatever we do, his men seem to turn up. They found us in Paris by tracking my phone. He must have security service resources.'

'What about the team in London?'

'If they were on Vadim's side, he would have found us already. The info Vadim has is general. He knows what area we are in, but not our exact location.'

Vance picked up the empty mugs and took them to the sink. 'What's your plan from here?'

'We need to keep Callum safe, and see what's on the USB stick we found. It's too risky to use any mobile phones or the Internet so we'll all have to go old school, keep our heads down.'

'Well, I'm about as old school as they come. I only have a landline: no mobile, no Internet. No one is going to track you here. You'll be safe until Frank's recovered. I can arrange access to a computer, so you can see what's on the USB stick, but we'll do that tomorrow. You need some rest.'

Porter yawned and stretched. 'That's the best idea I've heard in days. I could sleep for a month.'

'Pick any of the rooms upstairs, son. I sleep down here, in the back room.'

'Thank you, Mr Vance. See you both in a few hours.' He left the Kitchen and plodded up the stairs.'

'You should sleep, too, Ali.'

'I'm okay for now. I have trouble sleeping anyway, still can't relax after the prison.'

'I know the feeling. It usually takes me a good measure of whiskey or a bottle of wine before I drop off. You want another tea?'

'I'd love one, thanks'

Vance picked up the kettle and refilled it. Sinclair watched the way he moved. He'd obviously been injured at some point and still walked with a limp. She didn't really want to pry, but she had to be sure she could trust him. 'Frank said you know each other from Baghdad?'

'That's right. I was working in a hospital there. Well, not a real hospital, just somewhere we set up as one. We were mostly treating civilians who'd been caught by bomb blasts. One day we were hit by a bomb ourselves. Went from treating people to needing treatment in less than a second.'

'Where does Frank come into it?'

'He appeared from nowhere, ran into the building and started dragging people out. He got me clear just before the whole place collapsed. I owe him my life.'

Sinclair pointed at Vance's leg. 'Is that where your injuries are from?'

Vance tapped his leg. 'That's right. The ones you can see, and the ones you can't.'

'PTSD?'

'I couldn't work afterwards. That's when I left the army. Came to live here a few years later. I cope better here, it's quiet – no loud noises, no real drama.'

'Until we turned up.'

Vance smiled. 'Don't worry about that, anything for a friend.'

'Are we safe here? I don't want to put you in harm's way. If it's a problem, we'll move on as soon as Frank wakes up.'

'It's pretty tight-knit around here. It took me a while to be accepted into the community, but I help out the locals with some unofficial medical help. They'd rather come to me than travel all the way to the hospital. That makes me one of them. Any trouble and they would close ranks. Protect their own.'

'That's good to know, Gabriel. At least it explains why you have a fully stocked sick bay.'

'It's amazing what you can get on the black market, Ali, and please, call me Gabe, all my friends do. Tell me, where did you meet Frank? You seem close, he obviously means a lot to you.'

'It feels like a lifetime ago since we met, so much has happened since then. We were serving in Afghanistan. Frank and my brother, Connor, were best mates, they'd served together for years. When I arrived, we were like the three musketeers. We thought we were indestructible.'

Chapter 17

*A*fghanistan: ten years earlier.

Colour Sergeant Frank McGill and Sergeant Connor Sinclair exited the briefing and checked their kit. This was the last op before Four-Two Commando, Royal Marines, left Afghanistan and returned home, but they couldn't afford to be complacent. The operation was every bit as dangerous as anything they'd done in the last six months. This tour had been a nightmare. They had lost too many friends and colleagues, including their own troop commander, for it to be remembered as anything other than that.

Lieutenant Ali Sinclair let her eyes adjust to the darker conditions outside before she walked to where the marines were preparing to be picked up by a Chinook. This was the part she hated most: seeing them off, not knowing if they would make it back in one piece.

McGill gave a quick salute. 'Morning, ma'am.'

Sinclair returned the salute. 'Morning, Colours. Carry on.'

McGill continued securing his kit. 'How's the world of intel this morning, ma'am? I hope you guys are right on this one.'

'We've been up all night looking at it. The info's come from a reliable source. Taking this guy out could put the Taliban on the back foot in this region for years. Would be a bit of payback, too.'

'I'm all in favour of a bit of payback. What d'you reckon, Con?'

Connor Sinclair looked up. 'Be nice to get the bastard before we leave, Mac.'

Ali Sinclair stepped closer to her older brother. 'You take care out there, you hear me?' She stepped back. 'You look after him, Colours.'

McGill slapped Conner Sinclair on the back. 'I always do, ma'am. He can't do fuck all without me lookin' after him.'

'I mean it, Frank.'

McGill lowered his voice. Although Ali Sinclair outranked him, she was still his best mate's little sister. 'Don't worry, we'll be fine. We get this op out of the way and head home. You finish your tour and follow us in a month. The three of us'll be on the piss, down Union Street, before you know it.'

'I'm looking forward to it already, Frank.' She grabbed Connor's arm. 'Both of you be careful. I'll see you soon.'

Connor Sinclair nodded. 'Don't worry, sis. Put the kettle on, we'll be back in no time.' He gave her a wink then followed McGill up the ramp and into the Chinook that would carry them to their target.

The Chinook's twin rotors bit into the air as it lifted off the ground. Ali Sinclair watched as it disappeared into the Afghan sky and left her in a swirling dust cloud. She was uneasy about this operation. She wasn't sure if it was because they were all so close to going home, or if, deep down, she was worried about the quality of the intel they had received. She stood for a few minutes, her head tilted to one side, listening to the fading sound of the Chinook. When she could no longer hear it, she turned and walked away.

The Chinook pilot kept the aircraft at a good altitude until the last minute, and then dropped fast into the drop-off point, a mile from the intended target's compound. The pilot didn't slow the rotors as the marines poured out of the back; the Chinook was a big target and needed to be on the deck for as short a time as possible. Once the men had dismounted, the pilot lifted off and got high, fast, out of the reach of any small arms fire from anyone who fancied a pot shot.

The marines confirmed their location and target then set off. Intelligence had briefed them that a high-ranking Taliban Commander, who the Americans had been after for two years, was holed up in the compound they were heading for, and would be for the next two nights. Originally, the US wanted to obliterate the place, but the British Head Shed had decided that confirming the commander was there, and trying to take him alive, was more valuable to them. Besides, if it all went pear-shaped, they could still call in an air strike. They obviously weren't concerned about the possible cost in lives if it went wrong.

The troop took the difficult cross country route, staying away from roads and bridges where improvised explosive devices were more likely to be placed. That made it slow going. Crossing uneven ground in the dark, even with night-vision goggles, was difficult enough, without having to watch out for command wires and booby traps. The troop was led by marines with metal detectors to search for IEDs, but even they didn't pick up everything. Every inch of progress was torture.

As they approached the compound, McGill split them into three sections. His section took up a position in an irrigation ditch to the front, while the other two sections took a side each and worked their way around to the rear.

McGill checked the compound through his binoculars. There was no movement: no lights, no sentries; the whole area was in darkness. 'This place looks deserted, Con. If there was some high-rankin' Terry in there, there'd at least be sentries.' He pushed the button on his radio. 'Anyone else see movement?'

The other sections responded, 'Nothing here, Mac.'

'Okay, Con. Take a scaling ladder and three lads. Check it out.'

Connor Sinclair and three other marines kept low as they approached the nine-foot walls of the compound. They would use the scaling ladder, rather than the obvious door, to prevent them from being channelled into a booby trap.

McGill watched the eerie, green scene through his night vision. The four marines reached the base of the wall and raised the ladder. Connor started to climb, checking left, right and above with every step, while the other marines kept defensive positions around the ladder's base. One rung … two … three; the progress was slow but steady. Sinclair was two feet from the top of the wall when McGill saw movement.

The whole troop felt the blast wave as the front wall of the compound erupted in flame. The noise and the heat hit them, followed by a rainstorm of rubble and dust. They all knew instantly what had happened: they'd been set up. There was no high-ranking commander, the compound was full of Taliban, ready to die for the cause.

McGill watched in horror as multiple gunmen appeared on top of the other walls and opened up. Bullets were pinging around their position. The marines returned fire but were taking casualties. McGill screamed to his radio operator, 'We need CASEVAC and air support, NOW.'

McGill climbed out of the irrigation ditch and crawled over to Sinclair. 'Con, CON?' He checked for a pulse but knew he wouldn't find one. Sinclair's wounds were massive. He had to check the others.

Two of the marines were in the same condition as Sinclair but the other one was breathing. His left leg was missing below the knee and blood poured from the ragged stump where his right arm should have been, but he was still alive. 'Stay with me, mate, we need to get the fuck out of here.' McGill applied tourniquets to the younger man's arm and leg and gave him a shot of morphine. He dragged him out from under the rubble and picked him up.

The rest of McGill's section lay down covering fire while McGill ran back across the open ground carrying the injured marine. He reached the edge of the ditch and dived for cover just as the first missiles from the Apache helicopters struck the compound and lit up the early morning sky.

* * *

Ali Sinclair watched as medics carried the wounded from the Chinook and into the field hospital; she watched as the body bags were brought out and the survivors of the operation trudged down the ramp.

McGill was the last person to leave the helicopter. He was covered in blood, none of it his. His face was pale and streaked with dirt, his eyes vacant. The guilt he felt weighed heavily on him. Did he do anything wrong? Could he have foreseen the ambush? Could he have saved Connor? He looked at Ali

Sinclair and slowly shook his head.

Sinclair held her hand to her mouth. She looked at the body bags, her brother was in one of those. She started to tremble, tears running down her cheeks, she had to see him. She ran to where the casualties lay and looked for the one marked Sinclair.

McGill caught up to her. 'Don't, Ali.'

'I have to see him.'

'No, you don't. You don't want to remember him like that.'

Sinclair ignored him, searching the names.

McGill grabbed her arm. 'Ali. Don't.'

Sinclair pulled her arm away but McGill picked her up and carried her away from the Chinook. She kicked and struggled until McGill put her down. She spun around and hit McGill in the chest, pounding her fist against his body armour. 'You said you'd look after him. You said it would be okay.'

McGill wrapped his arms around her and pulled her towards him. She buried her face in his chest and began to scream. Her knees started to give way as the unbearable grief hit her. McGill held on to her, supporting her, as he watched the body bags being loaded into an ambulance. He gritted his teeth and blinked, holding Sinclair even tighter, as his own tears made tracks through the grime on his face and dripped onto her shoulder.

* * *

Sinclair had checked everywhere for McGill, but no one had seen him for a couple of hours. She'd checked his bunk space, the galley, and all around the perimeter. Now, she was worried. She felt guilty about shouting at him, he was suffering as much as she was. The only place left to look was a disused US Army B-Hut on the far side of the compound.

The American barracks hut had been damaged during an attack a couple of months earlier and hadn't yet been repaired. The Americans had reduced their numbers and didn't need the extra space, so it didn't get used for anything.

She pushed open the door and stepped in. 'Frank, you in here?' There was no reply. She let the door swing closed behind her. 'Frank?'

McGill was sitting on a desk at one end of the hut, his head bowed; in his right hand was a nine-millimetre Sig Saur.

Sinclair took a few steps towards him and spoke calmly, 'What are you doing, Frank?'

McGill didn't respond.

Sinclair took another step. This time she spoke like a drill instructor. 'COLOUR SERGEANT.'

McGill's head snapped up. His eyes were red and bloodshot and his face was still streaked with grime. He was wearing the same blood-stained combats he'd worn during the op. 'I should have gone. I should have gone to check the compound.'

Sinclair continued edging towards him, her eye on the gun. 'It wasn't your fault, Frank. Connor was doing his job, you both were.'

'I told you I'd look after him. I didn't.'

'I didn't mean what I said, I was in shock. I don't blame you.'

McGill raised the Sig Saur and rested the barrel under his chin.

Sinclair held out her hand. 'NO.' She had to think fast. 'Give me the weapon. THAT'S AN ORDER, COLOUR SERGEANT.'

McGill slumped and lowered his sidearm. Sinclair reached out and took it from him. She made it safe and tucked it into her waistband. 'What were you thinking, Frank?'

McGill rubbed his face and wiped his eyes. 'I can't do this any more, Ali. Con was like my brother. I can't live like this. I can't watch as the people I care about die in front of me.'

Sinclair grabbed the front of his jacket. 'Snap out of it, you selfish bastard. What about me? I'm one of the people who sent you both in there. How do you think I feel? Connor *was* my brother. After our dad died, he was the only family I had left. If you go, how do I get through this alone?'

McGill looked into her eyes. He had always promised Connor that, if anything happened, he would look after Ali. 'I'm sorry, my head's not right. I don't want to leave you on your own. That's not what Con would've wanted me to do. With him gone, you're all I have.'

'We're family now, Frank. We have to look after each other.'

McGill put his hands on Sinclair's shoulders. 'I promise you, no matter what, whenever you need me, I'll be there.'

Sinclair wrapped her arms around his neck and kissed his cheek. 'The same goes for me, Frank. No matter what.'

Chapter 18

It was just after dawn when McGill woke up and he felt like shit. The net curtains were blowing in the light breeze and the morning sun glinted off the fluid in his IV bag. He could only remember sketchy details of the last couple of days. The last clear memory he had, was Ali and Callum getting him off the roof and into the van. After that, it was a blur of flashing lights as they'd driven through the night, his old friend talking to him as his wounds were cleaned, and Callum sitting next to the bed, opening up to him about everything. He made a mental note to have a long talk with the young man, to thank him. Most of all, McGill remembered Ali sitting on the edge of the bed, holding his hand, willing him to be okay.

Sinclair was asleep in the chair on the other side of the room. She hadn't made it to her own bed, preferring to stay in McGill's room. Even asleep she looked worn out. The last few weeks had taken their toll on them all. They needed to rest, and formulate a plan to figure out how deep in the shit they were. First of all, he needed to get to a toilet – his bladder was bursting. 'Ali?'

Sinclair shifted in her seat, not wanting to wake up.

'Ali?'

Sinclair's eyes flickered open. Her neck and back were stiff and her head ached, but she was happy to see McGill fully awake. She sat up and stretched out the kinks. 'Morning, Frank. How do you feel?'

'A lot better than I did. Really need a piss, though.'

'Stay where you are, I'll be back in a minute.'

Sinclair left the room as McGill forced himself into a sitting position. He slid his legs off the edge of the bed, screwing his eyes shut at the sharp pain in his back and thigh. His calf muscle ached and it hurt to move his foot, walking wasn't going to be an option.

Sinclair reappeared, pushing a wheelchair. 'If we can get you into this, I'll push you round to the loo.'

With Sinclair's help, McGill managed to stand up. The pain wasn't as bad once he was on his feet, and he could probably have shuffled along the corridor, but he didn't want to risk ripping out his stitches. He sat in the wheelchair and Sinclair transferred the IV drip to a pole that was attached to the back.

Sinclair pushed McGill along the corridor to the bathroom and helped him stand up again. 'It's okay, Ali. I can manage the rest.'

'I'll close the door behind me, give you some privacy. Didn't realise you had a nervous bladder, though.'

'Get out before I piss myself.'

Sinclair laughed as she closed the door. McGill was fine. He'd be back to his old self in no time.

Vance came up the stairs and along the corridor. 'Morning, Ali. How's our wounded soldier?'

'He seems fine. Thanks for taking care of him, Gabe.'

'It's nothing. I'll give him a check-up and we'll see about getting him outside for some fresh air. How are you?'

'Bit of a headache and a stiff neck, nothing serious.'

'I'll give you something for that, but you need to relax, get some real sleep in a bed.'

'I promise I will, later. Now, how about I put the kettle on and you check on Frank?'

* * *

The smell of fresh coffee filled the kitchen and drifted up the stairs. Porter was busy making a large pan of scrambled eggs while Sinclair made slice after slice of toast and filled up the rack on the table. A small television was on in the background, which Sinclair looked at occasionally. She couldn't understand what was being said, but would have picked up if they were talking about them or what had happened in Paris.

Vance carried the wheelchair downstairs then helped McGill shuffle down, step by step. He pushed McGill into the kitchen and parked him next to the others.

Sinclair put down four coffees. 'Dig in, everyone.'

Porter served up the scrambled eggs. 'My speciality.'

Sinclair was already buttering some toast. 'Lookin' forward to this, I'm bloody famished.'

McGill grabbed his coffee. 'Me too.'

'Take it easy, Frank. You might not be able to keep much down.'

'Don't worry about me: iron-clad stomach. My mum always said so. Any mention of us on the news?' He pointed to the television with his fork.

Sinclair shook her head. 'I haven't seen any pictures that looked familiar. Maybe they're trying to cover it up.'

Porter looked at the screen. 'They did mention the flat earlier, but it wasn't the main story. There was definitely no mention of us or any other suspects.'

Vance walked towards the TV and reached to switch it off. 'That's enough of that for now. We'll check again later.'

'NO, WAIT.' Sinclair had jumped up out of her seat and was pointing at the screen. 'What are they saying? What is that story about?'

Vance turned up the sound. 'It's just some shit about a cabinet reshuffle back in London. Usual, boring stuff.'

'What are they saying, Callum?'

'Gabe is right, a cabinet reshuffle. Some junior minister at the Home Office has been promoted to the main job. He's the new Home Secretary. He's a bit of a rising star, apparently.'

McGill put down his mug and wheeled himself to where Sinclair was standing. 'What is it, Ali? What's wrong?'

Sinclair pointed at the smiling face of the politician in the news report. 'That's him. That's Vadim.'

Chapter 19

'We've got to let Simeon know. He and Danny could end up walking into a trap, or worse still, lead us into one.' Sinclair was pacing up and down in McGill's room.

McGill was back on the bed. 'Are you sure it's him?'

'I'll never forget his smug face. If I hadn't been in prison for so long I might have spotted him earlier. We could've avoided some of this shit.'

Vance and Porter were in the kitchen, they knew this was something McGill and Sinclair had to talk about.

'It's not your fault, Ali. What we need to do now is get back to London and retrieve Justin's file from the safe-deposit box. The evidence we need must be in there.'

'Vadim's the Home Secretary, for fuck's sake. He's got access to resources we can't match. We'll have every security and law enforcement agency in Britain looking for us.'

'It's not that easy for him. MI5 and GCHQ aren't his private army. The police won't come after us without reason. All he can do is push them to look for you as an escaped convict. He can't just launch a mission to take us out.'

'But look what he's managed to do so far. He must be using some of the organisations.'

'Okay, he's got influence, and he can use that to put people under pressure and get what he wants, but only up to a point. Getting the security services to kill us will take more than influence.'

'We need to see what's on that USB stick and get a message to Simeon without being tracked.'

There was a knock at the door and Vance peered into the room. 'Okay to come in?'

McGill waved him in. 'Of course, Gabe.'

Vance opened the door fully and stepped in. He was carrying a laptop, which he plugged into a socket by the bed. 'I've had this for a few months now. Keep meaning to write my memoirs but never got around to it. Anyway, it's not brand new but it works, and it's not connected to the Internet.' He placed it on the bed and powered it up. 'There's no password. Nothing worth stealing.'

'Thanks, Gabe. This will really help. Ali, have you got the USB stick?'

Sinclair passed the stick to Vance. He plugged it into the laptop and stepped away. 'I'll leave you to it. You can tell me later, if you want to, that is.' He left the room and closed the door behind him.

Sinclair dragged the chair to the bed and sat down. 'Right, let's see what's on this thing. Hopefully, we'll get some answers.' She clicked on the folder icon, which revealed a single video file. 'You think we should look at this without Callum?'

'There might be something on there that he won't want to see. We can let him watch it once we've checked it out.'

'Okay. Here goes.' Sinclair clicked the video file and sat back.

114

When the video started, it showed Wyatt, facing the camera. 'Hi, Callum. I wish I could be with you, but if you're watching this it means something bad has happened. If you're watching this then I'm probably dead. I just hope you're okay, and I want you to know that I love you and I always will.'

Sinclair and McGill looked at each other, feeling guilty at their intrusion on such a private moment.

Wyatt paused for a few seconds, clearly struck by the implications of what he had said. 'I want you to be safe, so I'm hiding all of this evidence,' he held up a stuffed, brown cardboard folder, 'in a place you know well. Think back to where we first met and you'll know what I mean. I've got one last piece of the jigsaw to find. This organisation is planning something big but I don't know what it is. I've got a lead on where I can find out, so I'm heading back to Geneva. It's risky, so, if anything happens, I need you to do something for me: get to the folder, you're the only one who'll find it. You need to get it to the authorities. Don't worry about my notebook, I put that together to help you get this far, it's the folder you need to bring down the conspiracy. I hope you have someone with you and you aren't alone.' He paused again and looked down, away from the camera, tears dripping from his chin. 'Stay safe and have a good life. I love you, Callum. Goodbye.' He reached out towards the camera and the video ended.

Sinclair closed the laptop. 'That's gonna be hard for Callum to watch.'

McGill nodded. 'I feel for him, but we need to know where Wyatt has put the folder.'

'I'll go and get him, we can watch it together.'

* * *

Watching the video had been uncomfortable for Sinclair and McGill but they couldn't imagine what Porter had gone through. When it was over, they left him alone and he sat in his room for the rest of the morning. When he walked into the kitchen, his eyes were red and bloodshot, he looked terrible. 'I smelled the coffee.'

Sinclair sat next to Porter and held his hand. 'Are you sure you're up to talking about this, Callum?'

Porter wiped his eyes. 'Yes. It's what Justin would have wanted.'

'It won't take long, we just need to know what Justin meant when he spoke about where you met and where you think he's left the folder.'

'Well, I've been thinking, and I can't believe it's this easy.'

'What do you mean?'

'When I first met Justin, I was working in a private bank in London.' He pulled out the remaining key that hung round his neck. 'This is the type of key they used for their deposit boxes. It can't be that simple, can it?'

Sinclair shrugged. 'It only seems easy because you know the answer. That's why Justin left you the clue.'

'It must be that then. I need to get to the bank and see what's in that box. I'll need the passport from the other box to get access to it.'

Sinclair looked at Vance. 'We need to get to London. As soon as possible.'

Vance pointed at McGill. 'You won't be going anywhere until Frank recovers. It's going to take a little while before he's fit to travel, never mind any action you find yourselves in.'

McGill tried to stand. 'I'm okay, let's go.'

116

Sinclair grabbed his arm and pulled him back into the wheelchair. 'Sit back down, Frank. Gabe's right, you aren't going anywhere just yet.'

McGill winced. The effort of standing had sent a sharp pain up his thigh and across his back. 'Shit.'

Sinclair patted his arm. 'Okay, Gabe, we'll stay for a short while, but how do we get to London when we're ready? We can't just jump on a plane or a ferry.'

'I'll start to make some arrangements, it shouldn't be a problem getting you into the country.'

'What's your plan?'

Vance walked across the kitchen; he leaned with both hands against the edge of the sink and looked out of the window. 'I haven't always stayed strictly to the letter of the law.' After a pause, he looked at Sinclair and McGill. 'Before I came to live here, I did some work for a guy in London who didn't want any police involvement when his employees got themselves shot or stabbed.'

Sinclair looked at McGill then back at Vance. 'You can't be serious? You want us to trust some gangster to organise our travel?'

Vance smiled. 'Let's face it, none of the three of us are squeaky clean, we've all broken the law at some point.'

Sinclair shook her head. 'Breaking the law because you have to is a long way from making a living out of it. What's this guy into, anyway? Drugs, prostitution?'

'Not that I'm aware, Ali. He's what some people might refer to as an old-fashioned gangster: protection, gambling, smuggling.'

Sinclair let out a short laugh. 'Oh, great, he sounds lovely.'

'Look, Ali, sooner or later you have to trust someone, and

117

Harry Nash isn't going to turn you in. He can help.'

Sinclair fidgeted with her mug, staring at the table. After a pause, she looked up at McGill. 'What do you think, Frank?'

McGill knew Sinclair well and knew she had strong principles. Breaking the law wasn't easy for her, she was the archetypal law-abiding citizen. It was only the events of the last few years that had conspired against her and led to their current situation.

McGill, on the other hand, was a different kind of animal. His childhood had been rough. An alcoholic mother and abusive father were nothing unusual in his peer group. For a lot of them, crime was the only career they could get into. As a teenager, he'd been sent to borstal for attacking a teacher, that was where the Royal Marines had recruited him, that was his way out. For him, the marines gave him the structure and discipline he'd needed, while also giving him an outlet for some of his more violent tendencies. Some of his friends weren't as lucky and ended up exactly like Nash.

When McGill's wife became collateral damage in a war between drug dealers, he'd stepped back into that world; it fitted him like an old suit, he was comfortable. Sinclair was the only reason he wasn't still in it.

McGill had no qualms about using gangsters to get what he and Sinclair needed. If Nash double-crossed them, McGill would deal with it. He was as bad as anyone Nash had working for him.

McGill leaned over and put his hand on Sinclair's. 'You know I've had dealings with these people in the past. If anyone has a reason not to trust these fuckers, it's me, but we need to get back to London and we need someone who isn't connected to the authorities.'

Vance nodded. 'You don't have many other options. Besides, Harry Nash may not be a nice man, but he owes me, and he'll honour that.' He gestured around the room. 'It was his money that paid for this place.'

Sinclair shook her head and pursed her lips. She still wasn't happy but could see the logic behind using Nash. 'I won't pretend I'm happy about this, but, I suppose you're right, we can't just rock up to the ferry like tourists. First, we contact Simeon. If he can find a better way to get us back in, we use it. Agreed?'

McGill put his coffee mug down. 'Okay, Ali, but if we can't get hold of Simeon, then I trust Gabe. If he says this gangster will get us in, that's got to be our best option.'

Vance drummed his fingers. 'Okay, we're agreed. First things first, you have to recover, Frank.'

McGill sat forward and leaned on the edge of the table. 'I'll be fit before you know it.' As he spoke, a muscle spasm snatched his breath from his lungs and he collapsed back into the wheelchair, wincing as pain shot up his back.

Vance checked the stitches in McGill's back. 'See. I told you, you're not ready. Give it a couple of weeks. There's no big rush. If you write down the message you want delivered to London, I'll sort it out. You lot need to rest.'

Sinclair patted McGill's knee. 'He's right, Frank. You just get better so we can get on with it.'

McGill gave Sinclair a fake salute. 'Yes, ma'am. I'll do my best.'

Chapter 20

The blue moped's engine whined and spluttered as it accelerated through London's rush-hour traffic. Car horns blared as it swerved in and out of the queueing cars, the pillion passenger holding on and leaning in to the turns. As the traffic lights switched to red, the moped mounted the kerb and sped along the footpath, scattering pedestrians as they jumped out of its path.

Simeon Carter was standing at the edge of the pavement, waiting to cross the road, as the moped approached. He considered diving out of the way but he was too old for that shit. He stood a better chance if he held his ground. The moped swerved around a young mother with a pram and headed straight for Carter; at the last second it braked and pulled up next to the crossing. As the pillion passenger shoved his hand inside his jacket, Carter tensed up. This was it, this was how he would meet his end. Before he could react, the passenger removed his hand from his jacket and held out an envelope. Carter hesitated before taking it. The passenger nodded to Carter, and the moped's rider sped off, leaving pedestrians coughing in a cloud of blue exhaust fumes as it accelerated and dropped back onto the road. It turned down a side street and was gone, followed by blaring car horns and a stream of obscenities from onlookers.

Carter watched the moped disappear then looked down at the envelope he had been given. It didn't look suspicious, just a normal white envelope. It was crumpled from where the passenger had been clinging on to it, but it wasn't bulky and it had no writing on it. He turned it over and opened the flap. Inside was a single sheet of folded paper, printed out from a computer, plain and anonymous.

He fished about in his jacket and found his reading glasses. He'd been meaning to get bifocals for years but never got around to it. He held up the note and read the message. 'This can't be …' He put the note back in the envelope and set off for Kinsella's flat.

* * *

Danny Kinsella was, as usual, sitting in front of his bank of computer screens, his glasses reflecting the glow that lit up the room. He was watching news reports and running various bits of data through scripts, looking for patterns and connections between events. When Carter walked through the door, Kinsella jumped up, almost knocking over his coffee, and switched on the lights. 'Simeon, I've found something. Something I think is really big.'

Carter held up the note he had received. 'Looks like you're not the only one, Danny. I've just been handed some info that raises the stakes massively. Tell me what you've got first.'

Kinsella pointed at one of his screens. 'I've been running all the data from the notebook through a script, and it doesn't really give us more information until you cross-reference it with other events, police reports and travel data.'

'What does that show us?'

Kinsella sat back down and tapped at his keyboard. Names and dates flashed up on the screens. 'At the time of each of the killings in the book, I can see the same group of people travelling alone to each location. Time after time: they arrive in a country, one of the names in the book dies, and then they leave. They are using multiple fake identities but it's the same group of names, over and over again.'

Carter sat down in front of the screens. 'If they're not connected, that would be one hell of a coincidence.'

'Exactly. What are these people up to if they aren't involved? Why the fake IDs? The whole thing stinks.'

'You're sure about all of this? I mean, can we link these identities to the killings?'

Kinsella nodded. 'I would say so. Sometimes they use one identity to enter the country and a different one to leave; I think, they pick up the new passport while they are in the country, after they've carried out the assassination. I've then tracked that second ID to another killing sometime later. It would take a lot of money to have fakes this good waiting for them. Money, or government involvement – or both.'

Carter slumped back in his chair. 'We know Vadim is high up here, but this points to other members of this conspiracy in influential government positions all around the globe. This is much bigger than we feared.'

Kinsella nodded. 'I reckon we've got five assassins travelling the world, carrying out the killings, supported by a group who can supply fake passports at the drop of a hat. Five assassins backed up by Vadim's foot soldiers.'

Carter was always amazed by Kinsella's ability to track things down and his talent for finding patterns and piecing things together. 'Do you have pictures? Can we identify any of them?'

Kinsella pressed another key and a series of passport photos appeared. They all had the classic look of the official identity photo. The subjects looked straight ahead, blank faces and lifeless eyes staring down the lens. Four men and one woman posed for the camera, different hairstyles and colours, some with facial hair and some without, but, undoubtedly, the same group of five people. 'These are the pictures from the fake passports. Obviously they can't change their appearance too much in the short time they spend in any particular country.'

'Do you know where they are now? Who's next on the kill list?'

Kinsella picked up a printout. 'That's the thing, Simeon, three of them have gathered in London. That's the first time I can find more than two of them in one place at the same time. The other two seem to be in Geneva. None of the targets in the notebook are in London or Geneva. I think they've abandoned the list.'

Carter could tell Kinsella was worried by what he'd found. 'Why would they do that? This thing all started in Geneva, what are they after there? Is that the team chasing Sinclair and McGill?'

Kinsella took off his glasses. 'I don't think so. These two,' Kinsella pointed at two of the passport photos, 'are still there.' He clicked on a newsfeed on a screen that showed a hotel preparing for a large group of visitors. 'There's a UN security summit due to be held shortly at this hotel, just outside Geneva. I think this is the big event they've been leading up to. They've dropped all their other plans to concentrate on this. An attack at the summit could kill several very big birds with one stone.'

Carter picked up the note he'd been handed earlier and read the text again. He hoped he was wrong, but he had a sinking feeling in his stomach. 'This has all the hallmarks of a coup.'

'What do you mean, Simeon?'

Carter let out a deep sigh. 'I've been in this game a long time. I've been involved in operations like this before.'

Kinsella had no experience in the world of espionage outside of reading about it in James Bond novels. 'I don't understand what you mean.'

'If you want to take control of a country, there are only a few ways you can do it. You can invade, but then you end up in a mess, like Iraq. You can convince the country's own military to rise up and overthrow the government, but then you end up with Cuba or Zimbabwe.'

Kinsella was fascinated that Carter had been involved in this kind of thing. He'd always taken the stories he'd heard with a pinch of salt. 'And what's the other way?'

The more Carter explained, the more he believed that this was Vadim's plan. 'You get rid of the government you don't want, covertly, and put your own puppets in at the top.'

'How do you get rid of a government "covertly"?'

Carter paused and looked straight at Kinsella. 'You discredit them with fake allegations of corruption or some other criminality. That way, their own people take them down. Or …'

Kinsella's heart was pounding. 'Or, what, Simeon?'

'Or you kill them and blame someone else. That way, everyone gets behind the new government.'

'Holy shit. They couldn't be planning that, could they?'

Carter took off his glasses and rubbed his eyes. 'A moped

nearly ran me down in the street today, and the passenger shoved this into my hand.' He held up the piece of paper. 'It looks like it's come from Sinclair and McGill, but god knows how they got it here.'

Kinsella was glad to hear they were still alive. 'They are both very resourceful. Are they alright? Where are they?'

'All it says is that they were compromised and tracked down in Paris. McGill has been wounded but is recovering. They have holed up somewhere safe and ditched all electronic devices.'

Kinsella nodded. 'That must have been the incident the French were talking about. I'm not surprised they've ditched the electronics, it's the best option. Whoever is after them has some serious resources.'

'You can say that again. Sinclair has finally managed to identify Vadim. You're not going to believe this, Danny.'

Kinsella took the note from Carter. 'Believe what?'

'Ali says Vadim is the Honourable Marcus Enfield, our new Home Secretary.'

The only noise in the flat was the sound of the fans inside the computers. The two men stared at each other in silence, incredulous. Kinsella was the first to speak. 'This is massive, Simeon. They're planning to bring down the government and take control. We have to tell someone.'

'We can tell Lancaster, but what do MI6 do without any evidence? Don't forget, McGill and Sinclair are off the books, we aren't working officially either.'

Kinsella turned the note around and held the text up to Carter. 'We need to offload the evidence. This is too big to sit on. We know too much now, Vadim will be after us as well. We have to assume he knows everything. We have to get out and go into hiding, try and help the others.'

Carter knew this could be the end for all of them. If Vadim pulled this off, he would be too powerful to stop. Vadim may have stopped everything else to concentrate on the coup, but he would still find time to kill them. 'Okay, give me copies of everything we've got and destroy any mention of Sinclair and McGill. We've got to give them the best chance we can if things go wrong here. I'll set up a meeting with Edward.'

Chapter 21

Hyde Park was full of tourists soaking up the sights and sounds of London while enjoying the fine weather. Kids ran around on the grass shrieking and giggling as office workers, glad to be away from their desks, sat and ate a sandwich or read a book. No one looked like they were taking notice of what was going on around them; no one obviously watching or carrying out surveillance. Everything looked perfectly normal. That was good, Carter wanted his meeting with Lancaster to be as public as possible. He didn't want to be suddenly bundled into the back of a waiting van, and disappear to some foreign black ops site with the rest of the terrorists. If Vadim could pull that off, Carter would never see the light of day again.

Edward Lancaster was standing just off the footpath next to The Serpentine, watching the ducks floating past. His suit jacket was folded and on the floor at his feet. Partly because of the temperature, but also because Carter had asked for it in his message. It wasn't that he didn't trust Lancaster, but you could never be too careful. Carter had to be sure Lancaster wasn't armed or wearing a wire.

When Carter approached, Lancaster looked around and behind him – he was checking for followers or eavesdroppers;

Lancaster wanted to ensure his own safety just as much as Carter did. These were dangerous times. 'Good to see you again, Simeon.' He held out his arms to the side. 'Is all this really called for? You know you can trust me.'

Carter put down his briefcase and took off his own jacket, laying it on the floor next to Lancaster's. 'I know I can, Edward, but it's really for both of our sakes. You never know what either of us could be threatened with to make us turn on each other.'

'It hasn't been like this since the Cold War, Simeon. You sounded serious on the phone.'

'It is serious, Edward. Powerful people want us taken down before we can do the same to them. We have no way of knowing who is on our side and who is part of the conspiracy. I've already destroyed my phone, so don't try and contact me on it.'

'That's a bit drastic, isn't it? It was an anonymous phone anyway.'

'With the information we've found out, you don't want any link between us, believe me. I have a feeling I'm going to be running for a while.'

Lancaster had another check around them and lowered his voice even though they were alone. 'What is it, Simeon?'

Carter told him everything: the notebook; the conspiracy; the assassinations and, worst of all, the new Home Secretary and the UN summit. 'I know it sounds far-fetched, Edward, but Danny has been working night and day on all of this.' He handed Lancaster a large buff envelope containing the sheets Danny had printed out. 'This is everything we have. It doesn't have any of our names in it, in case it falls into the wrong hands. I need you to keep it safe, we may need it.'

Lancaster folded the envelope in half and slipped it inside his jacket. 'How sure are you, Simeon? This could finish us all off.'

'I'd bet my life on it. In fact, I might need to.'

Lancaster looked around at everyone enjoying the park, blissfully unaware of any impending chaos that might befall them. 'Sinclair's sure about the Home Secretary?'

'She's in no doubt. Enfield was on the island with Bazarov.'

Lancaster put his hands in his pockets and stared at his feet. 'What do we do, Simeon? Is this evidence in the envelope enough for us to expose the conspiracy?'

'Not on its own. A lot of it is circumstantial. Enfield could argue it's all fake news, and the conspiracy is against him.'

'The slippery bastard would probably get away with it, too. End up with all of us in prison instead.'

Carter nodded. 'We need more, and we need Sinclair. I'm hoping she can get to the other folder they've mentioned and get here before it's too late.'

'Where's the other folder?'

'We don't know and Sinclair won't tell us. We just have to trust her.'

Lancaster lit a cigarette and took a deep draw on it, blowing out a cloud of smoke. 'I've been meaning to give these things up, not sure I'll manage it just yet. At least this explains the review.'

Carter looked behind him as a couple walked by on the footpath. He waited for them to be out of earshot before he continued. 'Review of what?'

'The new Home Secretary has asked to be briefed on all security operations, domestic and foreign. Obviously, he has started with MI5, they report to him, but I can see us being next.'

'What's he looking for?'

'He must be looking for Sinclair, trying to find out if any of us have had contact with her.'

Carter smiled. 'That's a bit ironic, isn't it? The mole trying to find out if he has a mole in his organisation.'

Lancaster picked up his jacket and the envelope. 'We have to stay away from each other until this is finished. It would be dangerous to assume that Marcus Enfield is the only member of this conspiracy to make it to a senior position within the establishment.'

'Do you think you can trust your boss?'

Lancaster paused. 'I've never been that sure of him, even before this lot started.'

'Has he done anything to make you suspicious?'

Lancaster shook his head. 'Nothing in particular, maybe I just don't like men like him.'

'Men like him?'

Lancaster stubbed out his cigarette. 'You know the type: public school, posh family, never been in the field. He only got the job because Daddy had friends in the service. He's a politician, not one of us.'

'We'll have to be careful, Edward. Sinclair and McGill are unofficial, but these things have a habit of leaking out. Someone, somewhere, knows you are working with an unofficial asset.'

Lancaster held up the envelope. 'I'll look after this, Simeon, and I'll pass on our security concerns to the Prime Minister and the UN. It'll have to go through my boss, unfortunately, but I can't just bypass him. In any case, Vadim won't come after me unless he has something concrete to go on.'

Carter picked up his jacket and briefcase. 'Let's just hope we're in time to stop whatever they've got planned in Geneva. Take care, Edward.'

'And you, Simeon. Watch your back.'

The two men parted and walked in opposite directions back through the park. Carter couldn't help feeling that the world would be a very different place the next time they met.

Chapter 22

Lancaster knocked on the door of the Chief of the Secret Intelligence Service. Known as 'C' to his subordinates, Kelvin Hadley had been the head of MI6 for three years, but in that time he hadn't managed to gain the widespread trust or respect of the service. There were too many stories from his past of how he'd treated people, throwing his own officers to the wolves so he could climb the ladder. The service didn't forgive behaviour like that.

Lancaster wasn't interested in the gossip and rumours about Hadley, he just didn't like the man. He always tried to avoid going to see his boss, but he had to push his personal feelings to one side and swallow his pride. Lancaster was a professional and had to escalate Carter's concerns over Geneva. He put his hand on the door handle and waited.

Hadley could see Lancaster through the glass of the door; he didn't like him. He didn't like the way everyone talked about him being a hero in the field during the Cold War. No one said it to his face, but he could tell they were suggesting that Lancaster should be head of the service, not a man like Hadley: a man with no front-line experience. It was jealousy, he knew he was destined for greater things. Hadley enjoyed making Lancaster wait, it made his otherwise mundane day a little more bearable. 'Come in.'

Lancaster walked into the office and closed the door behind him. 'Good afternoon, sir.' Lancaster spoke with undisguised contempt. 'Need to brief you on a possible security concern.'

'Have a seat, Lancaster.'

Lancaster sat down and looked around the office. The normally plain interior was decorated with shelves that were covered in mementos and awards, the man was displaying his ego for all to see. Anyone taking a closer look would realise all the awards had been given because of who Kelvin Hadley was, not for something he had done. Men and women who worked for him had risked, and in some cases lost, their lives in operations, while this prick soaked up the glory.

'What is it, Lancaster? I haven't got all day.'

Lancaster considered talking to the Prime Minister himself, but that wasn't protocol. 'We've had a tip-off about a possible threat to the UN security summit in Geneva. We believe it's a valid threat.'

Hadley looked up from the document he was reading. 'And where did this tip-off come from?'

'I'd rather not say at this time, sir.'

Hadley got up and paced around to Lancaster's side of the desk. 'You'd rather not say? Well, Edward, I'm afraid you'll have to say if you expect me to escalate this any higher.'

Lancaster couldn't drop Carter in it. He'd rather just walk out. 'It came from a trusted source; an operative I used to work with stumbled on the information.'

Hadley stood behind Lancaster. 'Would that be Simeon Carter by any chance? I know you've met with him a few times.'

Lancaster's heart skipped a beat. Had Hadley been following him? How much did he know already? 'Simeon and I are old friends. We meet up for coffee, occasionally.'

'Are you sure that's all it is, *Edward*?' Hadley put the emphasis on his name. 'Do you know anything about an ex-operative called Sinclair?'

Lancaster had to avoid giving away any more than he had to. 'I've heard the name, sir. There's a rumour in the office that she escaped from prison, again.'

'We've been asked to keep an eye out for her, by Mexico. She's not your source, is she?'

Lancaster shook his head. 'The source is unimportant. We need to pass on the possibility of an attack of some sort in Geneva. We have to tell the PM and the Americans.'

Hadley opened the office door. 'That will be my job, not yours. I'll talk to the PM at our regular meeting, tell him what I've found. I'll brief the Home Secretary, too.'

Lancaster didn't care about Hadley taking the credit, but now the Home Secretary would know they had found something; Vadim would know. He had to start putting things into place to protect himself and those around him who he knew he could trust. He got up and walked out without saying a word.

Hadley closed the door behind him.

* * *

The street lights were just beginning to come on when Carter got back to Kinsella's flat. He'd spent the time since his meeting with Lancaster putting some things in place in case he and Danny had to run: sending messages to old contacts to arrange travel and accommodation. Danny already had money in foreign bank accounts so that wouldn't be an issue.

He stepped into the lift and pressed the button for the top floor. He had been thinking about everything they had found out that day. He couldn't get rid of the voice that kept telling him something wasn't right. Every mole Carter had dealt with during the Cold War had been relatively low-level, hiding in the shadows. They had never had a mole who had reached the upper echelons of government before; a mole with such a high profile. Any security operative worth their salt would know to stay hidden. Call it gut instinct, but something didn't add up.

When the lift doors opened, Carter stepped out and turned right, heading for Kinsella's flat. He wasn't really paying attention to what he was doing, too many other things on his mind. When he pulled out the key it caught on the door handle and he dropped it. 'Bugger.' Carter reached out to steady himself and bent over to retrieve the key. As he leaned his weight against the door, it swung open.

The door was broken, the lock smashed. Inside, Danny's chair was lying on its side, his computer screens were dark. A cup of coffee had been spilled and papers piled up on the desk. Someone had searched the room thoroughly but hadn't finished.

'Danny? Danny are you okay?'

Two black-clad firearms officers appeared from the kitchen, shouting orders. 'On your knees. ON YOUR KNEES.'

Carter knew what was coming next. He dropped to the ground, arms in the air. More police appeared from the other rooms in the flat and up the corridor behind him. In a blur, he was down on the floor and handcuffed. He looked to his left, Kinsella was being brought out of the kitchen, flanked by two officers. Carter didn't want him to panic. 'It's okay, Danny. Don't panic, and don't say anything till you've got a lawyer.'

'I'm fine, Simeon. I've got a very good lawyer who'll look after both of us. We'll be out in no time.'

Two police officers picked Carter up and read him the standard police caution. 'Do you understand?'

'Yes, yes, I understand. Remember, Danny, you have the right to remain silent.'

The two police officers pulled Carter back into the hallway, and he and Kinsella were frogmarched down the corridor, out of the building, and bundled into the back of two separate police vans.

Chapter 23

The dim headlights of the beaten up old Land Rover lit up the front of *Maison des Fleurs* as Gabriel Vance reversed the 4x4 into one of the barns. He climbed out and grabbed two large shopping bags from the passenger seat, holding them in one hand as he swung the barn door closed. As he approached the house, the front door opened and Sinclair stepped out to meet him. 'Any news?'

He held up the bags. 'I got a few supplies. You lot are using up all my teabags.'

Sinclair tried again. 'Forget the bags; have you heard anything from London?'

Vance looked down at the ground, not wanting to tell Sinclair the news. 'It could be bad, Ali. Let's go inside and I'll bring you all up to speed.' He handed Sinclair one of the bags and they both headed for the house.

McGill and Porter were sitting in the kitchen chatting. Porter appreciated the older man taking the time to talk things through with him. On top of everything else, Porter was still grieving. McGill had become a stand-in father to him, listening to whatever Porter wanted to say; he'd become a shoulder for him to cry on.

McGill didn't need the wheelchair any more, and he no

longer had a drip in his arm. A few more days and he'd be good to go. Maybe not a hundred per cent, but good enough. He was tired of sitting around while Vadim's men tried to track them down. It wasn't in his nature to be the one running away. McGill wanted to be on the road, he wanted to be the one hunting them. It was the only way all of this would stop.

Vance put his bag on the counter top and sat down at the opposite side of the table. 'We've had contact from London. Your message was delivered to Carter, but the situation has ramped up.'

McGill stood up and paced around the kitchen, testing his strength. 'Ramped up more than it already has? That doesn't sound good.'

Vance knew McGill and Sinclair weren't going to like what he was about to tell them. 'Carter and Kinsella have been arrested on some trumped-up terrorism charge. Apparently, the police have said they have evidence of an active plot that Carter and Kinsella are involved in. They're on remand.'

Sinclair slammed her fist on the table. 'Surely no one believes that, can't they see it's Vadim stitching them up?'

McGill sat back down. 'That's the thing, though, Ali. They are involved in a plot and we've sent them the evidence to prove it. The police are just doing their job, following through on the evidence they've been given.'

'This is bullshit. They are with us, trying to stop the conspiracy, they're not part of it. Why can't everyone else see that?'

'It's a matter of perspective. We must assume Vadim has at least one senior cop on his payroll. Manipulating the evidence to show a different angle to the story wouldn't be difficult.'

'Why isn't Edward Lancaster doing something about this?'

'He can't. As soon as the authorities know he's involved, he'll be in as much danger as we are. He has to stay hidden for as long as possible. Fight this from the inside.'

Sinclair laughed. 'We really are fucked, aren't we?'

McGill paused. 'There's something else we have to consider, Ali.'

'Don't tell me there's more bad news, Frank. Things are bad enough.'

'While you were in prison in Mexico, Vadim tried to have you killed several times. What if that's his plan here? I don't think Simeon and Danny will be able to protect themselves like you did.'

Sinclair stood. 'We need to get to London, now.'

Vance held up his hands, palms towards Sinclair. 'Not so fast, Ali. I've put things into place, made some arrangements, but it'll take a couple of days to get to London. It's the fastest you can do it. Get your things together, you'll need some kit for when you get there. I'll sort that.'

Sinclair sat down again. 'I hate all this hanging around, we need to help Simeon and Danny. We can't let Vadim kill them.'

'You and Frank get ready to travel, I'll contact London and see what can be done to protect them.'

Sinclair gripped Vance's forearm. 'Thanks for all your help, Gabe. I really appreciate what you've done for us, what you're risking.'

Vance put his hand on top of Sinclair's and smiled. 'I owe my life to Frank. His friends are my friends. Anything you need, I'll do what I can.'

Chapter 24

The hotel *Maison de Jura* was situated in the centre of a one-hundred-acre estate in the mountains north of Geneva, close to the French border. Its isolated position, and the fact there was only one access road, made it a favourite for the organisers of inter-government conferences. The whole estate could be sealed off for weeks in advance and thoroughly searched before the heads of government came anywhere near the site.

Security presence at the hotel, which had gradually increased in the build up to the summit, was now at its peak, as the attendees arrived. Motorcades of black 4x4 vehicles made their way along the access road and through the security cordon. One by one, each VIP turned up with their own entourage and security detail. Last to make an appearance, as always, was the President of the United States.

Many Secret Service agents were evident around the perimeter and throughout the hotel. Local police were becoming increasingly agitated as their most important charge approached. Armed guards kept a discreet distance, but had effectively surrounded the immediate perimeter of the hotel gardens, and controlled access to the helicopter pad, where Marine One, with the President on board, would be touching down.

Intelligence from MI6, of a possible, though unspecified, threat, was treated seriously. The hotel and grounds had been swept again, prior to any VIPs arriving; no one was getting in who didn't belong. All staff had been vetted, once the dates of the summit were known, and everyone was confident that any threat was empty and had been neutralised.

Asil Balik watched the commotion from the window in the main ballroom. He was the hotel's handyman and spent his days working his way down the list of repairs and maintenance jobs the manager had given him. He had been living in Switzerland for twenty years, since he and his father had moved there from Turkey in the nineties. His father had worked in the financial industry for years and had jumped at the job offer from the Swiss bank. Asil's mother had died the previous year and his father wanted a new life for them, a fresh start.

The young Balik had loved his new home. He was proud of his Turkish roots but considered himself Swiss; he had integrated completely into Swiss society and taken up citizenship as soon as it was open to him.

His father's untimely death had hit him hard. He dropped out of university and descended into a general malaise that clouded everything. Drink and drugs became his normal way of life as he flitted from one dead-end job to another. That was, until he met Christina. She gave him a reason to change, a reason to stop wallowing in self-pity.

Christina was a local woman, who used to work at the hotel, too; they fell in love and were soon married. When a family followed, Christina gave up her job to stay at home and look after their two young children. His life had turned around, his life was perfect.

The two men who had come to Balik's house two weeks earlier weren't locals. They weren't friends or tourists. They were angry, violent men who had crashed into Asil's perfect life and turned it upside down. They wanted Asil to do something for them, something important, they'd said. They had given him a list of very specific actions that he must carry out. Instructions that he had to follow, to the letter, if he ever wanted to see Christina and the children again.

Balik looked down at the small metal box they had given him. It was the size of a cigarette packet and didn't look dangerous. He had no idea what it was, but he knew it couldn't be good. He had smuggled the box into the hotel as soon as the men had given it to him. He'd hidden it in his underwear; security wasn't as tight then and it hadn't been a problem. Now he needed to put it into position, in the air conditioning vent in the Lucerne Suite, as the men at his house had told him. He looked out of the window: everyone was watching the US President's arrival. All eyes were away from the hotel and no one was interested in anything he was doing. He picked up his small stepladder and toolbox and headed for the suite.

Balik unscrewed the louvered cover from the air conditioning vent and used adhesive pads to stick the metal box to the inside. He checked the time on his watch then pressed the red button on the edge of the box. A tiny green light came on and blinked every second. The countdown had started.

He closed the vent and folded up his ladder. His job was complete, the instructions followed. He opened the door an inch and checked outside, the corridor was empty. He slipped out of the room and headed for the kitchen, and the next job on his list.

Chapter 25

Vance's old green Land Rover rattled and shook as McGill drove through the rural back roads of north-western France, heading for the old fishing port of Douarnenez. Although the fishing industry in the area had all but died, it was still used by water sports junkies and occasional pleasure boats. Sinclair, McGill and Porter had been given directions to a jetty where they would board a fishing boat.

McGill wasn't happy about their forthcoming sea voyage. 'Couldn't we find a plane that could drop us off somewhere?'

Sinclair shook her head. 'Too risky, Frank. If we travel by boat we've got hundreds of miles of coastline to pick from. If we landed in a plane someone might spot us.'

'Couldn't we at least get a fast boat?'

'Fast boats attract attention. That's the last thing we, or the people who own the boat, want. Don't worry about it, just get us there.'

The Land Rover's engine spluttered as McGill changed gear to climb a hill. 'We'll be lucky if this thing lasts long enough.'

'We're just going to abandon it anyway, Frank. Leaving Gabe the camper was a good way to say thanks. He'll get good use out of it.'

'I suppose so. How far away are we now?'

Sinclair picked up the map from the dashboard and studied it. 'I reckon we're just about there. A couple of miles further on then hang a left. We should be able to see the jetty then.'

McGill put his foot down, which didn't have much effect, then turned onto a smaller road that led down to a private jetty. 'That old rust bucket can't be it.'

Tied up alongside the jetty was a medium-sized fishing trawler that looked like it wasn't far from breaking up and sinking. As they pulled up, an old man, who was as weather beaten as the boat, walked down the gangplank to meet them.

He held out his hand. 'You must be Ali. You can call me John.'

To their surprise he wasn't French. Sinclair took his hand. 'Glad to meet you, John. This is Frank, and Callum.'

'Good to meet you all. If you'd like to jump aboard, we'll get going.'

Sinclair and Porter got the bags out of the Land Rover while McGill stayed with John. 'Tell me, John, is this boat sea worthy?'

John chuckled. 'We use this jetty to run fishing trips for tourists. Some of them like to be on an old trawler. Don't let its looks fool you, though. The outside has been deliberately aged. Underneath, she's sound with a good engine and will do a steady 15 knots. There's plenty of up-to-date equipment on board to make sure we get to where we need to be.'

'Glad to hear it, John. I'm not the best of sailors.'

John laughed. 'You'll be fine, my friend. We'll get you there in one piece.'

Sinclair and Porter carried the bags up the gangplank, followed by John. McGill paused for a while, as if he was enjoying his last moments on dry land; he shook his head then followed the others.

* * *

McGill was in a bad way and it was nothing to do with his injuries, although they did still hurt; it was the way the trawler bobbed and rolled as it made its way across the English Channel. McGill hated the sea, he always had. He was lying on his back, staring at the stars as his stomach churned. He'd already vomited everything he'd eaten in the last twenty-four hours, but it didn't stop his body trying to expel more. He turned over and dry retched again, actually thinking that falling off that roof in Paris might have been the better option.

Sinclair came up the ladder, onto the upper deck and handed McGill a bottle of water. 'Have a drink, Frank. You don't want to get dehydrated.'

'Just shoot me and dump me here. Trust me, it's for the best.'

'Oh, what a wuss. Has mummy's little soldier got a poorly tummy?'

'If I could stand up without retchin', I'd kick your arse.'

Sinclair laughed. 'You'd try.'

McGill sat up and took the water. They could see lights flickering in the distance and one of the crew was lowering a semi-rigid inflatable boat into the water. 'Looks like we're leaving, Frank.'

'Thank fuck for that. You'd better go and get Callum.'

Sinclair went back down below to get Porter and their backpacks.

McGill climbed to his feet and walked to the guardrail. He

looked down at the inflatable as the crew member fired up the outboard motor. Flashbacks to previous jobs ran through his mind. He still felt shit but he had to switch on. With Vadim being Home Secretary, England was now enemy territory. They would be on everyone's wanted list. Vadim couldn't afford for any of them to turn up with a folder full of evidence and blow his conspiracy out of the water. He climbed over the guard rail and on to the rope ladder that hung down the side of the fishing boat. After checking below, he took a deep breath to overcome his nausea and stepped off the ladder.

Sinclair and Porter stood on the upper deck of the fishing boat with the three small backpacks Vance had sorted out for them. Each contained a change of clothes, water bottle, simple first-aid kit and a few snacks. Anything else, they would get once they were back in the UK. Sinclair threw the backpacks down to McGill then she and Porter climbed down the ladder into the inflatable. The crewman let slip the rope that secured the inflatable to the fishing boat then turned the throttle on the outboard and steered them towards the beach.

As the rigid hull of their boat skimmed over the waves, salt spray blew into their faces; Porter shielded his eyes but McGill was in his element. It was like being a commando again, making an assault onto a beach. He knelt at the front of the boat, his heart rate and adrenaline levels increased: he was ready for action. The crewman cut the engine and as soon as the bottom of the boat hit the pebbles, McGill was out and running up the beach. He looked all around for any signs of life, listening for any unnatural noise, looking for vehicle lights. There was nothing. The only sound he could hear was the waves lapping on the pebbles. He turned his gaze back to the sea and waved to the others.

Sinclair and Porter were soon beside McGill and they watched as the boat disappeared into the darkness. Throwing on their backpacks, they climbed the steepest part of the beach to the ridge that ran parallel to the shoreline. There were no street lights on this part of the road and there was no passing traffic. McGill pulled out a map and used a small torch to check their position. 'Just under two miles along the coast to the drop-off point for the car. We'll stay away from the road as much as we can. Remember, we don't know who our friends are here, we have to treat everyone as if they are against us.'

Sinclair nodded. 'Just don't hurt anyone until we know they are definitely working for Vadim. Some of the people after us will be regular police, just doing their job. They're as much a victim in all of this as we are.'

'I'm not too worried about the police, they have a responsibility to protect the public. If things get too hairy they'll back down, if coming after us puts the public at risk. It's Vadim's muppets we need to watch out for. Collateral damage won't worry them at all.'

Sinclair grabbed McGill's backpack strap and pulled him round to face her. 'But no killing unless it's unavoidable, right?'

'Okay, okay. We'll have to be careful, but don't take any risks.' He looked at Porter. 'Are you ready, Callum?'

Porter didn't know what he was supposed to be ready for. 'I guess so.'

'Good, let's go.'

McGill took the lead with Sinclair bringing up the rear. Porter, inexperienced in this kind of situation, stayed in the middle and went wherever he was told to. McGill kept them in the shadows between the ridge and the road, moving as quickly as they could but keeping away from any prying eyes.

After thirty minutes, they crouched in the cover of a copse of trees that overlooked a dimly lit car park. The car they were looking for was parked on its own at the far end of the rubbish-strewn tarmac, hidden from the road. All they had to do was pick up the keys that were on top of the front wheel and drive away, easy. The problem they had was that between them and their transport was a group of other cars, with people milling about around them.

McGill checked out the scene through his binoculars. 'If I were a betting man, I'd say those people are up to something that might attract the police.'

Sinclair shifted her position to try to get a better view. 'What is it?'

'Put it this way, some of the car windows are steamed up and there's a group of men looking in.'

'Holy shit. They've left our car at a dogging site.'

'Could be worse, at least they'll be too busy to notice us. Hopefully.' McGill put down the binoculars and took off his backpack. 'Stay here. I'll go and get the car and pick you up. Don't move out onto the road until I'm there.'

Sinclair put the binoculars into McGill's backpack. 'Be careful, Frank. You never know how people are going to react when they get caught out doing something they shouldn't.'

McGill kept low, and made his way down to the edge of the trees and around the perimeter of the car park. The target car was parked in the spot furthest away from the only working light, in almost complete darkness. McGill approached it from the rear and looked through the back window to make sure it was empty. Dropping to his knees, he turned on his torch and checked under the car for anything suspicious. He hadn't mentioned the possibility of a car bomb to the others, but it would be an easy way to take them out.

The keys were sitting on top of the driver's-side front tyre in a plastic sandwich bag. He had no way of knowing how the car's alarm was wired. If he'd been prepping the car to be picked up, he would have disabled the alarm and just used the key to open the door. He couldn't risk that here, it might set off the alarm. He had to use the key fob.

As soon as he pressed the button, the indicators blinked twice and a loud 'blip' echoed around the car park. 'Shit.'

'What you up to, mate?'

The voice came from behind him. McGill stood up slowly and turned around. The man was in his mid-thirties, muscular and heavily tattooed. McGill smiled at the man and pointed at the car. 'Just pickin' my car up, buddy. Don't wanna disturb anyone.'

'We don't like outsiders sneakin' around and taking pictures of us. You a reporter?'

'I'm nobody, mate. I'll just get in my car and drive away. Leave you people to it.'

The man took a step towards McGill. 'It's too late for that. Give me your wallet. I wanna see who you are.'

McGill had promised Sinclair he would avoid trouble, and he really was trying. 'Walk away, mate. You're out of your depth.'

The man clenched his fists and took another step towards McGill. 'I said, give me your wallet.'

'Not gonna happen, buddy. Walk away, I don't want any hassle and, believe me, you don't either.'

The man wasn't in the mood to back down. He took another

step towards McGill and raised his fists. Unfortunately for him, the last step took him within striking distance. McGill raised his right foot and smashed it into the man's kneecap. The man went down immediately, clutching his knee and screaming. McGill patted him on the head. 'Deep breaths, mate. You'll be okay in a couple of days.'

The rest of the group were now paying attention to the commotion on the other side of the car park. Some had decided it was time to leave, but a few were now shuffling towards McGill like a zombie horde.

McGill jumped into the car and fired up the engine. He put the headlights on main beam, to blind the approaching zombies, and sped out of the car park.

When McGill stopped the car, Sinclair jumped in the front seat and Porter got in the back with the backpacks. Sinclair looked at McGill with a grin. 'You took your time. What did you do, stop to watch?'

'Don't ask. Bloody doggers.'

* * *

They drove for an hour before pulling into a layby on an A road outside the M25. McGill switched off the lights and the engine then turned around to tell Porter to get some rest, but he was already asleep. 'Dead to the world.'

Sinclair looked in the rear-view mirror. 'He's lucky. I wish I could fall asleep that easily.'

'You and me both, Ali.'

'We need to check the boot, Frank. See what our friends have left us before we get into London.'

'I'll do it, you look in the glovebox.' McGill got out of the car and walked round to the boot. Inside, there was a small suitcase, the type people use as hand luggage on flights. He unzipped it and checked the contents: three Glock 17s, spare magazines and ammunition, sound suppressors and a change of clothes. Behind the suitcase were two boxes of bottled water and a bag full of food: crisps, chocolate, packets of sandwiches – things they could eat on the move. He took three bottles of water and the bag of food and walked to the front of the car.

Sinclair was closing the glovebox. 'What did you find?'

McGill put the food and water on the back seat, next to Porter, and helped himself to a sandwich. 'Everything we asked for – food and water for the trip, weapons in case we hit any trouble before we get to the safe house, and a set of fresh clothes. It looks like Gabe's gangster friend can be relied on after all. What about you?'

Sinclair pointed to the contents of the glovebox, which were now arranged along the dashboard. 'Three Oyster cards, that'll make it easier to get around, three mobiles, directions and keys to the safe house, and a shit load of money.' She was holding up a plastic bag with thick wads of twenty pound notes in it. 'About ten grand in used twenties, I would say.'

'This guy must really owe Gabe.'

'I hope so. We might need to use him again. Let's get to the safe house before it gets light, and then we'll ditch the car.'

McGill started the engine. 'Sounds like a plan.' He pulled out of the layby and they headed for London.

Chapter 26

The UN summit was in full swing at the *Maison de Jura*. The heads of government had welcomed each other and posed for the obligatory photo to show how united they were; as usual, they were anything but united. Old rivalries rose to the surface and left the photographer with the unenviable job of herding them all into a group they were happy with. The Americans wanted to be centre stage but didn't want to stand next to the Russians; the Germans and the French were inseparable, and the situation between India and Pakistan was best left unsaid. People wandered off or had to take a phone call; it had taken almost an hour to get the single photo that was called for.

After the opening speech in the main ballroom, about how they should all work together to solve the world's ills, the delegates adjourned to their individual suites to blame the others for everything, discuss the morning's events and have some lunch. The UK delegation, led by the Prime Minister, filed into the Lucerne suite and descended like a plague of locusts on the five-star buffet that had been left for them. The PM and the Foreign Secretary went straight for the pork pies, while the Chancellor, who had more expensive tastes, made a beeline for the smoked salmon.

Junior MPs and parliamentary secretaries mingled with the civil servants as they waited for the big boys to load up their plates. They all helped themselves to glasses of fresh orange juice or mineral water and sat down to congratulate each other on how well they had done so far.

As the UK's political elite sat and chatted, the green light on the small metal box in the air conditioning vent stopped blinking and turned red. The end of the countdown, the start of the chaos.

* * *

Asil Balik had sneaked out of the hotel. It wasn't difficult, the security agents were looking for people trying to break in, not break out. He arrived at his little cottage, in the nearby village, twenty minutes later. He and his wife could never have afforded to buy a place like this: his father had left it to him when he died. They had discussed selling it and using the money for something else, but they were doing okay and it was such a lovely place to bring up the children.

He pulled up in the driveway hoping his family were okay and that the men who had threatened them were gone; he hoped they could get on with their lives, whatever was happening at the hotel.

As he approached the door, he could see it was slightly ajar. Would the men have left it open? A shiver ran down his spine. He pushed the door all the way open and paused, not wanting to go in, afraid of what he might find. 'Christina?'

There was no answer from inside. He stepped through the door and walked across the entrance hall towards the kitchen. The first thing he noticed was the spray of blood on the wall, the second was his wife's leg sticking out from behind the cupboard.

Balik ran to his wife. 'Christina …'

It was no use. Christina Balik was dead. A single gunshot had ensured she wouldn't be talking to the police.

Balik panicked. Where were the boys? He ran back to the hall and up the stairs, two at a time. The boys were lying on their beds, seemingly asleep. The only evidence otherwise was the neat nine-millimetre hole in each of their foreheads.

'NOOOO.' Balik scooped up his precious sons and hugged them to his chest. Why had they done this? He had done everything they asked. He rocked silently back and forth as his mind tried to deal with the sudden waves of horror that threatened to tip him into insanity.

The man who appeared next to Asil was quick; he grabbed his hand, placed a gun it and put the muzzle into the grief-stricken man's mouth. Asil knew what was going to happen but he didn't fight. He didn't want to live without his family. Before his assailant could finish the job, Asil Balik pulled the trigger himself.

* * *

In the Lucerne Suite, the inhabitants paused from their buffet at the sound of the small explosive charge detonating inside the metal box. It sounded like a single gunshot. The police bodyguards inside the room instructed everyone to stay where they were while they checked things out. Ultimately, that was what sealed their fate.

The charge ruptured the glass vial of nerve agent and dispersed it in a cloud into the air vent. The cloud blew out of the vent and on to the UK delegation who were now gathered at one end of the room. The first person to show any sign was a junior minister at the treasury. He started to have difficulty breathing and his heart raced. He grimaced and clutched his chest before collapsing backwards onto the floor.

It happened quickly after that. A second junior minister collapsed, followed by the Chancellor and the Foreign Secretary. Two civil servants frothed at the mouth as they crawled towards the door. The PM started to feel light headed. 'Everybody out. Get out of the room, NOW.'

Panic set in as those who were able to ran for their lives. The bodyguards reappeared and started pulling people out of the room, until they too were overcome. The fire alarm was set off and the whole building evacuated. Delegates poured out of the other rooms and joined the throng of people trying to get out; UK civil servants being helped by those from other countries, spreading the contamination. US Secret Service agents, alerted by what had sounded like a gunshot, were rushing the President to his helicopter. The rotor blades were already spinning and the US VIPs were quickly in the air, heading for safety.

A tsunami of panicking people burst out of the doors and onto the lawn in front of the hotel. It soon became apparent that symptoms were pointing towards a chemical attack, but not before first-aiders and those trying to help had already been contaminated.

Medical resources, which had been pooled on the estate next to the hotel, swung into action; the organisers had anticipated and planned for several possible scenarios. A chemical attack was seen as a distant, very remote possibility.

No one really expected it to happen – a bomb was much more likely.

Paramedics in protective suits were soon treating the victims and the hotel was sealed off. The dead were left inside, the living categorised by the severity of their symptoms and separated from those who needed immediate medical help. Other survivors began the process of being decontaminated – forced to undress and be scrubbed down inside hastily erected shower tents – some complained at the humiliation, but the majority were just happy to be alive.

Within an hour, the access road to the hotel was packed with military vehicles and ambulances ferrying people to hospital. Those who had been more seriously affected were loaded into a seemingly endless queue of air ambulances, which hovered above the helipad, awaiting their turn to land and load up.

By the end of the day, the statistics were being flashed around the world: thirty-seven dead, twenty-eight critical, and another one hundred and eight with mild symptoms. The UK delegation made up most of the dead: the Chancellor of the Exchequer, the Foreign Secretary, junior ministers and civil servants, bodyguards – thirty people dead. Among the critically ill were several more UK delegates, including the Prime Minister.

Within hours of the attack there were expressions of sympathy and solidarity, with the victims and the UK, from around the world. The US were calling it an attack on democracy that the President was lucky to survive. The United Nations issued a statement deploring the use of violence, and the EU offered help and support to anyone affected.

Within the UK, rolling news channels showed little else,

while social media was full of expressions of solidarity alongside the first calls for a swift investigation and, ultimately, retribution against the guilty – some media posts already suggesting who the guilty were, amid calls for military action.

Back in London, Vadim smiled and drained his glass of scotch. He called his driver and prepared to leave for the office. Today had been a success, now he had to prepare for phase two.

Chapter 27

The safe house was in the East End of London. Everyone in the area knew who it belonged to, they weren't going to stick their noses in or pry, it was none of their business. Besides, most of the local residents and the members of Nash's gang had grown up together. Nash was one of their own and they always looked after family. Those who came from outside the area were more concerned about avoiding the wrath of a gang leader who had a reputation for brutality.

No one had seen the new occupants of the two-bed terrace arrive the previous night, so couldn't describe them to the police – even if they'd wanted to. McGill had dropped off the others and the kit at four o'clock in the morning. He had switched off the headlights when they were still one hundred meters from the house and pulled up twenty yards short of the door to check for any watchers.

Sinclair and Porter took the backpacks and suitcase inside, before McGill drove the car to a multi-storey car park and left it where the instructions had told him to: on the top floor with the keys on top of the front tyre. Within minutes of him leaving the car, it was driven to a scrapyard where it would be crushed and all record of it destroyed.

By the time McGill got back to the house, people were starting to appear on the street; early morning deliveries were arriving at newsagents, market traders were setting off to get ready for another day selling their wares. Cafes that catered for the early risers, alongside taxi drivers who had worked the night shift, were opening and preparing for an influx of hungry customers.

McGill walked round to the back of the house and, after looking up and down the alley, opened the door that led to the house's backyard. He tapped on the back door and waited.

Sinclair watched from the bedroom window, checking that McGill hadn't been followed, before she went down to the kitchen and opened the door. 'Is everything okay, Frank?'

'Yeah, no drama and no followers. All went to plan.'

'Good. I've put the kettle on, we'll have a cup of tea and get some rest.'

* * *

They'd all grabbed a few hours' sleep and were up and ready to go. They were keen to get to the bank and pick up the folder, but it couldn't be rushed. First, they had to assess what the security situation was and how easy it would be for them to move around unimpeded.

Sinclair turned on the television and immediately knew that all their plans were down the pan. Every channel ran the same story: the attack at the hotel in Geneva. 'For fuck's sake, can't we get at least one break before the world decides to shit on us again?'

Porter sat on the couch. 'Why does that cause us a problem?'

'It doesn't cause you a problem, Callum. You're fine. Me,

on the other hand. I'm an escaped convict that the Home Secretary wants to kill. This gives them an excuse to up the threat level to critical and put troops on the streets. And, of course, there is the possibility that it was Vadim's goons that carried out the attack.'

Porter looked back at the television. 'Do you really think he would do something like this?'

Sinclair nodded. 'He's power crazy. He tried to blow up the world a few months ago. This is well within his scope. With half of the cabinet dead, he's the next in line to be PM.'

'We're fucked, aren't we?'

Sinclair smiled. 'It's a situation I'm beginning to get used to, Callum. Seems I spend most of my life being fucked-over by Vadim. This'll make things difficult but it doesn't change what we need to do.'

'So, we need to get to the bank and get Justin's folder as soon as possible.'

McGill pointed at the screen. 'Security is going to be as tight as a duck's arse from here on in. We have to be very careful.'

'I could go to the bank on my own. I know exactly how to get there, it would only take a couple of hours.'

Sinclair shook her head. 'Not a chance, not this soon. I'm not letting you out on your own. What if someone at the bank recognises you and realises you're using fake ID? It's too risky.'

'No one will recognise me. The bank was bought out and we were all made redundant. The new owners wanted to bring in their own people. No one I worked with is there any more.'

Sinclair looked at McGill for some backup. 'It's still too

risky. Vadim might know about the bank. He could have people there right now, just waiting to pick us up.'

'Ali's right, Callum. We can leave it for a day or two, until we figure things out. This operation isn't going to be a quick hit.'

Porter was disappointed. He'd thought if only he could go to the bank and get the file, all this would end. He reluctantly agreed. 'Okay then. You're the experts, but I still think we could pull it off. We could wear sunglasses or something, so no one recognises us. It wouldn't be that—'

Sinclair cut him off. 'NO, Callum. This isn't a game. I owe your dad a big favour and I'm not going to blow it by watching you get killed.'

Porter sat back, and sank into the couch like a naughty child.

Sinclair felt guilty. Porter was so far out of his comfort zone he wasn't thinking straight. He had no experience to draw on, to tell him what the best thing was to do. 'I'm sorry, Callum. You'll just have to trust us. Okay?'

Porter smiled. 'Okay, Ali. I understand.'

'Me and Frank will go and recce the route to the bank, see if there are any roadblocks or checkpoints – any extra security that might get in our way.'

'You think there will be?'

'There's just been a major terrorist attack against the UK government, I'd say there's a good chance.'

'I could help with that.'

Sinclair pointed at herself and McGill. 'We can pose as a couple, blend in. Three people would stand out more, raise suspicions. You just hang on here, Callum. Put your feet up, watch TV. We'll be back soon.'

McGill threw a baseball cap to Sinclair. 'Here you go, Ali. Tie your hair up and put that on. The police won't be looking for us right now, they've got bigger fish to fry, but it's best not to take the risk. That'll make you fairly anonymous.'

'What about your disguise?'

'I don't really need one, I'm not an escaped convict. Besides …' McGill put on a pair of sunglasses. 'I'll just be cool in my shades.'

Sinclair shook her head. 'Okay, let's get on with it. Lock the door behind us, Callum.'

They slipped out of the back door and into the alley behind the house; it was deserted. They picked their way between the wheelie bins, rubbish sacks and a discarded sofa, to where the alley opened out on to the main street, and paused for a moment. They saw nothing unusual, just ordinary people going about their business. As always, the everyday person on the street refused to panic, or change what they did, despite recent events. Sinclair and McGill waited for a group of teenagers to pass the entrance to the alley then slotted in behind them; just a couple out walking, hand in hand, without a care in the world.

For the first mile, Sinclair chose a route that zig-zagged and snaked around the local area, as McGill kept a watch for anyone following them. They changed direction frequently, stopped to sit on a park bench for a few minutes, and at one point, doubled-back and headed around the corner they had just turned. Once they were happy that no one was following, they made for the underground.

The atmosphere at the bottom of the escalator was completely different. There had been no sign of any increased security above ground, but when they reached the ticket hall, armed police were manning the barriers. More police with dogs stood to one side, while other officers searched people at random.

Sinclair and McGill stood at the back of the queue for one of the gates. They couldn't turn and leave, it would arouse suspicion. They each held one of the oyster cards they'd been given and hoped they worked first time and weren't stolen. The last thing they needed was to end up being arrested for something stupid. If Vadim found out they were being held, their lives would be worthless.

Sinclair was first to reach the barrier. She held her Oyster card to the reader, the gate opened and she walked through, no problem. As McGill reached out to scan his card, a police officer stepped forward. 'Could you step out of the line, please, sir?'

McGill did his best to look innocent. 'Anything wrong, Officer?'

'Just a routine check, sir. Please stand over here.' The officer guided him away from the rest of the passengers. 'Stand with your legs shoulder-width apart and arms out to the side.'

McGill did as he was told. 'Just to let you know, I came off my bike a few days ago and I've got stitches in my back and legs. Could you be careful, please?'

The officer carefully patted down McGill and lingered over the area where his bandages were. 'Can you show us the stitches, please? Just to be sure.'

McGill lifted his T-shirt at the back and turned around. The police officer whistled as McGill moved the dressing aside. 'That's a nasty looking one, mate. I've come off my bike a few times. I know how it feels.'

'Doesn't help when you fall off in your own driveway.'

'How did you manage that?'

'Well, it started off as a quiet night in the pub ...'

Sinclair tapped her finger on the screen of her phone, trying not to look too worried that McGill had been stopped. If things went bad, she would have to leave Frank and carry on alone. She watched out of the corner of her eye as he was searched, and sighed with relief as the police officer started laughing at whatever story McGill was recounting. It looked like Frank had used his charm to get out of another sticky situation. He was good at that.

McGill was taken to the front of the queue and he swiped his Oyster card. The police officer winked at him. 'Take it easy, mate. Don't burst your stitches.'

Frank smiled and nodded. 'I'll try not to. Thanks.'

He quickly caught up with Sinclair and the two of them walked down to the trains. 'That was too close for comfort. I think we'll avoid using public transport from here on in.'

'Definitely. It looks like paranoia has well and truly set in.'

'And it'll only get worse, the closer we get to the city. At least it looks like they aren't doing any checks on people leaving London.'

They walked onto the platform just as the train pulled in and stopped. The voice from the loudspeakers told them to 'mind the gap' as they stepped into the carriage. The heat was stifling: too many bodies crammed into a small space with no ventilation. Sinclair took off her jacket and tied it around her waist. She pulled a tissue out of her jeans and dabbed some of the sweat from her face. 'Why is it always too bloody hot down here?'

'I thought you'd be used to it, with all your time in Mexico?'

'I've never loved the heat, Frank. You know that. It's okay

165

when you're on the beach, with a pina colada, but in places like this, and in a Mexican prison, it's just shit.'

They'd changed trains three times on their way in to the centre of London, more anti-surveillance techniques to uncover any followers, and were walking along the concourse at Waterloo Station.

McGill ducked into a newsagents and came out with a street map and an I Love London hat. 'This'll make us look like tourists. We can wander about and take photos. We'll look just like everyone else.'

'Let's swing past the bank first, see what CCTV and security they've got in the area. Where is it?'

'On the other side of the river, close to the police station.'

Sinclair tried not to sound too sarcastic, but it was proving difficult. 'Oh, that's fantastic.'

'We do it quick, no one'll notice us. Take lots of selfies and smile, just another couple of tourists. We know there'll be a load of CCTV along the Strand, but we need to check security in the bank itself.'

'Okay. Then we figure out a route back to the safe house that doesn't include police checkpoints.'

'Agreed. Let's get on with it.'

They exited the station and turned left towards Waterloo Bridge.

Within a few minutes they were standing on London's Strand. It was, as always, busy, but it now had the addition of extra security. Armed police and military stood on corners in amongst the tourists and office workers who competed for space on the crowded pavements. The cycle couriers seemed a little more cautious than usual, as they zig-zagged between pedestrians and traffic. The security level had been increased to critical and news reports were saying another attack could be imminent. People didn't outwardly look worried, but they were.

Sinclair and McGill made their way towards the bank, which was sited away from the Strand and down a side street. They stopped on the corner and checked for cameras. All of the monitoring in the area was concentrated on the main road. There was one CCTV camera mounted on the outside of the bank, pointing at the door. The outer door was dark blue with a white number three painted on it. On one side of it was a frosted glass window, protected by ornate, wrought-iron bars. On the other side was the only indication of what the property was; a brass plaque read: Brown & MacMillan. Private Bank.

'We need to see inside, Ali. Get an idea of what we're walking into. Make sure it hasn't changed since Callum worked there.'

'I'll go in and ask about prices for a deposit box. You have a walk and see if there's another entrance.'

McGill nodded. 'Okay.'

Sinclair turned the handle on the outer door and stepped in to the bank's reception.

The inside was as anonymous as the outside. Anyone seeing a photograph of it wouldn't think it was a bank. A young woman sat at the small entrance hall's only desk. The walls were lined with mahogany panelling and brass wall lights. There was one other door out of the hall, behind the desk. The young woman smiled. 'Can I help?'

Sinclair scanned the walls and ceiling for cameras – she could only see one. 'Wow, this place sure doesn't look like a bank.'

'We like to keep it traditional. We've been here for nearly two hundred years and a lot of our customers prefer it this way.'

Sinclair smiled at the young woman. 'I was just looking for some information on your safe-deposit boxes. Price, security; that kind of thing.'

'It's all in here.' The young woman handed Sinclair a glossy A4 brochure. 'We do require references before we take you on as a client, but, if you decide that you like what you see, you can book an appointment with us.' She flashed Sinclair another smile.

'Could I just have a quick look at your vault? Just so I know how secure it is.'

'If you'd like to book an appointment, we can show you around then. After we've got your references, of course.'

Sinclair could see that she wasn't getting any further into the bank. This woman's job was obviously to put off casual enquiries. This was the sort of bank that catered for the rich and their associates – recommendation only. 'Okay.' She held up the brochure. 'I'll have a read of this and get back to you. Thank you.'

Another fake smile spread across the woman's face. 'You're welcome.'

Sinclair left the bank.

McGill was standing outside. 'Only a fire escape around the back. Nothing that will help us. Anything inside?'

'No, no help at all. There's one camera in reception but I couldn't see any of the rest of the bank. It's all mahogany panelling and brass fittings.'

'A bank for people with money then?'

Sinclair held up the brochure. 'The receptionist gave me

this. She said I needed references if I wanted to become a client.'

'How the hell did Justin get a box here?'

'Don't forget, Callum's family are very well-off and seriously connected. I would think that, combined with Callum working here, would be enough.'

'Not a bank for the likes of us then.'

Sinclair smiled and put the brochure into her jacket. 'Well, definitely not you.'

McGill shook his head. 'I'll give that remark the damn good ignoring it deserves.'

Sinclair pushed McGill's shoulder. 'Let's get out of here. We need to go and check Danny's flat. See if there's anything there that can help us.'

* * *

Porter had waited, just like Ali said. He had watched TV and waited, drunk tea and waited; now, he paced around the living room of the safe house with his fake passport in his hand, mumbling to himself. If he got to the bank and picked up the evidence in the deposit box, he could save Ali and Frank from any more problems. He could finish this on his own. Ali and Frank wouldn't be in danger any more, and everyone would know what Justin had done – how heroic he had been. All he had to do was get a taxi straight to the bank, open the deposit box, and bring the folder back here before anyone noticed he had gone.

He dropped the passport onto the table and ran his fingers through his hair. He was being stupid. What if something happened? He knew he shouldn't leave the house, Ali had told him to stay here, but he wanted to help. He slumped on the couch and picked up the TV remote, surfed the channels and waited some more.

It was no good. He turned off the TV and picked up the passport. His mind was made up. He phoned a cab, put the passport in his pocket and left the house.

As Porter got into the taxi, the motorcycle courier who had been watching the house, put on his helmet and started the bike's engine. His instructions were to follow anyone he saw leaving the house and report where they went. As the taxi pulled away, the courier merged with the traffic and followed at a distance.

Chapter 28

D S Zoe Gardner pushed the record button and waited for the long tone to stop. 'My name is Detective Sergeant Zoe Gardner' She looked at her watch. 'It's ten twenty-five, on Monday the twenty-third, and this is an interview with ...'

Simeon Carter looked tired. He hadn't slept properly since his arrest and was sick of playing these games. What he wanted to do was say nothing, but he didn't want them to think they were breaking him. He cleared his throat and sat forward slightly. 'Simeon Carter.'

DS Gardner nodded. 'Also present in the room are ...'

The man to the left of the DS straightened his back. He was getting as tired of these interviews as Carter was. 'Detective Constable Keith Lawton.'

Gardner pointed toward Carter's solicitor. 'And ...'

Carter's solicitor worked for a very old, very expensive practice in London. One of the perks of Kinsella's success was that he could afford the best. The solicitor looked and sounded exactly how an expensive solicitor should: immaculate three-piece suit, gold rimmed glasses and a privately educated accent. He took a file out of his equally expensive briefcase and placed it on the desk. 'Peter Fawcett.'

In an adjacent room, Detective Chief Superintendent Nicholas Thorpe studied the CCTV images of Simeon Carter, looking for some sign of weakness. Thorpe wanted to be the one interviewing the old man, but the rules didn't allow it. He would have to watch as his DS took the lead on this. He glanced sideways at the man who sat quietly in the corner.

Edward Lancaster brushed some lint from his trouser leg but didn't look up. He didn't want any facial expression to give away his relationship with Carter.

Thorpe looked at Lancaster with disdain. He didn't like the intelligence monkeys interfering in his work. What was he doing here, anyway? This wasn't anything they needed his help with.

Lancaster finally looked up, aware Thorpe didn't want him in the room, but determined to let the DCS know who had the higher rank.

Thorpe lowered his eyes and went back to watching the images. The DCS's hatred of Lancaster burned inside him. He gritted his teeth, muttering something under his breath.

Back in the interview room, Gardner began her questions. 'Now, Mr Carter, today we're here to continue your questioning about the attack on the UK government in Geneva. Tell me what you know about it.'

Carter sighed. 'I've told you already, Danny Kinsella and I had nothing to do with it, you're barking up the wrong tree. You should be—'

Gardner held up her hand and cut Carter off. 'I wish I could believe you, Simeon, I really do. Unfortunately for you, we've found evidence that shows you were aware of a conspiracy to launch an attack.'

'Being aware of a conspiracy is a lot different to being

involved.'

Lancaster shifted in his seat. 'I've seen the evidence, Chief Superintendent. It isn't that compelling.'

Thorpe stared at Lancaster. 'It was enough to get these two locked up on remand, Mr Lancaster.'

Lancaster smiled. 'Getting people locked up isn't difficult, in the current climate. I do hope you have something else to go on.'

Thorpe shook his head. Who did Lancaster think he was dealing with? He wasn't some rookie detective who could be intimidated. He was in charge, not Lancaster.

Gardner continued. 'It really would be better for you if you cooperated, Simeon. You're going down anyway.'

Carter sniffed. 'It's Mr Carter to you, and I was doing this kind of shit before you were born. If your evidence is so good, you don't need me to help.'

Gardner tapped her pencil on the desk. 'Where are Sinclair and McGill?'

'I don't know who you're talking about.'

Lancaster butted in again. 'Sinclair was one of ours. She is on the run, probably still in the US. If she was here, we would know; unless you've got evidence of that, too?'

Thorpe hated spooks, they always looked down on people like him. Carter and Lancaster were cut from the same cloth and Thorpe knew they had worked together before.

Gardner opened a cardboard file and spread several printed sheets out in front of Carter. 'We have evidence to show that you have been in touch with Ali Sinclair, an escaped convict, and Frank McGill – a man suspected of helping her and someone who is guilty of a great many things.'

'If he's guilty of something, why isn't he in prison?'

Fawcett interrupted. 'I don't see what this has to do with the allegations against my client.'

Gardner nodded at Fawcett then looked back at Carter. 'Who is your contact within MI6?'

'I retired from MI6 some time ago, DS Gardner. I don't know what you're talking about.' Carter gave Gardner his best smile.

Lancaster, once again, disturbed Thorpe's concentration. 'Any questions you have regarding past or present MI6 operations should be addressed to me, Chief Superintendent.'

Thorpe was becoming agitated at Carter's coolness and Lancaster's constant interruptions. He looked at his watch. 'This is getting us nowhere.' He stormed out and opened the door to the interview room. 'Interview suspended. Gardner, with me.'

'Sir?' DS Gardner looked confused at the sudden interruption. 'Interview suspended eleven fifteen.' She pressed the stop button on the recorder and followed the DCS into the corridor. 'SIR?'

DC Lawton looked embarrassed, unsure what to do. After exchanging glances with Carter, he cleared his throat, checked his watch, then excused himself and hurried out of the room.

Fawcett put his file back in his briefcase. 'They'll keep trying this, Simeon. They're trying to wear you down. You're innocent and the evidence is circumstantial, so keep your chin up. I'll make sure this all stays in the public eye and then they can't make you disappear to some secret facility out of the country. How's Danny coping?'

'Being remanded was a shock for him. He really wasn't expecting to end up in prison. Have you spoken to him?'

'Gardner and co have interviewed him in the same way

they've interviewed you, but I'm worried he might say something stupid if put under enough pressure. He doesn't have your experience.'

'I'll keep an eye on him, Peter. At least they let us share a cell.'

Fawcett shook Carter's hand. 'Stay strong, Simeon. We'll beat this thing.'

Lancaster looked along the corridor then entered the interview room, staying by the door and out of the view of the CCTV camera. 'How are you doing, Simeon?'

'I'm okay, Edward. Listen, we don't have much time. Have you heard from Sinclair?'

'There have been a couple of incidents, which we think are them, but nothing concrete. She and McGill need to stay in hiding. The police are convinced you all had something to do with the attack. Someone is planting evidence against you. My boss is pushing for more MI6 and military involvement in the manhunt – I think he sees it as a way of climbing the ladder; I reckon he's got political ambitions. I don't trust him at all.'

'Does he suspect you?'

'Not yet. After Sinclair's last escapade he knows she's somehow connected to MI6, but he doesn't know it's me. I told you before, Simeon. I didn't tell anyone I was using you and Sinclair as a team. I'll protect you as much as I can, but, sooner or later, he'll find out you're working for me.'

'You need to protect yourself, Edward. You need to find evidence that identifies Vadim. Just in case Ali doesn't make it.'

'I'm doing everything I can. You stay safe, Simeon. I'll try and get you both out.'

A prison officer opened the door. 'Okay, Carter. Let's get you back to your cell.'

* * *

Several senior military and police officers were filing out of the Home Secretary's office when Thorpe arrived to give him his briefing.

'Ah, Thorpe, come in.' Enfield waved him into the room. 'Thank you, gentlemen. Keep me informed of any developments.'

The rest of the senior figures still in the room, stood and left; some a little annoyed that Thorpe seemed to have a privileged position with the new Home Secretary. They could all sense the big changes that were about to happen. People were positioning themselves to climb the ladder. Not all of them would still be in post when the dust settled.

Enfield gestured towards a chair. 'Have a seat, Chief Superintendent.'

Thorpe sat down, feeling a little uncomfortable – like a schoolboy in the headmaster's office. 'Thank you, sir.'

Enfield checked that everyone had left the room and the door was closed. His mood changed. His demeanour became darker, more conspiratorial, and he lowered his voice. 'Why are Carter and Kinsella still causing me problems? Didn't I tell you I wanted them dealt with? Wasn't I clear when I said I wanted them gone?'

Thorpe ran his fingers around the inside of his collar. 'It's not that easy, sir. Too many people know they are in the system. There would be awkward questions if they just disappeared. We have to follow the law.'

Enfield slammed his palm down on the desk, an action that created a louder noise than he'd expected or wanted. He checked through the office's glass wall to make sure it hadn't attracted anyone's attention. He turned back to Thorpe. Once again, he lowered his voice, but the menace was still there. 'I don't give a shit about the law. I want them buried in a deep, dark hole. Better still, I want them dead. Find a way.'

Thorpe was sweating, rivulets running down his back. 'I will, sir. You can rely on me.'

'I hope so, Chief Superintendent, for your sake and mine.' Enfield adjusted his tie and composed himself. 'What about Sinclair and McGill? What about the American boy? I haven't heard any good news about them. They are the only people, other than you, who can identify me. I want the evidence they have, and I want them all taken care of.'

'We're doing all we can, sir. We're monitoring ports and airports. I'm sure they'll be heading for London. I've got people watching CCTV and using facial recognition. We'll find them.'

The Home Secretary slammed his fist on his desk and sent a pen holder crashing to the floor. This time, people outside the office did take notice. Enfield didn't care any more. 'What you're doing isn't enough. Do I need to remind you what will happen if we are found out? It's more than your career that will die.'

Thorpe could see his career – his life – coming to a sudden stop. Enfield was losing it on a regular basis. People were starting to talk about the pressure getting to him. It was only a matter of time until he blew up in public. 'You can trust me. I'll—'

'Get out. Don't come back until you've got good news.'

Thorpe crept out of the room, closing the door behind him. People in the office were looking at him, wondering what he had done to annoy the Home Secretary like that. If they hadn't been worried about their own careers, they might have said something, raised some concerns.

DCS Thorpe loosened his tie and dabbed at his face with a handkerchief. He had to do something to get back in Enfield's good books. If he didn't, it wasn't just his life on the line – his family, friends and colleagues were all in danger, too. Other than Sinclair, everyone who had met Enfield and knew his real identity was already dead. Thorpe knew he would be next, as soon as he was no longer useful.

As he walked down the corridor his phone started to ring: a call from the team he had monitoring the CCTV. Maybe this was the break he needed. 'DCS Thorpe.'

DS Gardner sounded excited. 'Sir, we've found them.'

Thorpe's heart raced. 'Are you sure?'

Gardner couldn't conceal her excitement. 'Yes, sir, as sure as we can be. I've looked at the CCTV pictures and I'm convinced it's Sinclair and McGill.'

The DCS closed his eyes and took a deep breath, a feeling of relief, of hope, washed over him.

Gardner thought the line had gone dead. She checked her phone still had a signal then held it back up to her ear. 'Sir?'

Thorpe opened his eyes. People were still looking at him. 'Where are they?'

'They're on the Strand, close to Charing Cross Police Station.'

'Well done, Zoe. I'm on my way.' He hung up and dialled another number. 'Sinclair and McGill are on the Strand. I'll stall the police response, get there now and pick them up.

Look for the boy, too.'

'We're on it.' Three of Vadim's assassins had been in London since before the Geneva attack, ready to move at a moment's notice. Ready to take care of anyone, anything, their boss wanted. They packed their weapons into paint-spattered tool bags and walked out of the old house they had been living in. The three of them jumped into an old, white, builder's van, which they'd been using to get around in, and headed for Charing Cross. They would be lucky to get there before their targets left, but they had to give it their best shot. They couldn't risk upsetting their boss.

* * *

Sinclair and McGill were already walking away from the bank and back across Waterloo Bridge towards the tube station when the white van pulled to a halt on the Strand. Two of the occupants climbed out and scanned the crowds that made their way along the pavement. As they'd expected, Sinclair and McGill were nowhere to be seen. With this many people on the street it was unlikely they would have spotted them anyway. The CCTV camera that had picked them up was mounted on the corner of a building, pointing parallel to the buildings, but there was no way for them to tell which way they had gone.

As they watched tourists milling about, one of them spotted a passenger climbing out of the back of a black cab. Vadim's assassin checked the photo he had been given and compared it to the passenger. It was Callum Porter.

The man handed the photo to his colleague, pointed towards Porter and signalled the driver of the van. Porter didn't spot anything, he wasn't looking for threats. He didn't spot the two men following him, or even the old, white, builder's van creeping along the street behind him. As Porter turned the corner towards the bank, the two men grabbed him and bundled him into the back of the van; the door slid closed and the driver put his foot down. The van sped off in a cloud of black, oily smoke.

The motorcycle courier, who had followed Porter's taxi into the city, was watching as the two men grabbed the American. There was nothing he could do to stop it, he had no training for that. He watched as the van pulled out into the traffic; he put his phone away and followed on behind.

Chapter 29

When Carter got back to the cell, Kinsella was lying on the top bunk reading a book. He put down the book when he saw Carter and sat up. 'How did it go?'

'Same questions, again and again, Danny. All we have to do is stay quiet and give Sinclair the time she and McGill need.'

'I'm not sure I can keep this up, Simeon.' He looked around at the blank walls of the cell. 'Not sure I can survive in here long-term.'

Carter was worried about Kinsella. He'd had a protected childhood; he went to a private school and then to university. He'd never experienced anything outside that world, he wasn't streetwise. The noise of the prison, the threats, the bullying, must be playing on his mind. 'You'll be okay, Danny.'

Kinsella slowly shook his head. 'When I was in the room, Gardener was quite nice to me. She kept saying my sentence would be shorter if I came clean, said I might even be let out if I told her everything.'

'Don't believe her, Danny. She'll tell you anything to get you to talk.'

'Was she friendly towards you, too, Simeon? When she was asking you questions?'

Carter smiled. 'Not really, but she's just asking the questions her boss wants her to. Thorpe's the one we have to be wary of.' Carter didn't want to tell Kinsella that they were targeting him, that they saw the younger man most likely to break. 'I think I annoyed them. Thorpe dragged gardener out of the interview.'

Kinsella jumped down from the bunk. 'I don't think it's a good idea to antagonise them.'

Carter shrugged. 'What are they going to do? We're already locked up.'

Kinsella sat down on the bottom bunk, elbows on his knees. 'I suppose you're right. It just feels like everyone is against us. Who's on our side, other than Sinclair and McGill?'

Carter put his hand on Kinsella's back. 'Edward was there. I managed to have a few words with him. He's a friend, even if he can't say so.'

'What did he say? Can he get us out?'

'He's doing everything he can, but it takes time. There are too many people either covering their arses or trying to climb the slippery pole. If they think that seeing us locked up forever is in their interests, they won't help.'

'But we didn't do anything, Simeon. How can they think we were responsible for killing so many people?'

'It's all planted evidence, Danny. The only chance we have is for Sinclair and McGill to come up with something that brings the whole conspiracy crashing down around their ears.'

Kinsella paced what little floor space there was. 'We don't even know if they're alive. What are we going to do if—?'

Kinsella's question was unfinished, as two other inmates appeared at the cell door. One kept watch as the other entered the cell and pulled out a knife. 'Right, you two. Out. Now.'

Kinsella retreated as far as he could. 'What do you want?'

The inmate with the knife had been giving them trouble since they'd arrived at the prison, but he hadn't threatened them with a knife before. This was something new.

'I said, out.' The inmate signalled towards the door.

Carter was, as ever, cool and calm. He knew someone else was pulling this little shit's strings. It was unlikely he would try and kill them there. 'It's okay, Danny, just do as he says.'

Knifeman put on a whining voice, 'Yeah, Danny. Do as I say.'

The lookout laughed. 'Let's go.'

Carter beckoned Kinsella to the door and they squeezed out passed the two inmates. Knifeman gave them directions and they walked along the cell block, followed by the henchman.

At the end of the block, in an alcove, was an old steel door that led to the old boiler room. The machinery that provided heating to the old Victorian prison had been updated and relocated, but the old boilers were still there. There were no cameras in that room and none of the guards ever used it. This was a place where scores were settled, away from prying eyes. Knifeman turned the handle and pushed the green, flaking surface of the door. 'In.'

The door swung open and Carter and Kinsella entered the dimly lit space.

The henchman stayed at the door while Knifeman forced Carter and Kinsella along a corridor and into the darkest corner of the boiler room. Plaster from the crumbling ceiling littered the floor and a rat scurried away as they approached. Knifeman pointed to the far side of the room. 'No one's gonna find you two till it's too late.'

183

Kinsella took half a step forward and put his arm in front of Carter in an attempt to shield him. Kinsella was terrified but wasn't going to let this arsehole see it. Carter was family, and if they were going to die then it wouldn't be on their knees. 'Why are you doing this?'

'You got a price on your heads and I need the money. Got debts. Nothin' personal.'

'I can give you more money than you can imagine. Just walk away.'

Knifeman shook his head. 'Can't do, mate. You don't take a contract from these people then walk away. I could end up as next on their shit list. Anyways, if I don't kill ya, someone else will. Just accept it.'

Carter took two steps back then worked his way sideways, trying to outflank the inmate.

Knifeman waved the knife at Carter. 'Where d'ya think you're fuckin' goin, grandad? Get back in the fuckin' corner.'

Kinsella took a chance and grabbed for the knife. He gripped Knifeman's wrist with his left hand and drove his right shoulder into his chest. The two men fell and wrestled on the floor, both trying to control the knife. Carter took a step and swung a kick at the inmate's head but didn't make full contact. The inmate pushed Kinsella off him and managed to stand up, grabbing Carter by the throat. Kinsella started to get up but the knife was already travelling towards the old man's chest.

None of the men in the room were expecting what happened next. A hand the size of the bucket on a digger grabbed Knifeman by the face and propelled him into the wall. His head crashed into the brickwork and the knife fell from his hand. The little shit slid down the wall, bleeding heavily from a wound on the back of his head.

Carter looked at his rescuer. He was an enormous man they knew only as Grizzly, on account of his massive size and huge beard. He picked up the little shit with one giant paw and held him so their faces were level. The smaller man's feet dangled at least a foot off the ground. 'No one touches these two, right? Anyone tries, they have to deal with me. Got it?'

Knifeman knew Grizzly's reputation – he knew who he worked for. He nodded, blood dripping from his chin. 'Okay, okay, I don't have no beef wiv you.'

Grizzly threw the man to the other side of the room, where he lay unconscious and bleeding.

Carter helped Kinsella to his feet. They were both shocked by what had happened. Carter held out his hand. 'Thank you.'

Grizzly ignored the offered handshake and stroked his beard. 'Anyone bothers you, you tell me. The word has been put around that you aren't to be touched.'

Carter was grateful, but still confused. 'I thought there was a price on our heads?'

'There is, but people in here fear my guvnor more than anyone who's taken out a contract on you.'

'And who is your guvnor?'

'Let's just say, Harry Nash doesn't want you harmed.'

Chapter 30

Sinclair and McGill sat on a bench in the communal garden opposite Kinsella's flat. There didn't appear to be a police presence – uniformed or otherwise – outside the building. In the thirty minutes they had been watching, no one had entered or left through the front door. They had been sitting there as long as they could without looking out of the ordinary, and now they had to make a move; they either went in and searched the place, or left to return another day.

McGill put his arm around Sinclair, as if they were a couple enjoying a snatched moment together. 'What do you think, Ali? What should we do?'

'We need to go in sooner or later, but we take it easy. No violence, no drama. Any sign of a police presence and we turn around and leg it. We get back to Callum.'

McGill handed Sinclair a set of keys. 'Danny gave me these before I went to Geneva, just in case. They'll get us in.'

'Right. No time like the present.'

They checked both ways then crossed the road. Sinclair opened the front door and they both went in. Using the only lift was too risky – the noise would advertise their arrival, and they had no way of knowing who would be standing in the corridor waiting for them when the doors opened. McGill pushed open the entrance to the stairs and listened for footsteps – there were none. They entered the stairwell and started the climb to the top floor.

The exit at the top of the stairs was at the opposite end of the corridor to Kinsella's flat. McGill pushed it open far enough to check the hallway was empty, then they stepped through and crept towards the front door.

They didn't need the key for the door, the lock had been smashed during Carter and Kinsella's arrest and still hadn't been fixed. They pushed it open and entered the flat.

The heavy curtains were closed and, without Kinsella's usual six monitors to light up the room, the flat was in darkness. Sinclair used a small torch, which she shielded with her hand, to look around the flat. All of Kinsella's computer equipment had been taken by the police. 'Nothing left here for us, Frank.'

McGill pointed at a power socket on the other side of the room. 'Check that socket. Danny told me it was a last resort that he'd put in place in case this happened.'

'What did he mean by that? Did he know they were coming for him?'

'I've no idea, maybe he just knew they'd come eventually. Check it anyway, you know how sneaky Danny is.'

Sinclair knelt next to the power socket and ran her fingers around it; it felt normal. She pulled and twisted it but it wouldn't move. She pulled out a metal multi-tool from the leather pouch on her belt and unfolded the screwdriver. Working quickly, she unscrewed the front of the double socket and pulled it away from the wall.

Instead of seeing power cables behind the socket, attached

to the back was a metal tray – almost the same width as the socket and about ten inches long. The tray housed what looked like a portable hard drive. Its power lead ran to the back of the supply for the socket itself and a single blue LED glowed on its front. Sinclair removed the power lead and pulled out the hard drive, showing it to McGill. 'You're right. He is a sneaky bastard.' She placed it in her pocket and slid the now empty tray back into the hole. She had just finished fastening the socket into place when they heard a floorboard creak outside the door.

McGill stepped behind the door just before a uniformed PC shone his torch into the room. 'Who are you? Stand up and turn around.'

Sinclair did as she was told, her hands in plain sight. 'I'm a friend of the owner, I just wondered where he'd got to.'

'Then why are you in the dark?'

Sinclair shrugged her shoulders. 'Didn't want to frighten the cat.'

'Is that the best you can come up with? You'll have to come down to the station with me.'

Sinclair sighed. 'Don't hurt him too much.'

'What's that supposed to—'

The rest of the police officer's question remained unsaid, as McGill's arm tightened around the young man's neck and cut off the blood supply to his brain. The officer struggled and tried to escape, but McGill was too good at this kind of thing. The officer was unconscious in seconds.

Sinclair switched off her torch and put it away. 'Let's get out of here in case there's two of them. How is he?'

McGill checked the PC's pulse. 'He's okay. He'll wake up in a few minutes with a headache, but we shouldn't be here when he calls it in.'

They left the door to the flat open and went back down the stairs to the entrance. Outside in the street was a police vehicle, with another, older officer sitting behind the wheel. They were now trapped between the young officer, who would wake up in a matter of minutes, and the vehicle parked outside. McGill kicked the bottom of the door. 'Shit. Now what?'

'We get back upstairs, quick.'

They both sprinted back to Kinsella's flat. As they entered, the younger PC was just waking up. McGill grabbed him and pushed him face down on the carpet, kneeling on his back.

Sinclair knelt beside the PC and spoke clearly. 'If you do as you are told, you'll be okay. Do you understand?'

The officer nodded as well as he could in the position he was in.

'That's good. If you try to do anything else, I'll let this guy fuck you up. Do you understand that?'

Again, the PC nodded.

'Let him up.'

McGill sat the PC up and stayed behind him with his arm around his throat.

Sinclair moved and knelt directly in front of the now terrified officer. 'Get on the radio and get your colleague in here, now.'

The PC pressed the transmit button on his radio and spoke into the mic. 'Sarge, you need to get in here.'

The voice that replied was quiet and tinny. 'Can't you do anything on your own? What is it?'

'Trust me, sarge. You need to be in here.'

The tinny voice sounded more annoyed. 'For fuck's sake.

I'm on my way up. This had better be good.'

'Sorry about this, mate.' McGill tightened his hold and, once again, the PC was unconscious.

They left the flat and stood beside the lift; they'd assumed the older officer would come up that way, but wanted to be sure. They heard a mechanical clank as the lift descended to the bottom floor, and watched as the numbers glowed in turn as it headed for the top floor.

As soon as the lift was half way up, Sinclair and McGill ran down the stairs and stopped at the front door. McGill checked outside, the police vehicle was empty and the street was quiet. 'That's it, let's go.' He pushed open the door and they both slipped out, unnoticed.

* * *

The safe house was empty. Sinclair and McGill had searched it top to bottom to ensure Porter wasn't there. When they'd arrived back from their recce trip, they'd found his simple note:

Gone to the bank. Back in an hour. Callum.

'Stupid.' Sinclair screwed up the note and threw it across the room. 'What does he think he's doing?'

McGill sat on the couch. 'We can't go looking for him, he could be anywhere. It was a big enough risk just going into London today. We'll have to wait a while and see if he makes it back on his own.'

They waited: one hour; two; three. Sinclair started to fill a backpack. 'That's long enough. Something's happened. I'm going to find him.'

McGill packed his own bag: clothes, money, weapons;

things that would be useful, but not heavy enough to slow them down. 'Okay, but we do this properly. We do it my way.'

'What are you planning?'

'I've had enough of this sneaking about shit. Constantly hiding and waiting for Vadim to come and find us. We go on the offensive, hunt these fuckers down and get Callum back.'

'With Simeon and Danny in prison we'll be on our own.'

'I think it's time to contact Harry Nash. See what else he can do to help us out. No matter what we think of what he is, he must have a network of people who can move us around, watchers who'll know if there's anything out of the ordinary going on. He's our best bet of finding Callum.'

'What if we're too late? Without the evidence, the authorities won't believe us.'

'Then we bury Vadim and his whole organisation ourselves. We kill everyone who gets in our way. We take out Vadim and finish this once and for all. Agreed?'

Sinclair nodded. 'Okay, let's get on with it.'

McGill used the details they'd been given to leave a message for Nash and waited for a return call. Within twenty minutes a meeting had been arranged for the next day. All they had to do was get there.

They put on their packs, had one last check to make sure they had everything, and left the house. Out in the street the streetlights were just coming on; they had twelve hours to get to the meeting. There was no traffic and no one walking about, it was going to be harder to blend in than it had been earlier in the day. Public transport wasn't an option as they couldn't risk being stopped by police when they were carrying weapons, that was going to make it a difficult trip. They would need to stay off the roads where police could have checkpoints. Stop and search powers were being used liberally by anti-terrorist officers as they tried to pick up anyone they saw as a threat. An escaped convict carrying a gun would definitely fall into that category.

The only option Sinclair and McGill had was to take an indirect route that kept them away from as many public roads as possible. They would have to stick to using paths that crossed parks, and moving through gardens that lay between rows of houses. Car parks, tow paths and underpasses – anything that was out of public view. As they got closer, they would have to use back alleys and roof tops, crawl through the sewers if they had to. Whatever it took. They had to treat this like a covert mission behind enemy lines. With Vadim and the police looking for them, that's what it was.

* * *

When Porter woke up he was lying on his back on a mouldy, stinking mattress in the corner of a darkened room. The stench of urine was overpowering and he gagged as he took in a breath. He rolled onto his side; a thin sliver of light was coming from underneath the door, opposite where he lay, but not enough for him to see what, or who else was in the room.

Porter sat up, his head pounded and his tongue was stuck to the roof of his mouth. He couldn't remember much about the last few hours or how he'd got there. He remembered the white van pulling up and somebody grabbing him, but after that, everything was a jumble of lights and colours flashing through his memory.

He climbed to his feet, his legs like jelly, and staggered towards the door. He tried to open it but, unsurprisingly, it was locked. He ran his hands up the wall beside the door until, at shoulder height, his fingers brushed against what he was looking for: a light switch. He turned it on and immediately regretted it. When the single, bare lightbulb flickered into life, it was like someone had poured hot sand into his eyes. He screwed them tightly shut as he tried to adjust to the sudden assault on his senses. His head pounded even harder and waves of nausea attacked his stomach. He staggered back to the other side of the room and lost his balance, falling back onto the mattress where he curled into a ball.

Through the pain that filled his head, Porter heard a padlock rattling as someone unlocked the door. When the door opened even more light flooded into the room, making him curl into an even tighter ball. He heard someone walk across the room to the mattress and put something down beside him. 'Something to eat and drink, Callum. The drugs will wear off soon, you'll feel much better. Just try and get some sleep. We'll all talk in the morning.'

Porter tried to open his eyes to see who his captor was, but it was no good. He couldn't see anything but a bright, blinding light. 'Who are you? What do you want?'

The voice was calm and quiet. 'You don't need to know who I am, Callum. Just drink some water and sleep.'

Porter listened to the man's footsteps as he walked back out of the room, switching off the light as he left.

Porter waited until he heard the door close and the padlock rattle before opening his eyes. The pain in his head and eyes was now a dull throb. He grabbed one of the plastic bottles his captor had brought in and took a long drink, spilling some of the water on his chest. He lay back down and stared at the light under the door, thoughts running through his head.

What the fuck was he doing here? Why hadn't he stayed in the house like Ali had told him? He'd been stupid to think he could take care of things himself, stupid. He knew the only reason he was alive was because whoever had him locked up wanted the folder. He had no doubt they would force him to get it for them, but then what? Would he end up like Justin, another suicide from a bridge? Maybe something even worse. Where were Ali and Frank? Would they come and get him? He didn't want to be here any more, he didn't want to be involved in any of this. He wanted to go home, he wanted to see his family again. He closed his eyes and began to sob.

Chapter 31

The Black Lion was at the centre of an area that estate agents would describe as up and coming. Traditionally, it was an area of crushing poverty. Most of the residents worked in manual jobs at the docks, or at one of the small manufacturers that littered the area. In more recent years, they'd watched as neighbourhoods closer to the city were given over to high-value office blocks and housing – part of the capital's financial district. There was a spreading wave of development, funded by the billions that poured into the city in the eighties, but progress was slow. It wasn't until the millennium that the Black Lion had started to see signs of investment around it.

The area was now enjoying the effects of the massive investment that had accompanied the 2012 Olympic Games. It was an easily commutable distance from the heart of the city, and modern, high-value properties were being built in neighbouring boroughs. Property prices were on the up, a large part of the reason Nash had stepped in and snapped up the pub when the previous owner had died.

From the outside it still looked a little run down. The exterior was surrounded by a cage of scaffolding, where Nash was having the crumbling brickwork renewed and the windows replaced. By the time the work was finished, it would look as good as new, but it would still have its historic appearance.

On the inside no changes had been made, yet. It was still an old-fashioned, spit and sawdust boozer. Bare, oak floorboards, with some questionable stains, ran in front of a classic mahogany bar; the once glistening brass fittings that adorned it, were now tarnished and dented with some missing altogether.

Nash's plan was to rip out the old mahogany and replace it with a modern bar and food counter, selling craft beers, flavoured gins and various snacks. The floorboards and wooden furniture would be cleaned up and kept, and a coffee bar would be built in the corner. The walls were to be stripped back to the brick and some industrial lighting fitted. Everything that millennials and hipsters wanted from a pub. Of course, the regulars wouldn't be happy, but they'd get used to it.

Sinclair and McGill opened the door and walked up to the bar, watched every step of the way by two men who sat in a corner booth nursing mugs of coffee. An old woman, in her seventies, cleaned glasses behind the bar and placed them on a shelf above the taps. She smiled at McGill. 'We're not serving alcohol at the moment, my love, but I can do you both a cup of coffee and a bacon roll, if you'd like one?'

McGill returned the smile. 'I'd love a bacon roll and a coffee. Thanks very much.'

'You both look like you need one.'

McGill and Sinclair were looking rough. It had been a long night, zig-zagging their way to the pub from the safe house. They had crawled through hedges and hidden behind several wheelie bins on the way, and now sported a covering of twigs and bits of leaves. They both had smudges of dirt on their faces and looked like they had slept on the street.

Sinclair tucked some stray hair behind her ear. 'We're here to meet with Harry Nash. We're Mr and Mrs Johnson.'

'I thought you might be. I knew you weren't local, never seen you around here before.' She nodded to the two men who were nursing their pints. In unison, they took a mouthful of beer and went back to their game of dominoes. 'I'm Barbara, I was told to expect you. Now, if you follow me, I'll take you upstairs.'

Sinclair and McGill followed Barbara, as she led them through a doorway at the end of the bar and up a narrow flight of stairs. At the top was an equally narrow hallway that had several doorways leading off it. Barbara opened one of the doors and walked through.

On the other side of the door was a double bedroom, easily big enough to accommodate the king-size bed that was under the large sash window in the middle of the wall. On the right-hand side was a fitted wardrobe that covered the full length of the room, floor to ceiling. Barbara walked to the window and closed the curtains; she opened another door that led to an en suite bathroom. 'There you go, my loves. Get yourselves cleaned up and make yourselves at home. There are clothes in the wardrobe that might fit you both. Take your time, I'll go and make some coffee.'

Sinclair dropped her backpack on the bed. 'Thanks, Barbara.'

The old woman left the room and closed the door behind her.

Sinclair looked at McGill. 'Well, she was nice. Bit of a cliché, though. Do you think she's actually like that?'

'You mean the typical East End barmaid? Salt of the earth. Went to school with the Kray twins, cor blimey, apples and pears.'

Sinclair laughed at McGill's attempt at a cockney accent. 'Maybe she puts on an act for any tourists that drop in.'

McGill nodded. 'Yeah. I'm sure this place is a stop off on all the open-top bus routes.'

Sinclair was rifling through the wardrobe looking for something she could change into. She went for her typical jeans and T-shirt. 'These'll do. Right, me first in the shower.' She ran to the bathroom, smiling at McGill as she closed the door.

McGill shouted after her, 'How old are you, twelve?'

* * *

It took a little under an hour for the two of them to get cleaned up. McGill opened the curtains but the light was blocked by the scaffolding. 'Lovely view.'

'How long do you think he'll keep us waiting?'

McGill shrugged. 'Maybe he wants to show us who's in charge. Maybe it's a—'

McGill was cut short by a knock on the door.

Sinclair reached out and opened it. Barbara was standing in the hallway, smiling at them. 'Are you ready?'

McGill smiled back. 'As ready as we'll ever be, Barbara. Lead the way.'

The old woman headed along the hall, followed by McGill. Sinclair closed the door behind her and quickly caught up. At the end of the hallway was another door, identical to the one they had gone through into the bedroom. Barbara turned the handle and pushed it open, waving them into the room. 'Here you go, my loves. I'll put a pot of tea on for you and bring it through in a minute.'

McGill stepped to one side to let her leave. 'Thank you, Barbara.'

Inside the room, a woman in her mid-forties sat at a plain pine desk, typing on a laptop. She wore light brown trousers, and a white shirt with the sleeves turned up at the cuff. Her dark hair was gathered up in a bun and she wore horn-rimmed glasses. As Barbara closed the door, the woman looked up and removed her glasses. 'Thanks, Mum.'

Sinclair and McGill looked at each other. They weren't sure what they had expected to find in the room, but this wasn't it at all. McGill wondered who she was – Nash's PA? Did gangsters have PAs? The woman stood and waved them towards a pair of old, brown, leather sofas that had been placed on either side of one of the tables brought up from the bar. 'Have a seat, we'll have some tea in a minute.'

The door opened and Barbara reappeared with a tray full of cups and a teapot. 'There we are.' She put it on the table and, once again, left the room.

McGill couldn't believe how surreal and banal this all felt. 'We came for a meeting with Harry Nash. Is he here?'

The woman poured out three cups of tea. 'I'm Harry Nash, kind of. Please, help yourselves to milk and sugar.'

Sinclair took one of the cups. 'You're not what I was expecting.'

The woman smiled. 'I'm Harriette Nash. My friends call me Harry. Same name as my dad, different reputation. Where are my manners?' She stood and held out her hand. 'It's good

199

to meet you both.'

McGill shook hands but looked confused. 'So, it's your dad who's the gangster?'

'My dad is still the head of the organisation, but he's mainly retired now. I stepped in to run things two years ago, after he had his heart attack. Too much good living and excitement, I imagine. I changed the whole set-up. We're more of a legit business these days, or we're trying to be; stocks and shares, property development, that kind of thing.'

Sinclair took a sip of her tea. 'You've got some shady contacts for a legit business.'

'It's only been two years since my dad retired and he cast a big shadow around here. His name still counts for a lot, but there are people who would like to see him dead. I have to protect my family, and that means employing some guys with a questionable history. Most were here when Dad was running things – some of them are leg breakers from the early days. I like to look after them. After all, where else would they go?'

McGill didn't try to hide the sarcasm in his voice. 'So you're a charity now?'

Sinclair glared at him. 'You'll have to excuse Frank, he doesn't play well with others.'

'It's okay, I know it sounds a bit strange.' Nash poured herself another cup of tea. 'Look, my dad is ... was, a hard man – brutal, some would say – but he had to be. When he started out, the Krays were at their height. He had to make sure he didn't step on their toes, and at the same time, protect his little bit of territory, violently in most cases. I'm a different generation, I've been trying to change things for years. I finally convinced him you can make more money with a laptop than through illegal gambling and smuggled fags.'

'So, he became a business man?'

Nash shook her head. 'Dad hasn't changed at all. He's still an old-fashioned cockney gangster. He doesn't take any shit, and if someone gets out of line they get a slap. But he's getting on a bit now and things have changed. There's a new breed of criminal here now, that doesn't play by our rules. Eastern European gangs, heavily into drugs, people smuggling and prostitution. Dad was never involved in anything like that. Mum would never have allowed it.'

McGill was starting to warm to Harriette Nash, she reminded him of some of the women he'd grown up with. Streetwise and smart with a fierce sense of loyalty, they weren't afraid to break the law, but deep down they were good people and looked after their own. 'Your dad sounds like someone I would get along with.'

'I'm sure you would, Frank. I'll introduce you to him when I can. He spends most of his time at our country house, doesn't like the city any more. Since I invested in this place, Mum travels in now and again to give me a hand, she's a big help. I'm hoping that in five years we'll be completely legit, and won't need to be involved in guns or violence any more.'

Sinclair put her cup on the table. 'I hope you achieve that, Harry, I really do, but I'm afraid the help we need now is going to involve both.'

Nash leaned forward, her elbows on her knees. 'When Gabriel Vance asked us for help, he knew my dad wouldn't say no. Gabriel saved my dad's life when one of the other firms had him shot. Kept him alive till the ambulance arrived. We owe him a lot. So, if he wants me to help you, I'll do everything I can.' She sat back again. 'What do you need from me? I assume you need help rescuing your friend?'

Sinclair sat up straight. 'Callum, yes, but how did you know?'

'I had one of our young guys watch the safe house, in case anyone came snooping about. He saw Callum leave and he followed him to the Strand. He said three men in a van picked him up.'

'We were on the Strand yesterday, he must have been going to the bank; we must have just missed him. Do you know where they're holding him?'

Nash walked to her desk and picked up a page ripped from a notebook. 'This is the address. I've got someone watching it.'

Sinclair took the note and looked at the address. 'We'll get over there, now.'

Nash shook her head. 'Not so fast, you don't know the area. Give me a minute and I'll get someone to go with you.' She picked up her mobile and tapped the screen. 'Ask Luke to come upstairs, please, I've got a job for him.'

Chapter 32

Callum Porter didn't feel any better than he had the previous evening. His head was still throbbing and he was unsteady on his feet, staggering around like a Friday night drunk. They had questioned him for hours, late into the night. He'd tried to resist, he really had, but in the end he couldn't take any more pain. He'd told them everything: the notebook, Shawford's memoir folder, the safety-deposit box. His body was bruised and his ribs ached. He had taken punch after punch, only his face was unmarked. Justin had died rather than tell them anything, but Porter couldn't take it. He felt ashamed.

When he woke up they gave him some clean clothes and a couple of paracetamols; they hadn't kicked in yet and he felt sick. He tried to shield his eyes from the daylight, as he was frogmarched down the path and into the van, but no matter what he did, the light found a way to jab at his eyes.

One of his captors, the one with a beard that made him look like Captain Haddock, handed him a pair of cheap, red plastic sunglasses. 'Here, put these on. The shit feeling will ease off in a little while.'

Porter put on his new eyewear and climbed into one of the front passenger seats, next to the driver. The third man, who he had seen the previous day, had left the house early. 'Where are you taking me?'

The captain climbed in beside him and closed the door. 'Today, Callum, you're going to take us to where the evidence is. We're all going to the bank to make a withdrawal.'

Porter felt that his betrayal of Justin was now complete. He was going to hand everything to them. Ali and Frank couldn't help him now. Vadim's men were about to get hold of the only thing that could stop all of this. He bowed his head and clasped his hands together in his lap. He knew it would also mean his death, they didn't need him any more. The driver put the van into gear and pulled away.

Brown & MacMillan had just opened its doors when the van pulled up outside. The driver stayed where he was while Captain Haddock helped Callum climb out onto the pavement. 'Just do everything I tell you, Callum, and you'll be fine.'

Porter paused and looked at him. 'That's not true, is it?'

The man looked Porter in the eyes. 'It'll go better for you if we get what we want. Do you understand that?'

Porter nodded. 'Yes.'

'Good. Let's go.'

The receptionist had only just made a coffee and sat down when they walked in. She was hoping for a little time to fully wake up before having to deal with any customers. She had been at an old friend's birthday party the night before, and her head still felt a bit muggy, like it was packed with cotton wool. She put down her cup and flashed her best smile. 'Good morning, how can I help you?'

Porter didn't respond, he just stood still, head bowed. The bearded guy stepped forward and handed the receptionist a piece of paper and Porter's fake passport. 'You'll have to excuse my nephew, he's a little under the weather this morning. He'd like to access his deposit box, please.'

The receptionist took the passport. 'It's okay, I feel a little rough myself, to be honest.' She typed some details into her keyboard and checked that the passport matched. 'Everything looks good, if you'll follow me.'

Porter and his guard followed the receptionist down to the basement and, after checking in with the security guard, went into the vault.

The receptionist put her key in the front of the box and turned it. 'I'll leave you two alone. Just put your key in to get access. Let the security guard know once you've finished.' She walked out, heading back up the stairs.

Captain Haddock turned Porter's key in the lock and slid the box out, placing it on the table in the middle of the vault. 'Time to see what all the fuss is about.' He opened the box and they both looked in.

Sitting alone in the box was a book. Not a notebook, or a folder full of information, but a dog-eared edition of *The Count of Monte Cristo.* Captain Haddock picked it up. 'What the fuck is this? Where's the folder?'

Porter shook his head. 'I don't know. I thought it would be here.'

Haddock threw the book against the wall and kicked the table. 'Fuck.'

The security guard stood at the door. 'Is everything okay, gentlemen?'

Porter picked up the book, tucking it into the waistband of his jeans.

Captain Haddock grabbed Porter's arm and pushed him

towards the stairs. 'Everything's just fucking dandy. We're leaving.'

Porter was pushed through reception, out of the front door and back into the van.

The driver put down his newspaper. 'Everything good?'

Captain Haddock got in and slammed the door. 'No, everything isn't fucking good.'

'What happened?'

He gestured at Porter. 'Fucknuts here said the folder would be in there, but all we found was some stupid book.'

The driver started the engine. 'What do we do now?'

'We get back to the house. I'm gonna have to phone Vadim and try and explain why he shouldn't just have us killed for fucking up.'

The driver turned the wheel and pulled away from the bank. 'You ever met this guy, Vadim?'

Captain Haddock shook his head. 'None of us have. He's just a voice on the phone. From what I've heard, meeting him shortens your lifespan.' He swiped the screen of his phone and pressed the only number stored in it.

Chapter 33

The Home Secretary stood at the despatch box and confirmed that, after internal party meetings, he would be stepping into the role of prime minister during the current crisis. 'I can also confirm that the PM is now under the care of our own wonderful doctors and nurses and is receiving the best of care. He has not recovered consciousness, yet, but doctors are hopeful he will very soon. I look forward to welcoming him back into the house, once he is fit and well, and handing back the leadership to him.'

Shouts of *here, here* echoed around the chamber. The Home Secretary sat down and shuffled his papers, nodding as he acknowledged the expressions of support.

The leader of the opposition stood and waited for the noise to die down. 'I would also like to express our wishes for a speedy recovery and a quick return to the house.'

More cries of *here, here* accompanied the Home Secretary's return to the despatch box. He checked his papers and cleared his throat. 'It is with a heavy heart that I come to the House today. The security services have, this morning, briefed me on the evidence that has been gathered regarding the despicable attack on our democracy. It seems the perpetrator, Asil Balik, was part of a much larger conspiracy that appears to have had the backing of the Turkish government.'

There were gasps of disbelief at the thought of a fellow NATO member being involved in such an atrocity. The Home Secretary held up his hand to quiet the chamber. 'I have communicated with the Turkish Prime Minister and let him know, in no uncertain terms, that Her Majesty's Government expect their full cooperation in catching the rest of the conspirators.'

'Here, here.'

'We have the full backing of the other members of NATO and I spoke with the President of the United States this morning. He has pledged their unconditional support.'

'Here, here ... here, here.'

The Home Secretary nodded again and turned over his sheet of notes. 'We must consider the possibility that the Turkish government will refuse to give up the other conspirators. In that situation, we, as a government, as a country, must bring these people to justice ourselves. The decision to send our brave men and women of the armed forces into harm's way must never be taken lightly, but we believe it will be necessary to protect the citizens of the United Kingdom from further terror attacks. I will be having meetings in the coming days with the leaders of the other parties, and Her Majesty, in the hope that this can be concluded diplomatically. However, we must be ready in the event that military action is unavoidable.'

'Here, here ... here, here ... here, here.'

The Home Secretary sat back down, the House's enthusiastic endorsement ringing in his ears. Outwardly, he looked grave and statesman-like, but on the inside he was laughing. Things couldn't have gone better. He would be moving out of his relatively humble town house and into Downing Street, before the year was out.

* * *

William Darby had only been a member of parliament since the last election, two years ago. He was still, very much, learning the ropes. He had never imagined that he would have to vote on military action, on whether the country went to war. He still hadn't decided which way he was going to vote. He didn't consider himself to be a pacifist. If he was honest, he had never given it that much thought. A lot of the other back benchers were in favour of going to war, if it was necessary, and he was pretty sure a couple of them were in favour even if it wasn't. He was more worried about his reputation and his career prospects. The front bench would see it as betrayal if he voted against them, but he didn't want to be judged by future generations for committing the country to a disastrous, costly war. He had friends whose sons were in the military. How would he be able to look them in the face if something happened?

His mind wasn't on what he was doing as he sauntered down the road, briefcase in hand, towards the underground. He didn't hear the gunfire and was never aware that he had been shot. He died instantly. He would never know about the other people who panicked and ran as he crumpled to the floor. He wouldn't see the aftermath of the attack, the number of other people who were shot by the sniper in the next ten minutes. He wouldn't see the news reports from the scene, or the families who suffered. William Darby was the first of many to die that day.

Chapter 34

They were all sitting in a black people carrier, parked behind a large hedge on the corner of the street. Sinclair and McGill were sitting together in the back. Nash sat in the driver's seat with Luke Durand next to her. From where they were parked, they could just make out the van, and the house where Porter was being held. They had watched the van return, and the two men lead Porter back into the house, and decided to wait to see if the third henchman came back. As they heard the news of the Westminster shootings on the radio, heard about the loss of innocent life, they realised where the third man probably was.

Sinclair was clenching her fists, seething. 'When is this fucker going to stop? How many people is he willing to kill to get what he wants?'

Nash turned around. 'Do you really think it's the same guy that's doing all of this?'

Sinclair nodded. 'There's no doubt in my mind. You don't know him like we do.'

McGill put his hand on top of Sinclair's. 'Ali's right. Vadim is trying to create fear on the streets. He's trying to whip up the population so they'll back his call to arms.'

Nash spoke to Luke Durand. 'Then we'd better do everything we can to stop him. Are you ready for this, Luke?'

'Whatever you need, boss.'

Luke Durand wasn't the name he'd been born with, he hadn't used that name for years. Not since his twenty-first birthday party, the night he had stabbed his stepfather to death. He'd always blamed him for his mother's suicide, after the years of abuse she had suffered. Harry Nash senior had hidden him, got him a new passport and smuggled him out of the country, he would always owe him for that.

Alone in a foreign country, and not knowing the language, there weren't many jobs he could get. He'd begged, and worked as a labourer and a street trader, but never for long. He had to keep moving. It was the recruitment poster in Marseille that had convinced him to join the Foreign Legion. The training and service under a notoriously brutal regime had taught him a lot. He had learned to fight. Not just on the battlefield, but to protect himself from some of the other legionnaires. They were a brotherhood, but a violent one.

After five years, and with his brand new French name and ID, he had travelled the world working as a mercenary and a bodyguard, but he'd never forgotten Nash's kindness. Once he was back at home, battle weary and ready to settle for a more stable life, there was only one job he was interested in.

Durand turned to McGill. 'It's your show, chief, just tell me where you want me.'

McGill checked his weapon and put it back into his jacket. 'We need you to walk up and knock on the front door. They won't know who you are, it'll give us the edge. We just need a distraction; give us some time so we can enter the house from the back.'

Durand nodded. 'I can do that, no problem.'

'Okay, we know there are only two of them in there, so it shouldn't be a problem, but be careful. We have to make sure Callum is safe. Harry, you stay here and watch for us coming out, we might need to leave in a hurry. If anything looks bad, or if the other guy comes back, give us a long blast on the horn. Everyone ready?'

They all nodded.

'Good. Let's go.'

They left the people carrier; Sinclair and McGill worked their way to the back of the house while Durand crossed the road and walked up the path to the front door.

McGill and Sinclair were in the rear garden of the house. The sloping lawn and flower beds were overgrown and an old three-seater settee was propped up in one corner. It was a mess, but it fitted in with the neighbours' gardens on both sides. The windows at the back of the house were boarded up, apart from one. There was a grimy, cracked pane of glass above the single-storey extension that wasn't.

McGill checked through a one-inch gap in the boards covering the window next to the back door. He could see the two men sitting in the kitchen, eating. McGill raised two fingers, signalling to Sinclair. Porter must be on his own upstairs.

Sinclair climbed up the drainpipe and onto the roof of the extension. They were running the risk of being seen, but people in this area tended to mind their own business, unwilling to get involved in anything that might be gang or drug related. This house had all the giveaway signs that showed it might belong to a dealer.

She checked the un-boarded window. One corner of the glass was broken and covered with a supermarket carrier bag.

She moved the bag to one side and looked in. The window was at the end of a long hallway. She could see right through to the front of the house, there were no signs of movement. She was about to open the window and climb in when a man appeared from a doorway on the left-hand side of the hallway. Shit, there were three of them. The Westminster sniper had somehow got back into the house without them seeing him. She held up a finger towards McGill.

Luke Durand knocked on the front door. The two men in the kitchen immediately drew their weapons. The man upstairs did the same and moved to the window that overlooked the front door. Durand was standing with his back to the door and his hands in his pockets. He spun around and knocked again, louder.

McGill watched the two men in the kitchen. They nodded to each other and one of them moved out into the hallway. McGill aimed at the man left in the kitchen and held up three fingers on his left hand.

Sinclair aimed her weapon at the man upstairs and watched for McGill's signal.

The second man from the kitchen walked down the hallway and looked through the spyhole in the front door. If they all stayed quiet, their visitor would walk away. Everyone waited.

Durand knocked a third time. The man behind the door holstered his weapon. He was going to have to get rid of this prick. He unlocked the door and swung it open. 'Whatever it is you want, you're in the wrong place.'

Durand looked past the man and down the hallway. 'Is Dave in?'

'There is no Dave here, fuck off.'

Durand put his hands back in his pockets. 'Come on, mate.

Everyone knows Big Dave. I want to buy some gear off him.'

The man stepped out of the door. 'There's no Dave here, you prick.'

McGill counted down with his fingers: three, two, one; he and Sinclair fired simultaneously, each of their targets dropping where they stood. The man at the door spun round at the thud of the bodies hitting the floor. Durand stepped forward and clamped his left hand around the man's mouth, slicing open his throat with the butterfly knife that had appeared seemingly from nowhere. He pushed the man into the hallway, entered the house and closed the door behind him.

Upstairs, Sinclair had climbed in through the window and made sure her target was dead. She found the key to Porter's room and opened the door.

Porter sat up on his mattress, he thought he was hallucinating. The figure framed in the doorway looked just like Ali Sinclair. He rubbed his eyes and looked again.

Sinclair turned on the light. 'Callum. Let's go.'

Porter managed to stand, although he struggled to stay upright – his legs were weak and one of his knees was swollen. His face was bruised and bloody. With no need to go to the bank again, the three thugs had seen no reason to hold back. He held out his arms and staggered towards Sinclair.

Sinclair grabbed him and held him up. 'Callum. What did those bastards do to you?'

Porter was in tears. 'I knew you'd come for me, Ali. I dreamt you would, you and Frank.'

Sinclair shouted down the stairs. 'Frank. Get up here.'

McGill had kicked open the back door and fired another shot into the man in the kitchen, just to make sure. He heard

Sinclair shout and ran into the hallway. He jumped over the man Luke had killed and bounded up the stairs. Durand kept watch through the front door spyhole.

Sinclair was struggling to hold up Porter when McGill arrived. 'Help me, Frank.'

McGill grabbed hold of Porter and lifted him onto his shoulders. 'Right, everyone out.'

McGill carried Porter down the stairs, followed by Sinclair; Durand opened the front door and waved to Nash, who had the engine of the people carrier running. She let off the handbrake and turned the corner. As soon as she arrived at the end of the path, the other three left the house. Durand took the lead, checking both ways along the street before running to the car and jumping in the front. McGill followed carrying Porter, with Sinclair bringing up the rear after she had closed the front door of the house. Once they were all inside, Nash floored the accelerator, the wheels screeched as she pulled out and sped away from the house.

Chapter 35

Lancaster walked along the anonymous corridors of Vauxhall Cross towards another meeting with Kelvin Hadley. This time he would have to be conciliatory, he would have to pander to his boss's ego to get what he needed. It wasn't going to be easy, but Carter and Kinsella's survival could depend on it. There had already been one attempt on their lives, Lancaster had to get them out of prison and somewhere safe. Once again, he knocked on the door of C's office and waited. This was the game they always played – Hadley letting Lancaster know who was in charge.

'Come in.'

Lancaster opened the door and walked into C's office.

Hadley looked up from the papers on his desk. 'Edward, come in and close the door.'

Lancaster took off his coat, hung it on the back of the door and sat down.

Hadley closed the folder on his desk and looked up at Lancaster. 'So, Edward, what can I do for you? You said it was important.'

Lancaster took a deep breath. Hadley was already winding him up, suggesting that whatever they normally had a meeting about didn't matter. 'Yes, sir, very important. It's about

Simeon Carter and Danny Kinsella.'

Hadley sat up at the mention of their names. 'Have you found new evidence, Edward? I knew they were guilty all along.'

This was going to be more difficult than Lancaster needed it to be. 'No, sir, no new evidence and they aren't guilty of anything.'

'How do you know?'

Lancaster let out a small sigh. 'Because they work for me.'

Hadley stared at him, his anger rising. 'WHAT? You mean to tell me that these … terrorists have been working for us, all this time, and you never mentioned it?'

'I couldn't be sure who to trust. We had no idea of Vadim's identity, he could be any one of us.'

Hadley calmed down a little. 'Okay, I can understand the logic, but you still don't know who Vadim is, do you?'

Lancaster paused. He didn't want to tell anyone what Sinclair had said about the Home Secretary until he was in a position to do something about it. With Vadim killing off anyone who could identify him, the fewer people who knew who he was, the safer they would all be. 'No, sir. We don't know who Vadim is, yet.'

Hadley shook his head. 'Maybe we need to bring in someone else to do the job.'

Lancaster was seething. He gritted his teeth and pushed the anger away. 'That's your decision, sir, but I'm here to talk about Carter and Kinsella.'

Hadley grinned, he had won that round. 'What do you mean when you say they work for you? They don't work directly for us, do they? I don't want any of this traced back to me.'

Lancaster couldn't believe it. With everything that was going on, all he was worried about was his own arse. 'You don't have to worry about that, they were working unofficially.'

'Well, that's one thing. What were they doing for you?'

Lancaster swallowed. The next part might go down even worse. 'They're part of a team. The team I put together with Sinclair. They're Sinclair's backup.'

Hadley slammed his fist on the table. 'Holy shit, Lancaster. I knew someone was helping Sinclair, but I never thought it would be you. She's an escaped convict, for Christ's sake.'

Lancaster's anger was going to get the better of him. 'She's a wrongly convicted, former intelligence officer. One of our own who we abandoned in a world of shit.'

Surprisingly, Hadley was suddenly the one who was contrite. He held up his hand, palm towards Lancaster. 'Okay, okay. I appreciate she's had it rough, and she helped sort out that business with Bazarov, but she's still on the run. Do you know where she is?'

'Not exactly, sir, but I'm sure Simeon Carter can get a message to her.'

Hadley sat forward, his elbows resting on the desk. 'What is it you want me to do, Edward?'

Lancaster sensed that, for once, Kelvin was open to being helpful, at least, it appeared that way. Whether Hadley was genuine or not, Lancaster needed to take advantage of any favours he could get. 'We need to get Carter and Kinsella out of prison. Their lives are in danger.'

'And what can they do for me?'

There was the old Kelvin, only thinking of himself. 'Sinclair knows the location of a folder of evidence that proves the conspiracy – proves who Vadim really is. She'll only give it to us if Carter is safe.'

Hadley nodded. 'And if Carter dies, we lose Sinclair and the folder.'

'Yes, sir. If Carter and Kinsella die, Sinclair will disappear and take the folder with her.'

Hadley stood up and paced around the office. 'We can't allow that, Edward. We need that folder, we need to know what's inside.'

Lancaster didn't turn around to look at Hadley, another part of the game. 'They are back in court tomorrow afternoon. It would be in all our interests if they were granted bail.'

Hadley returned to his desk. 'I'll make some calls, call in some favours, but you'll have to do something for me, Edward.'

Lancaster had known he would be made to pay for this. 'What is that, sir?'

Hadley sat down again. 'Once Carter is out of prison, I need Sinclair to come in. I need her to hand the folder to me. Can you arrange that?'

Lancaster knew that was going to be a tough ask. Hadley obviously wanted the credit. Sinclair wouldn't like that. 'I'm sure I can arrange something, but the meeting will have to be somewhere neutral. There's no way she's going to come here.'

Hadley slid a brown file across the desk. 'That's a report on three killings that took place yesterday. One of the victims appears to be the Westminster sniper. From witness descriptions, it looks like Sinclair and McGill were involved.'

Lancaster flicked through the pages; it looked like Sinclair and McGill's handiwork. 'I had no idea they were up to anything like this, sir, but it looks like they've done us another favour.'

Hadley drummed his fingers on the desk and slowly nodded. 'Look, Edward, we've had our differences in the past, and we haven't always seen eye to eye, but we're on the same side here. We can't have Sinclair and McGill running around London acting as judge, jury and executioner.'

Lancaster retrieved his coat from the back of the door. 'I'm sure, if we can convince her that we know she's innocent, I can talk her into coming in.'

'Okay, Edward, and let's keep this between us.'

Lancaster opened the door. 'Will do, sir.' He walked out and closed the door behind him.

Chapter 36

They were all sitting upstairs at the Black Lion; Nash was sitting at her desk, McGill and Sinclair sat on one of the leather sofas and Durand sat opposite them on the other. The door opened and Barbara showed Porter into the room.

Sinclair jumped up and went to help him. She guided him to the sofa and helped him sit down. His face was bruised but he had been cleaned up and had the worst gashes treated. His left hand was bandaged and his right knee was strapped up. Sinclair sat on the arm of the sofa and put her arm around him. 'How do you feel, Callum?'

He tried to force a smile but his face hurt too much. 'I feel a lot better after that night's sleep, but I'm still aching pretty much everywhere.'

'The bastards had no reason to do that to you.'

'They just kept asking me where the folder was, and I explained that we'd thought it was in the box. They didn't believe me, obviously.'

Harriette walked to the sofas and sat next to Luke. 'You'll stay here until you're well. My mum will look after you. She used to be a nurse.'

Porter nodded. 'Barbara's been fantastic. I wanna thank

you all for what you did. I really thought I was going to die.'

McGill put his hand on Porter's leg. 'You're our friend, Callum. I don't have many, so I need to look after the ones I've got.'

Sinclair walked to the desk and picked up a notebook. She read the notes she had scribbled down the night before. 'I've tried to work out where the folder might be, Callum, but it's no use. Justin left the clues for you. Can you figure anything out at all?'

Porter shuffled in his seat. 'Yeah. When we got to the bank there was just this in the box.' He handed the book to McGill.

McGill looked at the worn paperback. It had bloodstains on it now where Porter had clung on to it as he was beaten up. He opened it. Inside the cover was a simple inscription:

To Justin, love Callum.

'This was Justin's?'

'Yes, it was. I bought it for him shortly after we met. When I saw it in the box, I knew it was a message from him.'

McGill handed the book back to Porter. 'What's the message?'

'When we first met I worked at the bank, but we actually met at a second-hand bookstore. The first present I bought for him was that copy of *The Count of Monte Cristo*. He loved that book, he used to read it all the time. He wouldn't have left it there without a reason.'

Sinclair had discarded her notebook; nothing she had written matched what Porter was telling them. 'How does the book help us find the folder?'

'Have any of you read the book, do you know the story?'

Sinclair nodded. 'A long time ago, they made us read it at school.'

222

McGill grinned. 'All we read at my school was *The Dandy*. I think I've seen the film, though.'

Porter held up the book. 'In the story, Edmond Dantès is wrongly convicted and sent to prison.'

Sinclair pointed at the book. 'I know that feeling.'

'He escapes, and seeks revenge after retrieving a great treasure hidden on the island of Monte Cristo.'

McGill was listening but didn't see the connection. 'I remember that bit in the film, but how does it help us find the folder?'

Porter tried to sit forward but the pain in his ribs stopped him. He winced but carried on. 'The name of the bookstore was Monte Cristo Books.'

Sinclair placed a cushion behind Porter and helped him sit up. 'Do you think Justin hid the folder there?'

'Thanks, Ali. It would make sense. We spent a lot of time there, it has a little coffee shop next door. We got to know the owner quite well. If Justin had wanted to hide the folder somewhere only I would think of, that would be a good choice.'

'Did you tell the three arseholes in the house any of this?'

Porter shook his head. 'They didn't ask about the book, they thought it was some kind of joke, and I didn't make the connection until later. I only held on to it because it reminded me of Justin; made what they were doing to me a little easier to bear.'

McGill looked Porter in the eye. 'A lot of big, tough men would have buckled under that kind of torture, Callum. You're a brave lad. Never forget that.'

McGill's words meant a great deal to Porter. He had never considered himself brave or strong. He smiled. 'Thanks,

223

Frank.'

Sinclair rested her hand on Porter's back. 'Okay, Callum, you need to rest for a couple of days.' She looked at Nash. 'Do you know this shop, Harry? We need to check it out, see if anyone's watching it.'

Nash picked up her phone. 'Leave it with me.'

Chapter 37

The steel door of the prison rolled open and Simeon Carter walked out, followed by Danny Kinsella. They had both been surprised the previous day when their solicitor had told them they were being released. Carter knew how things like this normally worked: he knew he owed somebody; someone would be expecting something in return for this.

Kinsella looked up at the sky and took a deep breath. 'I told you they'd realise it was a mistake.'

'I wouldn't be so sure, Danny. I think Edward had a hand in this.'

'So, what do we do now, Simeon?'

Carter looked at a black Range Rover that was parked a few metres away from them at the side of the street. The car slowly reversed towards them and stopped in front of Carter. The driver lowered the passenger-side window and leaned across the seat. 'Mr Carter?'

Carter lowered his head and peered through the window. 'That's right.'

The driver sat back up. 'Harry Nash sent me to pick you up. I've been instructed to make sure you're okay and keep you safe.'

Kinsella looked at Carter quizzically. Carter shrugged. 'Okay.'

The driver raised the window and Carter opened the rear door. 'After you, Danny.'

They both climbed into the back of the Range Rover and the driver pulled away.

Carter looked around the inside of the car – it was spotless. Whoever Harry Nash was, he paid a lot of money for his cars and he kept them in good order. He looked at the driver; the man's neck was thicker than his shaved head and Carter could make out a tattoo sticking above the collar of his shirt. Judging by the man's broken nose, and the size of his shoulders, he hadn't always been a driver. 'Can I ask where you're taking us?'

The driver looked in his rear-view mirror. 'You have a meeting, sir. With a Mr Lancaster. I'm to take you there first.'

Carter had known it would be Lancaster who'd arranged their release, but who was this gangster Harry Nash, and how was he involved? This was all getting more confusing by the day. 'I don't suppose you know what's going on, do you?'

The driver looked confused. 'Sir?'

'Doesn't matter, I'm sure I'll find out shortly. Will it take us long to get there?'

'Not long, sir. Just sit back and relax, I'll have you there in twenty minutes.'

* * *

Edward Lancaster sat on the park bench where he and Carter had met many times before. It wasn't overlooked by any buildings and there was only one path up to it. If anyone was going to overhear them without being seen, they would need to deploy some serious technology. He took a sip of his coffee, a second cup sitting on the arm rest, steam rising from it.

Carter appeared at the end of the path and made his way to the bench. He sat down next to Lancaster as if they were two old friends, meeting for a chat. 'Hello, Edward.'

Lancaster handed Carter the cup. 'Hello, Simeon. Thought you might like a decent coffee, now you're no longer a guest of Her Majesty.'

Carter smiled. 'I knew it was you, how did you pull it off?'

'Your solicitor did a lot, he's the only one who had dealings with all of us: you, me, and Harry Nash.'

Carter pointed back towards the car with his thumb. 'How is Nash involved?'

'He's apparently a friend of one of McGill's contacts. Looks like more favours are being called in.'

'Thank God for Frank's dodgy contacts. If not for them, we'd have been dead inside a week. Who arranged for our release? That's above even your pay grade.'

'Let's just say I won't be able to slag my boss off in public ever again.'

Carter took the lid off his coffee and blew the steam from it. He hated drinking through the little hole in the plastic. He was looking forward to a good, strong coffee in a proper mug. 'Can I assume that we now have to do something for him in return?'

Lancaster nodded. 'You know the game so well, Simeon.'

'Give me the bad news, what's it going to cost us?'

Lancaster checked for anyone approaching down the path. 'He wants Sinclair and McGill to come in. He wants the folder handed to him personally.'

Carter laughed. 'Everyone wants the folder, Sinclair – us, Vadim, your boss – we don't even know if Sinclair's managed to get hold of it yet.'

'I hope she has, for all our sakes. The Home Secretary is trying to make a grab for power. In private, he's saying that the PM will never be fit enough to come back. He wants to mount a leadership challenge and he's got backing from MPs in the Commons.'

Carter remembered why he hated politicians. With the country on the brink of absolute chaos, some of them were more worried about positioning themselves to be close to the power. Some of them saw this as a career opportunity. 'What about Ali and Frank? Has anyone spoken to them?'

Lancaster shook his head. 'They dropped off the grid when they were in France, but there was an incident in London that has their hallmark stamped all over it.'

'They are resilient. When you say hallmark, I'm assuming deaths were involved?'

'Three, including the Westminster sniper. Quick, clean and efficient.'

Carter took a sip of his coffee. 'Yeah, that's them. I'll try and get Sinclair to come in but it's up to her. No one will make her do something she's not happy with. Tell your boss that it needs to happen somewhere neutral, somewhere she can see them coming. She won't feel safe otherwise.'

'I've already told him that, he'll let me know when he's got something in place. In the meantime, Simeon, don't tell me where you're staying. It'll be better that way.'

Carter looked back along the path to where the car was parked. 'I'm not sure I know myself.'

Lancaster stood up and held out his hand. 'You know my

number. Call me once you've contacted Sinclair. I'll arrange the meeting.'

Carter finished his coffee and dropped the empty cup into the bin beside the bench. He shook Lancaster's hand. 'Will do, Edward. Take care.' He left Lancaster and walked back to the car.

Chapter 38

Monte Cristo Books was situated on a quiet side street, not far from Pall Mall. From the outside it looked like a small bookshop that was being crowded out by more modern, much bigger businesses. What the casual passer-by didn't realise, what wasn't obvious from the outside, was that Monte Cristo Books covered four floors of the Georgian building and occupied the upper two floors of the neighbouring shops. With close to a million second-hand and antique books, the inside was like a maze where book lovers would come along to lose themselves for hours. The coffee shop next door also belonged to Monte Cristo Books, and was where McGill and Sinclair were sitting.

The street was a dead end and the shop could only be approached from one direction. Sinclair and McGill were sitting in the window seat of the coffee shop – Sinclair facing the bookshop's door and McGill watching the street. 'I don't like this, Ali. If they block off the end of the street, we've got no way out.'

Sinclair took a sip of coffee. 'We won't be here long. Callum goes in and talks to the owner, either the folder's here or it isn't.'

McGill ate his third biscuit. 'Still don't like it.'

Porter walked up to the front desk and smiled at the woman who was looking after the till. 'Is Oliver Marlowe here today? My name's Callum Porter, we've met before.'

The young woman returned his smile. 'He should be here, I'll just check for you.' She picked up a modern reproduction of a 1930s Bakelite telephone and pushed a button, waiting for an answer. 'Oliver, you have a visitor. A Mr Porter. Okay, I will.' She put down the phone. 'He said he'll be right down.'

'Thank you.' Porter looked at Durand, who was standing a few feet from him watching for anything suspicious, and nodded.

After a few minutes, a tall, thin grey-haired man wearing glasses walked through from the back of the shop. He had a stubbly beard and was wearing a tweed jacket that looked a little worn around the cuffs and elbows. He held out his hand to Porter. 'It's good to see you again, Callum.' He glanced at Durand. 'Is Justin not with you? It would be good to see him again, too.'

Porter shook his head. 'Can we talk, Oliver? Somewhere private? It's very important.'

Marlowe looked concerned. 'We can go in the back. Please, come through to my office.' He led them through a corridor of bookshelves to a set of three steps that dropped down to an old mahogany door. Durand stayed at the top of the steps, while Marlowe and Porter went through the door and into the small office at the back of the building. Porter had been in the office one time before, with Justin. It made him more certain that either the folder was there or Marlowe would know something about it.

Marlowe sat on a leather wing back chair, next to an old disused fireplace that now had a vase of artificial flowers in

231

it. He gestured towards an identical chair, opposite. 'Do sit down, Callum. Tell me, how have you been?'

Porter lowered himself onto the well-worn leather, keeping his damaged leg as straight as possible. He took off his sunglasses. 'The skin around his eyes ranged in colour from a deep purple to a sickly yellow. There was a cut on the bridge of his nose and his bottom lip had a deep gash in it. 'I've been better, Oliver.'

'Oh, my poor boy. What on earth happened to you? Were you attacked?'

'It's a long story, Oliver, but some nasty people want something that belonged to Justin. I wouldn't tell them where it was, so they did this.'

Marlowe lowered his voice. 'Is the man outside one of them?' He stood up and moved to his desk. 'We can phone the police. I could lock the door till they get here.'

Porter shook his head. 'It's okay, Oliver, he's here to protect me. There are two more of my friends in the coffee shop.'

Marlowe sat back down. 'What did the people who did that to you want? Who are they, and where's Justin?'

Porter knew that Marlowe had known Justin for some time. They had worked together in the shop and developed a close relationship. What Porter had to say next wasn't going to be easy – for either of them. He swallowed and took a deep breath. 'He's dead, Oliver. They killed him.'

Marlowe didn't move. His eyes were wide and his mouth hung open as he tried to process what Porter had said. He shook his head then sat forward and placed his hand on Porter's knee. 'I'm so sorry, Callum. I really liked Justin. I know you two were close.'

Porter nodded. 'Thank you, Oliver.'

Marlowe sat back; he'd genuinely liked Justin Wyatt and felt sorry for Porter. 'What happened? Why did they kill him?'

'It was the same people who had me beaten. They killed him because he had something they wanted, something important. I think he might have left it here, with you.'

Marlowe nodded. 'He did leave a folder here. He said it was nothing, asked me to look after it for him. I knew there was more to this than he told me.'

'So it's here?'

Marlowe walked to another mahogany door, in the opposite wall. He unlocked it and swung it open. Behind the door was an alcove that housed a large safe. 'For some of our more valuable books.' He entered the combination and pulled open the thick steel door.

The inside of the safe looked like a bookshelf; old leather-bound books and manuscripts lined its shelves. On the left-hand side, underneath a stack of manuscripts, was a plain brown folder. Marlowe slid it out and gave it to Porter. 'He told me it would be you who would come and get this. He told me never to give it to anyone else, no matter who they said they were.'

Porter took the folder. This was it, the information, the evidence, everything they needed to bring down Vadim. This simple cardboard folder was the reason so many people had died. 'Thank you for taking care of it, Oliver, it really means a lot.'

'I'm glad I could help you to help Justin, I hope it stops all of this. Here, I'll give you a bag to put it in.' He pulled a canvas courier bag out of another cupboard and held it open.

Porter slid the folder into the bag and slung it over his shoulder. 'Thanks. If anyone else comes looking for this, don't put yourself at risk. Just tell them you gave it to me. I won't be in any more danger than I already am.'

'Should I be worried about you, Callum?'

Porter shook his head. 'I've got some good friends around me, people who can take care of things. I'll be okay.' He held out his hand. 'We'll talk about this over a hot chocolate and marshmallows, one day, Oliver.'

Marlowe took Porter's hand. 'I do hope so, Callum. Look after yourself.'

Porter opened the door and went back up the steps into the corridor, where Durand was waiting. 'I've got what we came for, Luke. Let's get out of here.'

Durand nodded and led the way back to the shop.

McGill was about to bite into another biscuit when he noticed the car. 'Blue saloon at the end of the street. Two up, watching the exit. Three more coming this way.'

'We need to warn Callum and Luke.'

McGill took another biscuit then followed Sinclair through the connecting door from the coffee shop into the bookstore. Porter and Durand were just returning to the front desk, about to leave, when Sinclair walked through the door and pointed back towards the way they had come. 'We aren't going out the front, Frank's spotted some followers.'

Marlowe waved them all to the back of the shop. 'Follow me, I'll take you upstairs.' He looked at the woman behind the till. 'Don't take any risks, Sharon. Stall them, and then tell them you think I'm in the office.'

'Okay, Oliver.'

Marlowe unlocked a door in the back corner of the shop that led to a lift. He inserted a key into the lift call button and the doors opened. 'Right, everyone in.'

It was a squeeze getting five of them in the lift, but they wouldn't be in there for long. When the doors opened again, they walked out into Marlowe's penthouse apartment. McGill checked out the modern decor. 'Very nice, your shop must be doing well.'

Marlowe locked off the lift. 'The shop and a sizeable inheritance. My father didn't disown me, after all.'

'Well, that does help, I suppose. We aren't headed for the roof, are we? I don't like roofs any more.'

Marlowe led them through the flat to another lift door. 'Not the roof; you could take the fire escape down, but you'll only end up back in the street. This lift goes down to a basement garage shared by all the buildings in the block. There's a door down there that brings you out on the next street along.'

Sinclair and Durand got into the lift. Porter shook Marlowe's hand one last time. 'Thank you, Oliver. I hope we'll see each other again soon.'

Marlowe gripped Porter's hand. 'Good luck, Callum.' He looked at McGill. He didn't know who he was, but he looked like a man who was used to violence. 'I need you to hit me.'

'What?'

'It needs to look like you forced me up here. In case there's any suspicion that I helped you.'

Porter tried to get out of the lift but Sinclair pulled him back. 'He's right, Frank. It's the best way for him to be safe.'

'Okay.' McGill led Marlowe away from the lift, out of Porter's view. 'Are you ready?'

Marlowe nodded. 'Don't do too much damage.' He gritted his teeth.

McGill took a step to his side. 'After three. One …' McGill threw a right hook and Marlowe dropped to his knees.

235

McGill helped him to his feet. 'Sorry about that, I didn't want you to duck, might have hurt more. Are you okay?'

Marlowe took out a handkerchief and dabbed at the trickle of blood running down his cheek. 'I'll be fine. Go. Good luck.'

McGill got into the lift and the doors closed.

There were no electronic numbers to tell them which floor they were on, this was a private lift straight to the car park. McGill pulled out his Glock. 'Only one stop. Everyone be ready.'

Sinclair and Durand drew their weapons. McGill was first out of the lift as the door opened. The car park was deserted. 'The exit must be on the far side.'

The four of them ran between the cars to the exit. Durand took the lead. 'They don't know me, I'll act like someone who's just parked their car. If there's anyone out there, they'll hesitate long enough for us to deal with them.' He climbed the steps to the door and pushed it open.

The exit door couldn't be opened from the outside, so the man who was standing there had obviously been put in place to make sure no one came out; these people had done their homework and knew about the car park. As Durand stepped onto the pavement, the man outside shoved a pistol into his gut. 'Back inside.'

Durand shrugged his shoulders and spoke to him in French: the actions of an innocent tourist who'd taken a wrong turn.

'I said, back inside.' The man pushed him back through the door and down the steps. Durand walked away from the steps, away from where the others were crouching. The man wasn't expecting anyone else to be there and didn't turn around. He thought he had got there first, that he was in the perfect position to set up an ambush. He couldn't have been more wrong. As he stepped towards Durand, his weapon raised, McGill stepped out of the shadows and shot him.

Durand turned to face them. He wasn't trembling or freaked out in any way, what had just happened hadn't bothered him at all. He lit a cigarette. 'I think we should fuck off.'

Sinclair pushed Porter up the steps. 'My thoughts exactly.'

The four of them went up the steps and out onto the street. McGill took the lead and they disappeared into the throng of lunchtime pedestrians.

Chapter 39

Brantleigh House was an eighteenth-century country house, surrounded by mature gardens and rolling parkland. It was also surrounded by secure fencing, CCTV cameras, and security guards. Harry Nash senior had bought it in the late seventies from a bankrupt lord who couldn't keep up with the maintenance and running costs of such a substantial property. It wasn't out of the ordinary back then, some manor houses and palaces were opened up to the public, or even turned into attractions, to help pay their costs. Many an ancestral stately home had been snapped up by rock stars and Hollywood actors. Harry Nash buying the house wasn't unusual enough to raise any eyebrows. Over the years he had done a lot of work to bring it back to its former glory, and it looked stunning.

As the people carrier pulled into the entrance, the iron gates swung open and the two men in the small guardhouse waved it through. Sinclair looked out of the window at the imposing house at the end of the long, tree-lined driveway. 'My god. You said it was a country house, not a palace.'

Nash smiled. 'Just something Dad picked up when I was very young. It was going cheap, we couldn't afford to buy it at today's prices.'

McGill whistled through his teeth. 'I couldn't afford the taxi to get up the driveway.'

They were still laughing when the people carrier pulled up in front of the house. Luke Durand switched off the engine and they all got out. Porter hobbled around in a circle as he tried to get some feeling back into his damaged leg, and McGill stood beside the car stretching his back. 'That feels better. I was beginning to seize up in there.'

Sinclair watched as a man in his seventies with a walking stick slowly made his way down the stone steps to meet them. When he reached the bottom, Nash walked over and took his hand, helping him down the last step. The old man pulled his hand away. 'I've told you before, Harriette, I can manage by myself.'

Nash gave him a hug. 'Course you can, Dad. I just wanted to hold your hand.'

The old man smiled. 'How's my princess?'

'I'm good, Dad. Come with me, I want you to meet some new friends.' She guided Nash senior to where the others were standing. 'Dad, this is Ali.'

Sinclair held out her hand. 'Nice to meet you, Mr Nash.'

The old man took Sinclair's hand and held it up to his lips, planting a kiss on the back of it. 'Always a pleasure to meet a beautiful woman. My friends call me H.'

Harriette gently grabbed her father's arm. 'You can let go of her now, Dad. Sorry, Ali, he always thought himself a bit of a charmer, back in the day.'

'I'm sure he was, and still is.'

H smiled at Ali and patted her arm. 'I like this one.'

Harriette moved him along to the others. 'Dad, this is Frank, and this is Callum.'

He shook their hands in turn. 'Good to meet you both, make yourselves at home.'

'I'll show them around, Dad, make sure they settle in.'

The old man gave her a peck on the cheek. 'Thank you, princess, I'm going for a lie down now.' He shuffled back to the steps and, refusing any help, climbed them to the front door.

Once H had gone, Harriette turned to the others. 'My dad doesn't come out of his room much these days, but he still likes to welcome everyone to the house. Follow me and I'll get you settled in.'

They walked up the steps and through the double front doors into a huge, marble-floored, grand entrance hall. Two ornate staircases ran up either side and met at the top where they joined an equally ornate landing. There was a glass chandelier in the centre of the hall and oak doors led off to other rooms.

Nash led them up the stairs and to the left. 'We use the east wing for guests. I've had rooms made up for the three of you. You'll find everything you need in there – toiletries, clothes, once you've had a bit of a freshen up, I'll see you downstairs for something to eat.'

Sinclair nodded. This was more luxury than she had seen in a long time, but she could definitely get used to it. 'Thanks, Harry. Thanks for everything.'

'My pleasure. Anything for a friend of Gabriel's, and now you're all my friends, too.' She smiled at McGill then made her way back down the stairs.

Sinclair looked at McGill. 'I think you've got a new fan there, Frank.'

McGill looked a little sheepish. 'Don't be daft, she's just

being friendly.'

Sinclair and Porter burst out laughing. McGill shook his head and went into his room.

* * *

McGill knocked on Porter's bedroom door. 'Ready when you are, Callum.'

Sinclair stood next to the door, leaning against the wall. 'If we have to go anywhere, we should leave Callum here. Harry will look after him.'

'He won't be happy about that, he's become quite attached to you.'

'I think you're the one he's attached to, Frank.'

McGill raised his eyebrows. 'Really?'

Sinclair nodded. 'Yeah, I've seen you with him, talking him through all the shit that's happened to him. Maybe you're not such a rough 'n' tough bootneck after all.'

McGill shrugged. 'I feel sorry for the kid. Anyway, keeping *him* calm helped us. If he had freaked out on the road here, it would've made things a whole lot more difficult.'

Sinclair smiled. 'Yeah, yeah, that's what you say. I think you're just a big softy.'

McGill playfully shoved her along the hallway, just as Porter's door opened; he looked gaunt and tired. He closed his door and limped into the hallway.

McGill put his arm around the younger man's shoulders. 'You okay, mate?'

Porter nodded and smiled. He had the evidence folder clutched to his chest. 'Yeah, I'm okay. I'm just really tired and my leg hurts a bit.'

Sinclair took the folder from him. 'I'll carry that for you. You make sure you hold on going down the stairs, okay?'

'Thanks, Ali. I didn't want to let it out of my sight, after everything we've been through to get it.'

McGill patted Porter's back. 'Right then, enough of the chit chat, let's get some scran. I could eat a scabby horse.'

Sinclair was always light on her feet and she skipped down the stairs, reaching the bottom while McGill and Porter were still only halfway down. She looked up at them. 'Take your time, fellas.'

A double door between the two staircases opened and Harriette Nash walked into the entrance hall. 'We've rustled up a few snacks in here, and there are some people I think you'll want to see.'

Sinclair waited for McGill and Porter to reach the bottom of the stairs then followed Nash through the double doors.

The room was set out as an informal dining room. The long oak table, which would comfortably seat ten people, was now covered, end to end, in plates of sandwiches, sausage rolls, crisps, pork pies, and cakes. A buffet that would not have looked out of place at a wedding. As they walked in, Simeon Carter got up from his position beside the window. 'Ali, Frank, good to see you both in one piece.'

Sinclair gave him a hug. 'It's good to see you, too, Simeon.'

Carter was a little surprised, he'd never seen Sinclair show emotion to anyone other than McGill. He was glad she seemed to be more open and trusting around other people. It would be good for her, and vital for her mental health.

Sinclair hooked her arm around Carter's and led him to where Porter stood. 'Simeon, I'd like you to meet Callum Porter. A valuable member of our team.'

Porter looked embarrassed. 'I'm not sure about that, Ali.' He held out his hand. 'It's an honour to meet you, Simeon.'

Carter shook his hand then gestured towards Kinsella. 'Ali, Callum, I'd like to introduce you to Danny Kinsella.'

'Nice to put a face to the name, at last.'

'Enough of the introductions, let's eat.' McGill grabbed a handful of crisps and crammed them into his mouth.

For the next hour they all forgot the shit they had been through and the problems they still had. They laughed, chatted and ate sandwiches like they were at the local village fete. It was Nash who brought them back to reality. 'I'll leave you lot alone, now. I'm sure you've got things to discuss that I don't need to know about.' She left the room and closed the doors.

Porter patted the folder, which he'd placed on the table. 'Justin died for this. I don't want Vadim to get hold of it. I trust all of you to make sure that doesn't happen.'

Sinclair held his hand. 'We'll make sure of it, Callum.'

Kinsella stood and picked up the folder. 'The first thing we need to do is copy everything that's in it. If anything happens to this, we'll still have the evidence that's inside it.'

McGill held out the hard drive he'd taken from Kinsella's apartment. 'You might want to take this, too.'

'Thanks, Frank. My Christmas card list's on here. Don't know how I would've coped if I'd lost that.'

McGill laughed. 'You're an arse, Danny.'

Kinsella turned to leave. 'Harry has a scanner in the other room. I'll get started.'

Carter shouted after him. 'Quick as you can, Danny.' He turned to Porter. 'Callum, could you leave us for a few minutes, please?'

Porter looked at Sinclair and McGill. 'You're not leaving me, are you?'

Sinclair took both of his hands in hers. 'You knew we'd have to leave you, sooner or later. This is where it could really hit the fan. Frank and I need to be able to work without worrying about you. You'll be safe here.'

McGill gave him a reassuring look. 'Go and get some sleep, mate. We'll finish this off and then we can all relax and you can go home.'

Porter's shoulders dropped. He knew they were right. He wasn't cut out for this and wasn't in a fit state to even run away. He gave both McGill and Sinclair a hug. 'Please, look after yourselves. I don't want to lose you, too.'

Sinclair held him and rubbed his back. 'Don't worry about us, we've got this. When we get back, I want to meet your dad.'

Porter nodded, a tear starting to form. 'Harry told me she can arrange for a message to be sent to him. He'll know I'm okay.'

'You'll be back home before you know it.'

Porter paused and took one last look at Sinclair and McGill; then, with a deep sigh and a bowed head, he left the room.

Carter waited until the door was closed before continuing. 'You're not going to like this next bit.'

Sinclair faced him. 'Not liking the way things are going is normal, now, Simeon. What is it this time?'

Carter sat back down beside the window. 'Edward Lancaster's boss, the head of MI6, wants you to hand him the folder and turn yourself in.'

Sinclair stared at Carter. 'Well, Edward Lancaster can tell his boss to fuck right off.'

Carter held up his hand. 'I know, I know. I appreciate your concern, Ali, but we'll have to give it to them sooner or later. It's the powers that be that'll bring Vadim down, not us.'

'It's not just bringing him down that I'm bothered about, Simeon. I want to be there when the bastard gets what's coming to him, I want to see his face.'

McGill sat on the edge of the table. 'He's right, Ali. They need the folder.'

Sinclair rubbed her eyes. 'We don't even know if this guy can be trusted, what if he's in on it?'

'Not everyone can be involved in the conspiracy, Ali. You have to trust someone, sooner or later.'

Sinclair was wondering if the constant fear and being permanently on the run was getting to her. Was all this making her paranoid? She needed to have a serious talk with someone when all of this was over – if she made it that far. 'Okay, I can see you're right, but I still don't trust him.'

McGill helped himself to the last sandwich. 'We'll have to be careful, and we meet out in the open so we can see anyone trying to ambush us. That, or no deal.'

Carter nodded. 'I've already told them that you'll only meet somewhere neutral.'

Sinclair shrugged. 'Okay. I don't like it, but okay. Set it up.'

The door opened and Kinsella came back into the room. He handed the folder to Sinclair. 'I've copied everything that's in there. A lot of it is newspaper cuttings and photos, but about a quarter of it uses more code names for things. It mentions Vadim but doesn't use his real name. I'll have to do some digging, and cross reference it with the other data I've got so we can put all the proof together. Then we'll be able to bring down Enfield.'

Sinclair looked at the file. 'We've all risked our lives to get this far. Let's not fuck it up now.'

Carter got to his feet. 'I'll contact Edward, tell him to set things up; you two, get ready.'

Chapter 40

Sinclair and McGill were on the road before dawn, heading for a disused airfield to the north-west of London. They had agreed to the meeting, eventually, as long as it was outside London, and only the head of MI6 was there. Being outside London meant they avoided any police checkpoints between Brantleigh House and the meeting. They didn't need any more drama.

They arrived at the airfield as the sun was appearing above the horizon, and stopped the car half a mile from the runway. McGill climbed out and lifted the Barrett .50-cal sniper rifle, which Carter had somehow managed to get for him, out of the boot. He set off across the overgrown field and Sinclair drove towards the runway.

McGill found a spot in the long grass that had a good view of the whole area, and settled down for a long wait. He set up his rifle then pulled a cammo net over himself, so he couldn't be spotted from above. Drones were far too easy to get hold of these days and he didn't want to take any risks.

Sinclair drove to the middle of the runway and waited for Hadley to arrive.

After two hours, McGill picked up an approaching car through his scope. He put in his earpiece and pressed the call button on his phone. 'This is it, Ali. Vehicle inbound, one up, looks like him.'

Sinclair could see the car at the far end of the runway. 'Roger that. I'll leave comms open.' She slipped the phone into her top pocket and put in an earpiece. She got out of the car, leaving the door open, and walked around to the rear so the bulk of the vehicle was between her and the approaching vehicle.

Hadley was nervous, he didn't like being exposed like this. He had always been a man who preferred operating from the shadows. He wasn't used to this kind of operation; but, if he wanted the folder, he had no choice. Sinclair had made that perfectly clear. All he had to do was get Sinclair to hand him the evidence, so he could make sure it was kept safe, and then turn herself in. It wasn't a complicated plan, but he knew it was going to be difficult, there was plenty of opportunity to mess things up. He stopped his car and got out, ten metres from where Sinclair had parked.

Sinclair held up her hand to stop him. 'That's far enough. Take your jacket off and turn around.'

Hadley did as he was told. He took off his jacket and lay it on the bonnet of his car. He held his hands in the air and turned slowly through three hundred and sixty degrees. 'I'm not armed and I'm not wearing a wire.'

Sinclair held up the folder and placed it on the roof of her car. 'This is what you want; this is what all the fuss is about.'

'It's not just the folder, Miss Sinclair, it's you, too. You can identify people.' He looked around, scanning the area. 'Where's McGill?'

'Don't worry about him, he's nearby, watching. He'll only come in once I tell him it's safe.'

Hadley didn't like the way that sounded. The last thing he needed was a loose cannon like McGill messing up the operation. He lowered his hands. 'All I want is the folder in a secure place. As long as you hold on to it, none of us are safe. We need it to stop the conspiracy.'

Sinclair lowered her head and held her hand to her mouth. 'What do you think, Frank?'

'He's part of the establishment, they haven't exactly been good to us so far, but I suppose we'll have to trust one of the arseholes eventually. Just be careful.'

Sinclair considered her choices. She didn't know this guy and had absolutely no reason to trust him, but, on the other hand, Simeon Carter was right; all they could do with this info was release it to the media. No one would believe her; Vadim would shout it down and scream fake news; they would be back where they'd started. She looked around, reassuring herself there was no one else there. 'Okay, Kelvin, I'll give you the folder, but I'm not coming in.'

Hadley had suspected this might happen. Sinclair didn't seem to trust anyone, and MI6 hadn't exactly stood behind her when she'd needed them to. 'I need you, with the folder. You can help us validate it. Without you, it means nothing.'

Sinclair put the folder on the ground. 'I'll leave it here, you make sure it gets to the right people. I'll be watching, Kelvin. Mess this up and I'll be paying you a visit.'

Things weren't going to plan: Hadley needed Sinclair. He couldn't have her on the run, able to leak info. He needed to be in control.

McGill watched through his scope. He could hear what was going on and was ready to back up Sinclair as she left. In the distance, a cloud of dust attracted his attention. He focussed on a point, a mile past Sinclair; a blue van was hurtling towards the runway. 'Ali, vehicle inbound, assume multiple occupants, get out.'

Sinclair looked behind her and watched as the van came into view. She snatched up the folder and shouted to Hadley. 'We've been made, get out while you can.'

Hadley could see the van but didn't look worried. 'Ali, leave the folder.'

A shower of thoughts bombarded Sinclair's head. Was this a van load of MI6's men? Had they sent backup after all? Maybe she should just let them take her, at least she would be safe from Vadim. Her decision was made for her when the passenger in the van opened fire.

McGill squeezed the trigger. It was a moving target, almost a mile away, but McGill was good – very good. The front tyre exploded as the fifty-calibre round punctured it. The second round slammed into the engine bay, steam and smoke pouring out from under the bonnet. As the occupants of the van scattered out of the back, McGill picked off two of them before they could find cover.

Sinclair jumped into the car and started the engine as small arms fire started to ping off the runway. Her front wheels smoked as she floored the accelerator and sped past Hadley. She threw the car into a handbrake turn and spun around. With the car rocking on its springs, she hit the gas again and headed straight back to where Hadley was still standing, not moving.

The occupants of the van were getting closer with their shots. Hadley was hit in the shoulder by a ricochet and dropped to his knees as Sinclair screeched to a halt beside him. 'Get in the fucking car.'

Hadley looked across the airfield, the assailants were using the long grass as cover from McGill as they crawled to the runway. He clutched his shoulder, it was a minor wound and the bleeding wasn't bad.

McGill fired shots towards the occupants of the van but was unable to see them. He hit one purely by chance. He was screaming in Sinclair's ear. 'Go, go, go.'

Sinclair couldn't just leave Hadley. She leaned over and opened the passenger door. 'Move your arse.'

Hadley grabbed his jacket and got in beside her; the door slammed shut as Sinclair floored the accelerator and drove towards McGill's position.

McGill picked up his rifle and sprinted towards Sinclair, jumping into the back seat as she slowed to a crawl. As soon as McGill was on board, she accelerated.

McGill looked out of the rear window. 'What the fuck just happened?'

Sinclair lowered her window and threw out her phone. She looked at Hadley. 'This prick must have told someone where we were. Vadim must be tracking us. Ditch your phones, both of you.'

Hadley took out his mobile. 'I had to tell someone where I was, they don't just let me wander out of the office whenever I feel like it.'

'Whoever you told, leaked it to Vadim. You nearly got us all killed.'

Hadley looked sheepish. McGill was glaring at him, probably trying to decide whether to shoot him now or later. Hadley cleared his throat, beads of sweat running down his face and the back of his neck. 'I'm sorry, take me to Vauxhall Cross, you'll be safe there and I can arrange for the security services to come in and meet us.'

Sinclair smiled. 'Not a chance. My friends, the only people I care about and trust, are in real danger because of people like you and Vauxhall Cross. That's the last time I trust any of you.'

McGill pressed the quick dial for Carter's number and left a message. 'Simeon, Vadim is on to us, the meeting is blown … Watch your back, we're leaving.' He hung up and threw his phone out of the window.

* * *

Marcus Enfield wasn't holding back. His face was red and the vein in his forehead pulsed as he screamed down the phone. 'Why can't we kill any of these people? I thought we had experts dealing with this. Do you realise how vital it is to me that I get rid of them?'

DCS Thorpe could hear Enfield's rant without even holding the phone to his ear. He knew he'd fucked up, knew he only had one more chance. He had to get this sorted out, his life depended on it.

Enfield's bodyguard was watching for anyone who might overhear his boss's tirade. If anyone heard any of this, it would be very difficult to explain away.

The Home Secretary carried on haranguing Thorpe. 'I want this done NOW. I want that folder. I want Sinclair, and anyone who knows what's in the folder, DEAD. It's them or you. Do you understand?'

'Yes, sir, I promise I'll—'

Enfield slammed down the phone. 'We need to watch him. If he looks like he's losing his nerve, I want him to disappear.'

The bodyguard turned to face Enfield but stayed by the door. 'I'll take care of it, sir. Personally.'

Enfield nodded. His face was no longer red and his breathing had slowed, but he was still fuming. 'I'm glad I can rely on someone.'

Chapter 41

Sinclair headed north, away from London, away from Vadim's apparent power base. They stayed off the motorways as much as they could and stuck to the minor roads. It would make for a long journey but there were fewer CCTV cameras – less chance of being tracked.

They had stopped once, just south of Manchester, to fill up with petrol and wait until dark before carrying on. Now, with Sinclair snoozing in the back seat, McGill drove them through rural Cumbria towards the one place where he would feel secure: his family home, Rock Cottage.

As they approached Rock Cottage, Sinclair opened her eyes and sat up. McGill switched off the headlights and pulled the car into a layby within sight of the house. 'I'll go up and make sure it's all clear. You stay here. If I'm not back in an hour, get out of here.'

Sinclair got out and switched to the driver's seat. 'Be careful.'

McGill rubbed dirt into his face to stop any light reflecting off his skin, and pulled on a black woollen hat. 'It's okay, I know all the blind spots, if there's anyone up there, they won't see me coming.' He tucked one of the Glocks into his waistband and climbed the dry stone wall that marked the edge of his property.

Sinclair checked her own weapon and stared up at the house at the top of the hill. The roofline was silhouetted against the night sky but, even with the dim light from the moon, and her eyes fully used to the dark, she still couldn't make out McGill. He'd done shit like this too many times before to be spotted easily. Sinclair settled back into her seat and waited.

It took McGill forty-five minutes to check the house and get back down the hill. He climbed over the wall and walked back to the car. 'Keep the lights off, Ali, and drive up to the gate. I'll open it and let you in. Drive up the hill and straight into the barn, I've left it open.' He looked at Hadley. 'You can get out and walk up.'

Hadley wasn't sure that he wouldn't end up in a shallow grave, but, for now, he would do exactly as he was told. He got out of the car and followed McGill.

Sinclair waited until McGill was at the gate then she started the car and drove out of the layby. She revved the engine as she drove through the gate and kept in a low gear to make the ascent of the steep hill easier. Anyone trying to sneak up on them, up this hill, had their work cut out for them. The tyres slipped and the engine came close to stalling, but, after a couple of minutes she made it to the top and drove into the barn. She switched off the engine and waited for McGill to appear before she got out of the car.

McGill closed the barn door and switched on a red light that was hanging from one of the rafters. He opened the boot and took out his rifle and the two backpacks they had brought with them. 'We need to get some sleep before we do anything else. You go in the house and get your heads down, I'll take the first watch.'

McGill passed the next few hours checking the security of the buildings and the access routes up the hill; he had spent years installing sensors, trip wires and hidden cameras all around the farm. Some might say he was being paranoid, but he had pissed off a lot of nasty people in his time. People who would think nothing of tracking him down and making him suffer. If anyone came near the house, he wanted to know. He wanted to know who they were and what they were doing, before they got to him. By the time Sinclair took over the watch, everything was set up.

An ominous red sky hung above the fells as McGill came out of the house and joined Sinclair. He handed her a fresh coffee and sat down on the old garden bench that leaned against the barn. 'NATO standard coffee, as usual.'

'Thanks, Frank. You get any sleep?'

McGill took a sip from his cup. 'A little. I could've done with a few more hours, but we've got things to do. Maybe we'll have a holiday, if we live long enough.'

'What's our plan from here?'

He looked at Sinclair, she was tired. Time spent on the run and the constant expectation that something was about to kick off had taken their toll. 'We could keep running, disappear, start a new life, but, as long as we've got the folder, they won't leave us alone; Vadim will never leave you alone.'

'So, what do we do?'

'We have to hope that Carter and Lancaster can finish things off at their end. They've got a copy of the folder, they have to bring it all out, get it to someone we know we can trust.'

She nodded towards the house. 'Hadley?'

McGill shrugged. 'I don't know. Maybe, maybe not. I just don't like Vadim's men tracking us down when we go to meet

Hadley. It's too much of a coincidence.'

'You think he's in on it?'

'He may not be involved, but he's a threat to our security. He obviously can't keep his mouth shut.'

'What can we do to help Simeon?'

McGill looked at the surrounding buildings. 'We make a stand. We stop running and fight. Vadim wants you and the folder, we keep his attention on us and buy time for Carter and Lancaster to bring him down.'

'Here?'

McGill nodded. 'I've made a few modifications to the old place. It might look like it's falling down, but you'd be surprised. This is as good a place as any.'

'Okay, but we don't kill anyone who's innocent. If they send the police, the army, they're just doing their job, they aren't part of the conspiracy.'

McGill finished his coffee. 'We protect ourselves. If they try to kill us, we kill them first, it's the only way. Stopping Vadim is more important than any one of us or them. We have to give Simeon time to do something.'

Sinclair nodded. 'Let's just hope he gets it done quickly.'

McGill took Sinclair's empty cup. 'Right, time for some breakfast. Let's see what I've got in the cupboards.'

When they walked into the house, Hadley was just sitting up on the old, worn sofa that he had slept on in the corner of the room. He looked like he'd spent the night hiding in a bush. His normally immaculate clothes were creased and grimy, his hair stuck out at odd angles, and his unshaven face looked like it had aged overnight. McGill found it funny. The MI6 spook had obviously never spent any time sleeping in ditches or huddled under tarpaulins like he and Sinclair had.

257

Hadley was used to the finer things, the only places he spent the night were five-star hotels. 'You should've been in the RAF, mate, they're used to comfortable surroundings.'

Sinclair laughed. It was normal for the different arms of the forces to make fun of each other, it was part of their mentality, part of their brotherhood. Hadley looked confused – he came from a completely different background and didn't understand what they were laughing at.

McGill, still chuckling at his joke, walked to the stove. 'Right, who wants a brew?'

Chapter 42

The Home Secretary brought the COBRA meeting to order. Around the table were the heads of the security services, senior police officers, and minsters and representatives from various government departments. Enfield looked at the faces that were all looking to him for leadership. Some were new in their post, stepping in to replace those killed or injured in Geneva; some were old hands who didn't trust the Home Secretary at all, but were biding their time. All of them were waiting for him to speak.

Enfield shuffled his papers. 'Ladies and Gentlemen, I'd like to start by condemning the cowardly attack in Westminster, and expressing deepest sympathy to all of the families involved. The perpetrators of this outrage cannot be allowed to get away. We will bring them to justice.'

There were lots of nods and expressions of agreement. Some of the old hands thought the Home Secretary was just grandstanding, but they nodded, too.

'I'd also like to condemn the attempt on the life of the Chief of the Secret Intelligence Service, yesterday. He is a brave man, and was personally striving to gather evidence on the latest terrorist attacks against our country. We don't know his current whereabouts, as he has decided to stay in hiding for the time being. I will be asking the Counter Terrorist Command to take charge of the operation and ensure Hadley is safe.'

There were more mumblings of agreement.

Enfield waited for silence then continued. 'After the debate and vote in The House, we have cross-party support and agreement for military action if the Turkish government are not forthcoming with the details of those responsible for the attacks. Today we need to discuss what our plans are. General?'

The Chief of the Defence Staff put on his glasses and opened the file in front of him. The wall of screens at the end of the room showed a large map of the Mediterranean, with icons showing the positions of various military units. 'Thank you, sir. As of this morning, we have recalled several regular army units. However, this is just a precaution as we do not see an immediate need for boots on the ground, other than special forces, at this stage. The Royal Airforce are readying for air strikes and we are moving two Astute Class submarines into the Med. Initial strikes will be by TLAM.'

One of the newcomers raised his hand. 'Sorry, what's a TLAM?'

The General looked up from his notes. 'It's a Tomahawk cruise missile.'

The newcomer looked sheepish and nodded, looking back at the screen.

The General continued. 'The A-Boats,' he looked over his glasses at the newcomer, 'that's Astute class submarines, carry TLAMS and are also able to deploy special forces. Once the deadline has passed, we will be in a position to make the first strike.'

Enfield looked around at the faces in the room. 'Any questions for the general?'

Once again, the newcomer raised his hand. 'Sorry, Home Secretary, but Turkey is a member of NATO. Don't we risk damaging the alliance if we launch a military intervention against another member?'

A junior minister from the Foreign Office nodded and chipped in. 'If we hit Turkey, they will undoubtedly leave NATO, and leave the eastern end of the Med open to the Russians. Their influence is increasing in Turkey month on month as it is.'

Enfield looked annoyed. 'I appreciate your comments and your misgivings, none of us want the country to go to war. However, we have already had the debate and the House has voted. Once the deadline expires, we *will* be taking military action.'

Everyone was looking at the two junior minsters. They both wanted to argue against this but thought better of it.

Enfield closed his folder. 'If there's nothing else, I'm sure we've all got things we need to do to prepare. Thank you all for your support.' He got up and left the room.

Chapter 43

McGill sat in the kitchen of the farmhouse and looked at a large flat screen television that he had hung on the wall by the door. The screen showed the feed from twelve CCTV cameras that were positioned around the property. Every inch of the farmyard, the surrounding land and the access road could be monitored from the kitchen.

On a desk in front of the television were controls for each camera and an alarm panel. The panel was a steel box, which had two rows of six red LEDs that were linked to motion sensors on the cameras. If any sensor picked up movement, the LED would light and the corresponding camera could be zoomed in to check the area. The lights came on occasionally as the local wildlife moved around the farm; McGill checked every one of them.

The house itself had solid stone walls, two feet thick, and every window had steel shutters on the inside. Both doors into the main house had two steel poles braced against them on the inside. Each pole slotted into a metal socket cemented into the floor. The doors were two-inch-thick oak and had heavy duty hinges at three points. They would be almost impossible to break down without some heavy-duty hardware. He might be accused of going a bit too far, but he would say he was just being careful. He would also argue that today's events were proving his point.

It was early afternoon when McGill spotted the car. It had pulled up in the layby they had used the previous evening. There were three passengers who had, up to now, made no attempt to get out. Occasionally, a cloud of cigarette smoke billowed out of one of the windows; they were waiting for something.

Sinclair stood close to the screen. 'What do you think they're doing?'

Sinclair zoomed the camera in as far as he could. 'They're just watchin'. They have no idea whether we're here or not, they've just figured out we might have come here. Give 'em time. They'll come up and take a look sooner or later.'

'Are we ready?'

McGill looked at the kitchen table. In a steel box were two assault rifles, four nine-millimetre pistols, multiple magazines for each and several boxes of ammunition. He had brought the box up from the basement, where he had hidden it behind a false wall. He and Sinclair had spent the morning cleaning the weapons and loading the magazines. 'I think we've got the hardware for anything that comes our way, we just need to stay alert.'

Sinclair picked up one of the pistols and cocked it. She slipped it into a shoulder holster and put two magazines into her jeans pocket. 'Try to wait until they're close, give them the chance to surrender. If they're security services just checking us out, they'll back off. If they're Vadim's men, and we have to kill them, it'll be easier to hide the bodies if they're already up here.'

263

McGill didn't take his eyes off the screen. 'They only get one chance to walk away from this. If they choose not to take it, we have to defend ourselves.'

Sinclair nodded.

Hadley stood beside them. 'Shouldn't I have a gun, just in case?'

McGill looked at Sinclair and shook his head. Sinclair nodded her agreement. Although he hadn't given them any real reason to be suspicious about him, he hadn't given them a reason to trust him, either. Sinclair closed the lid of the box and locked it. 'You just stay here, we'll deal with this.'

As they watched the screen, the car's doors opened and the three passengers got out. One of the men stubbed out a cigarette then walked to the gate and climbed over. He walked up the track as if he were out for a walk, looking for directions. Sinclair and McGill left the house and split up.

McGill made his way down the hill, while Sinclair positioned herself behind the barn with a view of the approach to the house. She watched as the first passenger kept to the path. He wasn't trying to hide, he was being as noticeable as possible, even shouting 'hello' as he got closer. The second passenger kept low and swung around towards the back of the house.

McGill was tracking the third man as he moved left and kept down below the dry stone wall. If this guy made it to the top of the hill, he would be behind Sinclair. McGill would be taking him out well before then, but, for now, he waited for Sinclair to make the first move.

Sinclair was focussed on the second man who was trying to sneak around the back of the house. She could see the first man, standing at the top of the path, out of the corner of her eye, but he wasn't a threat, yet. The second man had reached an old feeding trough, twenty metres from the house, and was holding a pistol in his right hand. He nodded to the first man, who pulled out his own weapon from a shoulder holster, and stepped forward.

The loud bang and bright flash came from a small explosive charge that McGill had rigged to a trip wire. The first man didn't see the fishing wire strung across the top of the path and he walked straight into it. The charge wasn't enough to injure anyone, it was little more than a bird scarer, but it was enough to disorientate him.

Sinclair took aim at the second man, who appeared from his cover behind the feeding trough. 'DROP IT.'

The man had no intention of giving up his gun, he'd been sent there for one purpose, and one purpose only: to kill Sinclair. He brought up his arm and levelled his weapon.

Sinclair had given him a chance, now it was self-defence. She pulled the trigger. The man's head jerked back and he tipped forward into the feeding trough. The second man held his hand up to his left ear, the ringing in it was louder than Sinclair's shot and it caused him to hesitate. By the time he realised what was happening, Sinclair's bullet was entering his chest.

The third man had been startled by the explosion. He watched the other two go down and decided he wasn't getting paid enough: it was time to back off and call for re-enforcements. He climbed back over the dry stone wall and ran to the car, jumping into the driver's seat. He felt for the key to start the engine but it wasn't there. He knew he'd left it there, he always did in case they needed a fast getaway. That was when it dawned on him – they'd fucked up, they had underestimated their target. He looked in the rear-view mirror. McGill stood up from behind the car and fired a single shot through the window.

McGill drove the blood-spattered car back up the hill and into the barn. He and Sinclair loaded the other two bodies into the vehicle then closed the barn doors.

McGill checked the pockets of the two Sinclair had killed. 'They aren't carrying any official ID, Ali, just money, old receipts and other shit.'

Sinclair checked the coat that was on the back seat. She found a passport for one of the men. 'This one's South African, apparently. What do you reckon the chances are that it's a fake?'

McGill nodded. 'They aren't security services, they must be Vadim's men.'

Sinclair was relieved. She didn't find the taking of a human life as easy as McGill seemed to. The knowledge that their assailants were there to kill them made it easier to bear. 'Well, that's three less arseholes to worry about.'

They closed the car's doors and went back into the house.

Hadley looked away from the screen, he'd watched what had happened and was impressed. It was going to take more than a couple of hired thugs to get the better of these two. 'You always that effective?'

McGill was checking the cameras for any other threats. 'We've had to be.'

'You should come and work for me.'

Sinclair put down her Glock. 'No thanks, I've tried that already, it didn't end well.'

'Are you sure they were Vadim's men?'

McGill nodded. 'Definitely. None of them tried to identify

themselves and they weren't carrying any official ID.'

Sinclair looked at McGill. 'How do you think they found us so quickly?'

'They didn't know we were here. They must be checking everywhere we might be hiding.'

Sinclair sighed. 'They're going to keep coming, aren't they? They're never going to leave us alone.'

'We'll stop them. Vadim will need to send more than three idiots to take us out.'

Sinclair just wanted to rest, she was exhausted. 'They know where we are now, should we run, or stick with the plan?'

McGill pointed at the television screen. 'Looks like it's too late to run. Someone must've called it in.'

On one of the CCTV cameras they watched the arrival of the police. Lights flashed as the cars screeched to a halt opposite the gate and police officers ran tape across the road to keep away any prying eyes and members of the press.

Sinclair slumped down into a chair, staring at the black and white scene on the TV. 'This is it. This is where it ends, one way or another. I'm relieved it'll finally be finished.'

McGill put his hand on Sinclair's back. 'At least we'll end it together.'

Chapter 44

Danny Kinsella had barely slept since he had got his hands on the evidence in the folder. He was fascinated by how intricate the back stories of the undercover agents were. Right from the start, each sleeper had had every piece of official documentation they would ever need. Not just current, but expired and out of date documents. The kind of things that accumulate in the homes of everyday people: old passports, full of visa stamps to show they were enthusiastic tourists or dedicated business travellers; utility bills from previous houses; letters and postcards from non-existent friends, even photographs of family occasions and holidays past. Whole lives created out of nothing.

Justin Wyatt had done a brilliant job. His research had been painstaking. If he hadn't been murdered, he would have uncovered the whole conspiracy by himself. The documents Shawford had given him were just the start. They'd contained the details of each sleeper, except their names – the professor had kept those to himself, but Wyatt had cross-checked each of them, one by one. He'd tracked down family trees, births, deaths and marriages, and replaced each codename with the sleeper's new identity. Kinsella couldn't believe how high up in the establishment some of them went. The only identity missing, the one Wyatt had been working on when he was killed, was Vadim's. Kinsella felt he owed it to Wyatt to finish the job for him.

The Home Secretary valued his privacy and his personal details were a closely guarded secret. In the modern age of the Internet, and seemingly endless social media updates, that was unusual. Enfield went to great pains to make it as difficult as possible for anybody to trace his family history, but Danny Kinsella wasn't just anybody. He had access to databases and could hack into networks that other people just couldn't get near to. After two days he had built up quite a detailed picture of Enfield's past and his family. Now he just had to put it together with Vadim's profile from the folder. Once he had that mapped, the Home Secretary was toast.

There was a knock from behind him and Barbara opened the door. 'Is it okay to come in, Danny?'

'Course it is, Barbara, it's your house.'

Barbara was carrying a tray. 'I always like to give our guests a little privacy, my love. People here can be a little overwhelming sometimes. I've made you some coffee and a few sandwiches, keep you going.'

Kinsella jumped up from his seat and took the tray. 'Everyone here has been wonderful, it's been a bit of a surprise, to be honest.'

'Why's that, my love?'

Kinsella paused and tried not to look the old woman in the eye. 'Well, you're supposed to be gangsters.'

'That's all in the past now. Harry, my husband, has done some things in the past that he's not proud of, but he did them for us. He kept us safe and provided for the family. If I do say so myself, he was pretty good at it.'

Kinsella looked at his surroundings. 'You can say that again.'

Barbara smiled. 'Harriette is turning us into a proper company, that's more her thing. It's what she's good at. All she needs now is a good husband.'

Harriette Nash walked through the door. Barbara rolled her eyes. 'Speak of the devil.'

'What was that, mum?'

'Nothing, dear.' She patted Kinsella's hand. 'I'll leave you to it.' She walked past her daughter, smiling, and left the room.

'I hope she hasn't been telling tales.'

Kinsella shook his head. 'No, far from it.'

Nash watched her mother walking down the hallway, singing to herself. 'She notices more than she says.'

'Don't all mothers?'

Callum Porter shuffled in through the door. His injuries were healing well but he was still stiff. 'How's it going, Danny?'

Kinsella took one of the sandwiches and pointed to his screen. 'It's a slow process, but I'm nearly there. I'm just comparing the Home Secretary's background to Vadim's profile in the folder.'

'How does it look?'

As Porter finished his question, several lines of text scrolled up the screen. Kinsella put down his sandwich and tapped at the keyboard.

'That's funny.'

'What is?'

'There are some bits that don't match. Look.' He pointed at the screen. 'All of these are okay: age, hair colour, eye colour, all the physical stuff. But to be honest, they are all pretty generic. These bits match: rich family, private school, single

270

child.'

Porter leaned over the desk and looked at the screen. 'So, what's the problem?'

'It might not be a problem, it just looks a bit strange. These dates and locations are places where Justin has said Vadim definitely was, but Enfield was in a different location at the same time for more than half of them.'

Nash was now standing behind them, trying to make sense of the data. 'Does that mean the evidence is wrong?'

'Not necessarily. We have to allow for a few errors. All data contains some mistakes. I'll check it again. Do you want to stay and watch?'

Nash and Porter stood back. They both knew how many hours Kinsella could spend tapping away at the keyboard. Nash was already half way out of the room. 'Got to give Mum a hand with something.'

Porter was close behind her. 'My leg's aching a bit, better go and lie down.'

They both hurried out of the room and left Kinsella alone. He turned back to his screen, shaking his head. 'Suit yourselves.'

Chapter 45

Knapwood Manor was the ancestral home of Kelvin Hadley's family. He had been living there since his parents had moved there in the late sixties, and had inherited the house and land on their death in the nineties. Although the house had been renovated and modernised, from the outside it was still, every inch, a late nineteenth century gothic manor.

Lancaster turned his car into the entrance and stopped in front of the wrought-iron gates. 'This is it: Knapwood Manor.'

Carter lowered his window and looked up at the house. It reminded him of a haunted mansion, he was sure he had seen something just like it in a seventies horror film. All it needed was a bolt of lightning to complete the image. 'This must be what they mean by how the other half lives. It's some house.'

Lancaster pressed the intercom and waited. 'You can say that again. Apparently, he comes from a rich family. I'm surprised he's never run for office.'

'If he's that rich, I'm surprised he works at all.'

Lancaster smiled. 'Maybe he just likes the power.'

Sitting on Carter's lap was the copy of all the evidence in the folder. He opened it and flicked through the pages. 'Do you think he'll be here? McGill's message said they were leaving. We have to assume Hadley is with them.'

'We have to check everywhere he could've gone, before we assume anything.'

'He doesn't know about the Home Secretary yet, does he?'

Lancaster shook his head. 'I didn't want to reveal everything – until we had to – and the Home Secretary isn't his boss, anyway. He won't be happy that we didn't tell him all the details, but he'll understand. If he's with Sinclair, I'm sure she'll tell him.'

'I hope so, Edward. We need someone on our side.'

The wrought-iron gate clunked and shook as it opened. Lancaster put the car into gear and pulled forward onto the gravel driveway, heading for the house. 'Looks like someone's here.'

As they reached the top of the driveway, they could see another car parked to the side of the front door. Lancaster slowed down and stopped. 'Shit, what's he doing here?'

'What is it, Edward?'

Lancaster pointed. 'That's the Home Secretary's official car.'

'What do we do now, turn around and disappear, or blow his brains out? We could always go and live in the Seychelles.'

'As tempting as that sounds, we have to find out how much Enfield knows. He might think I don't know who he is. If he thinks it's only McGill and Sinclair who know about him, it could help us. Don't forget who he is – if we just kill him, we're the ones who'll end up running.'

Carter took a nine-millimetre Sig Saur from his jacket and racked the slide. 'It's a long time since I've had to do any of this shit.'

Lancaster checked his pistol. 'You and me both, Simeon.'

'I'll go around the back, look for another way in. I'll let you go and knock on the front door.'

'Be careful, Simeon, he probably knows you're with me.'

They left the car and split up. Carter went to the right and disappeared behind the conservatory. Lancaster waited a couple of minutes then walked up to the porch and knocked.

The Home Secretary's bodyguard opened the door. 'Come in, Mr Lancaster.'

As Lancaster stepped past him, into the entrance hall, the bodyguard stuck his head out and looked both ways. He obviously knew Carter had been in the car and was looking for him. He didn't make a comment. Anyone else would have just asked where he was, but the bodyguard didn't. He showed Lancaster to the study then walked out of the front door and turned left.

The study was a large room; cases of antiques, and original paintings lined the walls. Lancaster looked around at his surroundings, he'd never been in this room before. Enfield sat behind a large wooden desk nursing a glass of Scotch. He waved a hand at the paintings on the walls. 'It's like a museum, isn't it, Edward? How much do you think they're worth?'

'I'm really not interested in my boss's interior decor, sir.'

Enfield held up a decanter of whisky. 'Drink?'

'No, thank you, sir. I came here looking for Hadley. I need to speak to him on a matter of some urgency.'

'I'm afraid he isn't here, Edward.'

Lancaster sat forward, pretending he didn't know what had happened at the airfield. 'Do you know where he is, sir?'

Enfield walked around the desk. 'There was an attempt on his life yesterday. He went to meet with Ali Sinclair and

Frank McGill, against my wishes. Do you know anything about that?'

Lancaster sat back and crossed his legs. This was all a game: the two men probing each other for information, not wanting to give anything away. Not wanting the other to know how much information they had. 'All I know is, he left the office and didn't come back.'

Carter had found an open door at the back of the house, and was standing in the kitchen – at the far end of the hallway from the study. He checked for any sign of the bodyguard then crept up the corridor and stood at the study door, listening.

Enfield and Lancaster were still testing each other. Enfield topped up his Scotch. 'Do you know anything about a folder? Kelvin mentioned it to me in one of our meetings.'

Lancaster shook his head. 'I haven't been briefed on everything yet, sir. I'm late to the party.'

'Have you known Simeon Carter long?'

Lancaster was on edge, he didn't like the way this was going; he could tell that Enfield suspected him. He must know Carter was involved with Sinclair, he must know he and Carter were old friends. Lancaster had to take Enfield alive, it was the only way this was going to end. With the Home Secretary dead, someone else would step into his shoes and the conspiracy would continue. If he got away, with his resources he could disappear completely and never be found.

Carter struggled to hear the voices in the room but he knew things probably weren't going well. He closed his hand around the grip of his pistol and readied himself to enter.

The bodyguard came out of nowhere. He had done a complete lap of the house looking for Carter and arrived back at the front door. Carter held his hand to his lips and motioned for him to stand still, but the bodyguard kept coming, his hand inside his jacket. Carter immediately understood – how could the person who spent most time with the Home Secretary *not* be involved? He had to have driven him to every meeting, been in the room for every phone call, maybe even carried out some of the killings himself. He had to warn Edward. He turned the handle and pushed open the door. The bodyguard already had his weapon in his hand and shouted as he brought it up to aim. 'Protect yourself.'

Before the bodyguard could pull the trigger, Carter fired and shot him in the chest. He went down, falling on his side, badly wounded but still alive. Carter took the gun from the man's hand and put it into his own pocket.

Inside the room, everything seemed to happen at once: the door swung open and they heard the guard's shout, followed by the gunshot. Enfield threw his glass at Lancaster and pulled a Glock from the desk drawer. Lancaster was up on his feet but Enfield had him covered. 'Don't try it, Edward, you won't make it. Drop your weapon, turn around, and back towards me, slowly.'

Lancaster pulled his pistol from his holster and threw it on the sofa. When he turned around, Enfield grabbed the back of his jacket and placed the gun to his head. 'Give me the folder, Carter.'

'It won't do you any good, Marcus. It's just a copy.'

'I know it's a copy, Sinclair has the original, I don't give a shit. Give me it.'

Carter stood over the guard, making sure he didn't go anywhere. 'You'll have to come out here and get it yourself.'

Inside the room, Enfield was losing his patience. 'Give me the fucking folder or I'll blow his fucking head off.'

'Okay, okay. It's in the car, I'll get it.'

Carter backed out of the front door and towards the car. Enfield manhandled Lancaster out of the study and into the hallway. He stopped beside the bodyguard and looked down at him. 'Can you move?'

The man was bleeding heavily. He held up his hand, as if asking for help.

The Home Secretary bent down and took the car keys out of his bodyguard's jacket. He pushed Lancaster through the entrance hall and out of the door, his weapon pointing at Lancaster's head the whole time.

Carter retrieved the folder from the car and put it on the ground in front of the door. He took two steps back but kept his weapon aimed. 'You won't get away with this, we'll track you down.'

Enfield smiled. 'You people don't know who you're dealing with.' He aimed his gun at Carter and pulled the trigger.

Lancaster could see it coming; he pushed back as hard as he could and slammed them both backwards into the door frame. Enfield's grip loosened and Lancaster dived away from him, pushing Carter into cover. Lancaster picked up Carter's pistol and returned fire from behind a small wall where he and Carter had landed.

Enfield grabbed the folder and ran to his car. He started the engine and floored the accelerator, the wheels spinning and throwing up gravel as he took off down the driveway. The iron gates were old, and rust had eaten through part of the hinges; they were designed to stop people driving in, not driving out. Enfield hit the gates at speed, the weight of his official car pushed the gates open and knocked one of them off its hinges. The car's windscreen cracked and one of the

277

wing mirrors shattered as it accelerated through the gap in the buckled gates.

Lancaster watched as the car disappeared round a bend. 'We've got to get to the Prime Minister, get past his security, hope he's recovered enough to understand what we're telling him and can do something about it.'

They walked back into the house. Carter unloaded the bodyguard's weapon and dropped it beside him. 'Do you really think he'll hang around now? We know he's Vadim, surely he's going to run while he still can?'

Lancaster shook his head. 'Not a certainty, Simeon. Without evidence, we can't prove a thing. Sinclair has the original folder and won't be handing it over any time soon – if she survives, and Enfield has got our copy. We have to warn Danny, if anything happens to his copy, we're the ones who are fucked.'

'We have to keep this away from the media, Edward. We don't want to spook anyone who's working with him till we know who we can trust.'

Lancaster looked down at the bodyguard. 'I'd better get an ambulance for this piece of shit.' He took out his phone and pressed a quick-dial number.

Carter checked the man's pulse and shook his head. 'He won't make it.'

Chapter 46

Kinsella opened the window. He had spent nearly three days working in that room and the air was hot and stale. The computer he had wasn't up to the standard he usually used and it was overheating. He planned to run one more comparison, between the folder profiles and the data he had gleaned from the Internet, then call it a day. He looked out of the window at the extensive grounds and envisaged his route through the gardens. There was a cool breeze blowing and he closed his eyes, looking forward to the fresh air. He promised himself that he would get out more. He was spending far too much time staring at computer screens and needed to live a little, being in prison had convinced him of that.

As he stood, lost in his thoughts, the printer whirred into life behind him and started churning out sheets of paper. It meant his last comparison of the day had finished. All he had to do now was read through the results. He bowed his head and paused, he hoped this was it, he hoped this analysis showed that the Home Secretary was Vadim, without any shadow of a doubt. If it didn't, no one would believe them about the conspiracy. An ageing spook, a computer hacker, an escaped convict and a slightly unhinged ex-marine. Who was going to believe them above the Home Secretary? They were going to be on the run for a very long time. He took a deep breath then walked back to the desk.

He picked up the papers from the printer and put them down in front of his keyboard, Enfield's profile at the top. He picked up a highlighter and started to work through it: physical characteristics, check; family history, check; dates and locations ... 'Shit.' There was still a gap in the comparison. A handful of dates that didn't match. He threw the sheet to one side and picked up one of the others. This time he had run several other people through the comparison process, as he wanted to work out how many gaps there were, on average, so he could say that Enfield's profile was statistically the best fit. It would give them something to show that the comparison was valid. He started to work his way through the others and there were gaps in all of them, as he had expected. Some had the right dates but no family history, others had the physical aspects but not the dates. Enfield was still the closest match. He picked up the last sheet: physical, check; history, check; dates and locations, check. That couldn't be right. He looked at it again: check, check, check. He grabbed Enfield's sheet, knocking his coffee over himself in the process. He compared them side by side. 'Shit ... Shit. SHIT.' He grabbed all the paperwork and ran out of the room.

Harriette Nash and Callum Porter were sitting together next to the wood burning kitchen stove, chatting about nothing in particular, when Kinsella burst in. He was shuffling through the papers, a large coffee stain on the front of his jeans. 'We've got to get hold of Simeon, he needs to know right now. Why the fuck didn't I do this sooner?' He threw the papers on the table and ran his fingers through his hair. 'Shit.'

Nash grabbed Kinsella's arm. 'Have a seat and calm down, Danny. I'll get you a towel for your leg.'

Porter picked up the papers and looked through them but couldn't make much sense of them. 'What is it, Danny? Did you link Enfield to Vadim?'

Kinsella slammed his hand on the table then stood again, pacing the room. 'The folder has the evidence in it, all of the killings, everything Vadim has done. We have to stop him.'

Porter was a little confused. 'Now we know it's Enfield, surely we can stop him. Frank, Ali, Simeon, they're all working to bring him down. It's just a matter of time.'

Porter shook his head. 'The Home Secretary isn't Vadim.'

Porter looked at Nash. 'But Ali recognised him from the island.'

Kinsella picked up the papers again and picked out two sheets. He placed the first one in front of Porter. 'This is Enfield's profile. You see where I've marked down the bits that don't match?'

Porter nodded. 'You said that finding some errors was normal.'

'It is, but only until you find a perfect match.' He placed the other sheet down on the table. 'This profile matches perfectly.'

The explosion outside shook the windows in their frames. Nash ran to the window. 'What the hell was that?'

Luke Durand ran into the kitchen. 'Get away from the window and stay down.'

Nash was on her hands and knees, crawling towards the table where the other two were sheltering. 'What's happening, Luke?'

Durand crouched at the window, his pistol drawn. 'Someone's blown the gate. They're heading up the drive.'

'What do we do now?'

Durand crawled to the door and checked the hallway. 'The lads can hold them at the front. We're well protected for now, but we need to leave. If they've got explosives they'll get in eventually. Everyone out.' He crawled out of the room and ran towards the rear of the house.

Nash, Kinsella and Porter followed him out of the room and into the hallway. Nash stopped and looked up the staircase. 'My mum and dad. What about my mum and dad?'

Durand grabbed her arm. 'It's okay, they're already outside in one of the cars.'

Kinsella split from the group and headed for his computer room. 'I've got to get the hard drive, it's got everything on it.'

Durand pushed the other two towards the back door. 'Get out, and get in the car. I'll wait for him.'

Nash and Porter did as they were told. Neither of them was an expert at this and they were both beginning to panic. They ran down the hallway to the back of the house and out of the door.

Durand stood facing the front door, weapon aimed, waiting for anyone who tried to come in. 'Hurry up, Danny. We need to go now.'

Kinsella pulled the cables from his portable drive and put it into a carrier bag with his notes. He could hear the shooting outside and dropped to the floor when the room's window shattered. Bullets struck the back wall and slammed into the screen on the desk. Kinsella slithered through the broken glass and out into the entrance hall.

Durand picked him up. 'On your feet, Danny.' He pushed him down the corridor and out of the house.

Outside, the engine of the people carrier was already running. Porter, Nash and her parents sat in the back. Kinsella and Durand jumped in the front and Durand floored it, the spinning wheels sent a shower of gravel over the black Range Rover that carried Nash's men.

The two cars stayed in close formation as they sped through the woods at the rear of the estate. The Range Rover coped with the rough track better than the people carrier and made an effective shield from the gunfire that followed them. Nash's men in the four-wheel drive returned fire and forced their pursuers to stay back far enough to make their shots ineffective.

As the two cars rounded a bend, Nash clicked a button on a small remote control that was normally kept in the vehicle's centre console. Behind the Range Rover, a steel barrier slowly rose from the track, leaves and mud slid off it as it reached its full height. The lead chase car had no chance, it slammed into the barrier and burst into flames. The following car swerved and careered into the undergrowth, hitting a tree side on.

At the back of the estate was another gate. This one was solid steel and not normally used. Nash pressed another button on the remote and the gate rolled open. The people carrier and the Range Rover powered through the opening and fish-tailed as they hit the tarmac of the road. Mud and debris flew from their tyres as they accelerated, the occupants of both vehicles watching the pall of black smoke coming from the burning vehicle, as the house disappeared into the distance.

Chapter 47

The police command and control vehicle was parked diagonally, blocking the road, just out of sight of Rock Cottage. Inside, DCS Thorpe stood in front of a whiteboard, where a layout of the area had been sketched. 'This is a Counter Terrorist Command operation and I will be acting as silver commander on the ground. I am in direct contact with the assistant commissioner, who is gold commander in the CTC HQ in London. The whole operation will be overseen by the Home Secretary himself.' He pointed to the chief inspector beside him. 'This is Chief Inspector Andy Dawson, from the CTU in Manchester. He is bronze commander, and any reports should be directed through him. Any questions?'

A local Cumbria police sergeant raised her hand. 'Yes, sir. What are we up against here? We've all seen the news and had briefings on events in London, who are this lot?'

'Good question Sergeant. Intelligence has told us that these people are part of the terrorist cell that launched the attack in Geneva. It is believed they may have further stocks of nerve agent in the house and we can't run the risk of them escaping. It may sound heartless, but a nerve agent release here is only going to kill a handful of people and a few sheep. If they attack London, we would be looking at thousands.'

There were murmurings amongst the gathered police officers. They didn't like the suggestion that the people who lived there were somehow less important than those who lived in London. The sergeant raised her hand again. 'What precautions are we taking in the event of a release of any nerve agent? How do we protect ourselves and the local population?'

The DCS wanted to keep any witnesses to what might happen at the house to a minimum. His plan to worry the local police officers was working. 'All civilians will be kept back behind a cordon, and personnel who are not required to assault the house will stay with the command vehicle. We have indicators set up in the road to give us early warning of any release, and decontamination and medical teams are on standby. All armed officers approaching the property will be wearing protective clothing and respirators.'

'Does that mean we are definitely assaulting the house?'

Thorpe nodded. 'Plans are being drawn up, I'm awaiting the go ahead from Gold Command.'

'Do we know how many of them there are?'

Thorpe shook his head. 'We have no way of knowing. We suspect there are at least two and they may have a hostage. Whatever happens today, we can't allow the terrorists in that building to carry out any more attacks. This is a matter of national security. They must be stopped, at all costs.'

Standing at the back of the briefing was SAS Sergeant Mick Butler. Recently returned from operations in Syria, he was there to liaise and advise. If the CTC and the Home Secretary deemed it necessary, he would lead the Regiment's assault on the house. He didn't like the way things were going so far.

Thorpe was too keen to throw other people into the line of fire. Butler had met Sinclair and knew McGill by reputation, they weren't terrorists. It was time for Butler to contact his bosses back in Hereford. He stepped out of the command vehicle and pressed the call button on his secure phone.

* * *

The armed officers from the Counter Terrorism Unit checked their weapons and adjusted their protective suits. All exposed skin had to be covered up and respirators put on before the assault could begin. Each man checked the man next to him: gloves pulled on; cuffs taped over; respirator harnesses tightened; if the intel was right, they couldn't afford to take any risks.

McGill watched the officers through his binoculars. 'They're definitely putting on chem suits. They must've been told we've got nerve agent.'

'You think they're getting ready to come at us?'

'I'd say so. You wouldn't put a mask on and then hang around for hours, you know how uncomfortable they are.'

Sinclair nodded. 'Yeah, like trying to move about with your head in a bag. I thought they'd at least wait until it was dark.'

'Normally you'd assault before dawn. It's when anyone on watch is at their lowest point, makes it easier to surprise them. Vadim's obviously still pulling the strings, I think he wants this dealt with quickly.'

'Remember what I said, Frank.'

McGill lowered his binoculars. 'Yeah, I know. We don't need to kill them, they're just doing their job.'

Hadley didn't relish the thought of being at the centre of

a full-blown armed assault. 'Maybe it would be better if we handed ourselves in. I'm still the head of SIS, they'll listen to me.'

McGill didn't lower his binoculars. 'I wouldn't be so sure. Some arsehole is probably down there right now telling everyone that you're in on it. Probably fancies takin' your job.'

DS Gardner was uneasy with the way DCS Thorpe had been running things since they'd arrived. He seemed to have a gung-ho attitude and wasn't listening to any of the advice he'd been given. He wasn't even trying to talk to McGill and Sinclair. She stopped him as he left the command vehicle. 'Could I have a quick word, sir?'

'What is it, Zoe? We are a little busy at the moment.'

She pulled him to one side, out of earshot of the others. 'I'm a bit concerned that we're rushing things, sir. We haven't sent a negotiator in yet.'

'These are terrorists, DS Gardner. They don't want to negotiate.'

'I'm aware of what they are, sir. I'm also aware of how it will look if we unleash an armed team without giving the terrorists the opportunity to give themselves up. You don't want to end up in prison yourself, do you, sir?'

Thorpe wasn't happy, but Gardner was right. This was a high-profile case. They had to be seen to do everything right and he couldn't afford to fuck up again. 'Okay, Zoe, well volunteered. I want you to go up to the house and convince them to surrender.'

'Wait ... What? Me? But I ...'

'You can do it. Take them a radio, then at least we can talk to them. Okay?'

Gardner looked up at Rock Cottage then back at the DCS. 'Okay, I'll do it.'

Mick Butler watched the preparations, they were rushing into it. They hadn't done any recon to check the defences, they didn't even know how many people they were up against. Thorpe was pushing it too fast. He pressed the call button on his phone and waited for an answer. 'I'm not too happy with this, boss. There's somethin' about this guy, he's makin' everything sound as bad as he can. It's like he's trying to make sure the assault is as aggressive as possible, like he's tryin' to make sure no one in the house survives.' He nodded as he listened to the voice on the other end of the call. His concerns were being taken seriously, and noted, but, if he was ordered to, he would have to assault the house. People way above his pay grade would make that decision. He nodded again. 'Will do, boss.' He ended the call and put his phone away.

DCS Thorpe was talking to the firearms team lead. 'We know there are at least two terrorists in the house and we now know they have a hostage. They are both ex-military and one is an escaped convict. The priority is to disable them quickly and prevent them from setting off any devices or releasing any chemicals. Any evidence in there MUST be left for me to examine first. Good luck.' Thorpe walked away and left the team to do their job.

McGill had put down his binoculars and was watching events through the scope of his Barrett. One team of four were standing on the road by the gate making last minute checks. The other four-man team had disappeared off to the right and seemed to be working their way around to the other side of the house.

Sinclair was sitting in front of the CCTV monitor. 'We've

got a four-man team heading up the hill towards the barn.'

'The other team has spread out and are coming up the track.'

Sinclair zoomed in with one of the cameras. 'They're being a bit reckless, aren't they?'

'They're just getting into position, they won't come too close just yet. They'll have a sniper somewhere, waiting for us to make a move.'

'How do you think they'll play it?'

McGill put his rifle on the table. 'Once they're in position, they'll check for final approval. When they get that, it'll be fast. Probably tear gas through the windows and an enforcer through the doors.'

'Are we ready?'

'Yeah, I think so.' McGill lifted a steel box, the same size as the control for the cameras, onto the table. He turned on the power and three rows of ten red LEDs lit up. Each of the lights had a small toggle switch below it. 'They're all armed.'

Sinclair panned the cameras around. 'Looks like they're in position, as close as they want to get.' She focused a camera on a single woman who had walked through the gate. 'Someone's coming up the track.'

DS Gardner walked up the steep track, her arms held out to the side. In her right hand she carried a megaphone and in her left a radio. She stopped at the top of the track and lifted the megaphone to her mouth. 'Sinclair ... McGill ... My name is DS Zoe Gardner. I want to talk.'

There was no movement in the house.

'I want to get you out of there before anyone gets hurt ... Please.'

McGill swung open the steel shutter that was covering the window and watched Gardner through the net curtain. 'You think we should talk to her?'

'It might help. It'll certainly kill more time.'

McGill cracked open the window. 'Walk forward, slowly, no sudden moves.'

DS Gardner walked towards the house, keeping her arms to the side. When she was a few feet away she checked to her left and right. The armed officers were watching her, one of them gave her a thumbs-up. She took a deep breath, steadied herself, and approached the window.

The net curtain was blowing in the breeze and Gardner could just make out a figure standing at the other side of the window. 'Hello?'

Sinclair stepped forward. 'Hello, Zoe, I'm Ali Sinclair.'

Gardner was nervous, she'd never been in this situation before. 'I've been sent up here to negotiate your surrender and …'

Sinclair held up her hand to stop her. 'Forget the playbook, Zoe. Just talk to me.'

Gardner looked behind her, as if seeking approval from her boss. 'Okay. My boss, down there, is ready to order an assault on the house if you don't give up.'

'And what do you think? Are you comfortable with that?'

Gardner looked at her feet. 'Unfortunately, it doesn't matter what I think. My boss is in touch with Gold Command and they will be talking to the COBRA Committee. It's probably the Home Secretary that's giving the orders.'

'Listen to me carefully, Zoe. This is all part of a massive conspiracy that involves the Home Secretary and lots of others. Get in touch with Edward Lancaster, he works for MI6. He'll tell you the same.'

'I've met Lancaster. He was at an interview we were doing.'

Sinclair nodded. 'So you know he's genuine. Look, whoever is pushing you to finish this quickly, is probably involved.'

'But my boss is the one who's in charge.'

'Exactly. Has he been doing anything a little strange, a bit out of character?'

Gardner thought for a moment. 'Well, he does seem a bit on edge, and some of his decisions looked a bit flaky, but we're all under a lot of pressure. I'm sure if you gave yourselves up, we could get to the bottom of things.'

Sinclair smiled. 'We can't do that, we don't know who we can trust.'

Gardner remembered the radio in her hand. She held it through the gap in the window. 'Take this so we can contact you. Please think about coming out.'

Sinclair took the radio. 'Watch your back, Zoe, and do try and contact Lancaster. It's for your own good as well as ours.'

Gardner turned and walked back down the track. Sinclair closed the window and swung the steel shutter back into position.

* * *

The Home Secretary walked into the COBRA meeting and sat down. He looked a mess. Several people sitting around the room were shocked by his appearance and the smell of drink on his breath. He had a cut next to his left eye and his shirt collar had blood on it.

One of the junior ministers from the Foreign Office voiced everyone's concerns. 'Are you okay, sir?'

'Err … Yes, thank you. I was involved in a minor car crash this morning. I'll be going to hospital to get checked out as soon as we finish here.'

The others around the table exchanged glances, some concerned, some admiring his commitment. They carried on. The Chief of the Defence Staff was first to speak. 'As you all know, we have received no confirmation from the Turkish government that they are willing to meet our demands. For that reason, we have now finalised our preparations and the first air strikes will take place at zero six hundred tomorrow morning, unless we receive the order to stand down.'

Enfield was staring at the briefing notes he had been given. He wasn't taking in all the details, he needed another drink. 'Thank you, General. We all hope that the government of Turkey contacts us before then, but, if they don't, we must be willing to strike to protect our democracy.'

Nods and murmurs told Enfield he still had the support of the committee – even if some of that support was insincere. He looked at the Assistant Metropolitan Police Commissioner. 'I see on your brief you mention the events in Cumbria, can you give us an overview of the situation, Commissioner?'

'Yes, sir. We currently have an operation going on in Cumbria. These two people ...' He pointed to the wall of screens at the end of the room. Side by side were mug shots of Sinclair and old service photos of McGill. 'Frank McGill and Ali Sinclair are both known to the police and security services. The Intelligence Service has received intel that shows these two are involved, in some way, in the recent terrorist attacks. Unfortunately, we believe they are now holding the chief of the Intelligence Service as a hostage.'

Enfield nodded. 'These are grave times for all of us. How is the operation proceeding?'

'I'll be heading back to the CTC after this meeting, to take charge personally. We are expecting an armed unit from the CTU in Manchester to mount an assault very soon. I'll keep you informed, sir.'

'Yes please, Commissioner. You have my authority, do whatever it takes to ensure the safe return of Kelvin Hadley.'

'Will do, sir.' He stood up and left the room.

Enfield looked at everyone else. 'If no one has anything to add, I think I should get myself to A & E.'

Everyone around the table nodded, still concerned by the Home Secretary's appearance.

'Thank you all. With your support, we'll get through this.' He held on to the table as he stood then, unsteadily, walked across the room and out of the door.

Chapter 48

The radio that DS Gardner had handed to Sinclair was in the middle of the table. Every few minutes it crackled into life as Thorpe called them and told them to surrender. It had been ten minutes since the last call, and all three of them were staring at the radio waiting for something to happen.

McGill picked it up and checked the battery was still okay. 'Looks like they've given up on the idea of talking us out.'

Sinclair went to the screen and studied the grey images. 'They haven't moved yet, what are they waiting for?'

'They'll be checking for the final go ahead. We need to be ready.'

Sinclair opened the weapons box and took out more ammunition for her Glock. McGill unloaded his rifle and put the magazine inside the box. 'We don't need that, this'll be all up close.'

Hadley was still hoping he could talk them out of this, but wanted to be ready in case he couldn't. 'I'll need a weapon. To protect myself.'

Sinclair shook her head. 'They've already said on the radio that they think you're a hostage. It's probably why they haven't come after us already. You stay down on the floor, if they get in here, they won't shoot you if you're not armed.'

'But if none of us were armed, they would have to take us in. I could tell them everything that's happened.'

McGill took a pump action shotgun out of the box. 'I have a feeling they're going to shoot us whatever happens. It's a special request from the Home Secretary.'

Hadley shook his head. 'I still can't believe what you've told me. I've known Marcus for years, he's as committed as any of us.'

'But committed to who? We've got it in black and white.'

Hadley pointed at the folder. 'Is his name in there?'

McGill picked up the folder. 'It doesn't mention his real name, but Danny Kinsella will find the link.'

'If his name isn't in there, what makes you so sure that Marcus is this ... Vadim?'

Sinclair stared directly at Hadley. 'Because I met him. I'll never forget his face. He looked down at me and ordered Bazarov to have me killed. Ever since then he's been paying people to take me out. I've been beaten more times than I can remember. That prison was hell because of Vadim. The next time I see him, I'm gonna kill him.'

Sinclair was getting angry just talking about it. She stabbed her finger on the table top, her voice cracking with emotion. McGill grabbed her hand and squeezed it to calm her. 'Let's just say we have more than the folder. That prick is going down, no matter what.'

Sinclair had stopped trembling and was breathing normally. She patted McGill's hand. 'Thanks, Frank.' She looked back at Hadley. 'Frank's like a human form of Valium: he keeps me calm, stops me from doing something I might regret.'

Hadley knew Enfield could be a bit of a smug bastard at

times. Instead of getting the job done, he preferred to gloat – that would be his downfall. Enfield wasn't happy to stay in the shadows, out of the limelight, that's why he liked being the Home Secretary. A man like that could never be running a global conspiracy. Hadley was also in no doubt that Sinclair, given the chance, would kill Enfield rather than bring him in.

McGill panned one of the cameras. 'Looks like they're coming, Ali. Get ready.'

They could see the two four-man police teams cocking their weapons and starting up the hill. Sinclair and McGill grabbed their weapons and made a final check of the windows and doors; all were locked and the steel shutters were in place.

McGill pumped the action of his shotgun. 'Here they come.'

The first team approached from the front, quickly arriving at the house and crouching down next to the door. The second team paused at the barn before taking up a similar position at the rear.

Simultaneously, a member of each team stood back and fired tear gas through the window. At the same time, another team member sent in a stun grenade. Both projectiles broke the windows, but only got as far as the steel shutters before bouncing back and landing at the officers' feet.

The CS gas didn't affect the men as they were wearing respirators, but the concussive blast of the stun grenades blinded them and caused momentary deafness and loss of balance. Some of the men held their ears and managed to stand, but they were no longer able to attack the house.

Sinclair swung open the steel shutter behind the front window, McGill aimed his shotgun through the gap and pulled the trigger. The first beanbag round hit one of the officers between the shoulder blades and knocked him forward, onto his hands and knees. The second round hit another officer in the thigh and numbed his leg, causing him to fall to his knees.

McGill cleared the window and Sinclair closed the shutter. One of the front team members, who hadn't been as badly affected by the stun grenade, picked up the enforcer battering ram and swung it at the door. The door shook in its frame under the assault of the heavy steel battering ram, but, with the brace McGill had fitted, the door wasn't going to break down. McGill picked up the steel box covered in LEDs and flicked one of the switches.

Above the front door, McGill had installed a stun grenade of his own. The bright flash and explosive percussion made the officer drop the enforcer and he rolled away holding his head. The other three members of his team were lying or kneeling on the ground, in no fit state to do anything.

By now, the team at the rear had abandoned their assault and were making their way around to the front. McGill flicked two more switches and set off bird scarers at the front of the house to keep their heads down.

As the rear team arrived at the front, McGill swung open the steel shutter and took aim with the shotgun. Sinclair put her hand on the barrel and pushed it down. 'Leave them, Frank. Let them pull back. They're no threat any more.'

McGill pulled the shotgun in and closed the shutter. 'I don't think they were expecting that.'

Sinclair watched the screen as the two teams limped back down the hill towards their command vehicle. 'How long do you think they'll wait before they come again?'

McGill put down his shotgun. 'They won't come back again.'

Hadley came out from his hiding place in the kitchen. 'What do you mean? Surely, they won't just give up?'

McGill zoomed in on a figure they could just make out, standing close to the dry stone wall. He was wearing civilian clothes and had been watching everything. None of the police were attempting to move him on, and, as they watched, he lifted a phone to his ear. McGill tapped the screen. 'We just ramped it up to a whole new level. I would say, that guy there is Regiment. Right now, he's calling his boss back in Hereford. The next people to assault the house ... will be our friends from the SAS.'

* * *

Danny Kinsella looked out at the docks through a grubby window of the warehouse they were now hiding in. Nash had recently bought the warehouse and planned to turn it into luxury dockside apartments – that was going to take a great deal of work. In the meantime, Nash had arranged for some inflatable beds and sleeping bags to be brought, just in case their stay was extended. Kinsella switched on his phone and dialled Carter's number.

Carter looked at the number on the phone: he didn't recognise it, but only a handful of people knew his. 'Hello?'

Kinsella was pleased to hear Carter's voice. 'Simeon. It's me.'

Carter felt a wave of relief wash over him. He'd been worrying about Kinsella since he heard about the attack at Brantleigh House. He trusted that Nash would keep everyone safe, but it didn't stop him from thinking the worst. 'Danny, thank God you're alive. I really was worried.'

'I'm okay, Simeon, everyone is okay. We're in—'

Carter cut him off. 'Don't tell me where you are, Danny, I don't need to know.'

'Of course, right, I'm not used to this spy stuff.'

Lancaster was gesturing to Carter, trying to mime a folder. Carter nodded. 'Listen, you've all done as much as you can. You have to keep yourselves safe and look after your copies of the evidence. It's all we've got now. If anything happens to me, you must make this stuff public. Don't let Vadim get away with it.'

'I promise I won't, Simeon, but I've found something you need to know.'

Carter didn't like the sound of this. 'What is it, Danny?'

'I went through all of the profiles and compared them to known people, and I got a match. I've been thinking, why would Vadim risk everything by letting people know who he is? Why would someone as powerful as him be doing his own dirty work?'

Carter was puzzled. 'What do you mean?'

Kinsella watched as the rush-hour traffic picked up on the other side of the river. Regular people, getting on with their lives, oblivious of the nightmare being cooked up by the people they trusted to protect them. 'We know that Vadim hires people to get their hands dirty, so why go to the island to see Bazarov, why give Sinclair the opportunity to identify him?'

Carter's eyes widened. 'He wouldn't, he would send someone else.'

'Exactly. Enfield is nothing more than a straw man, put in place to take the heat off Vadim. A sacrificial lamb to give Vadim time to escape if it all goes wrong. Nobody knows who Vadim really is, not even the other conspirators.'

'Jesus, Danny, are you sure?'

'I've checked Enfield's background, he doesn't fit at all. I don't think the other conspirators even know he isn't Vadim. The cover is so complete, so perfect.'

Carter was stunned, it had never entered his mind that they were chasing the wrong guy. 'Do you know who he is, Danny?'

'I've found a profile that fits exactly. I'd bet my life that this is Vadim.'

Carter ended the call and looked at Lancaster. 'We need to get to the Prime Minister, now.'

Chapter 49

Visibility around Rock Cottage was getting worse. A fog bank had begun to roll up the valley and dark rainclouds obscured the sun. A flock of Herdwick sheep moved as one towards the relative shelter of the lee side of a dry stone wall, while birds and other wildlife disappeared into burrows, sets and nests, sensing the approaching storm. With nothing moving, and any remaining sounds deadened by the fog, the normal peace and quiet of the area was even more profound. This new silence, this new tranquillity, was broken by the rhythmic beating of a helicopter's rotor blades.

The Dauphin helicopter, from the Army Air Corp's 658 Squadron, appeared between the hills at the far end of the valley, skimming the trees and dry stone walls as it tried to keep below the level of the encroaching fog. The pilot hugged the ground and swung left and right, following the undulating contours of the Lake District's rugged landscape. The Herdwick sheep, huddled together and settled in their new-found shelter, scattered and ran from the aircraft's noise and downdraft.

Inside the helicopter, the co-pilot checked his map, and pointed to a field next to the road, in the bottom of the valley. The pilot nodded and gave a thumbs-up, turning his controls and heading for their landing spot. The co-pilot signalled to the passengers, telling them they were about to land. The passengers were members of the Special Air Service's Counter Revolutionary Warfare Wing, the most elite counter-terrorist unit in the world. They checked their kit and readied themselves to disembark. All their training, all the planning, had been leading to this point. It was time for them to go to work.

Mick Butler leaned on a rust-covered steel gate and watched the aircraft bank along the side of a hill, then slow, and descend towards him, touching down one hundred metres from the edge of the field. The pilot throttled back on the engine and the passengers began to climb out.

As soon as the police attempt to enter the house had failed, Butler knew it was only a matter of time until the rest of his team arrived. The counter-terrorist team were based at SAS headquarters at Credenhill, near Hereford. They had practised assaults like this time and time again, until it had become second nature. This was the time when that practice would pay off.

Butler had been sent ahead to liaise with the police and other civilian authorities, but at the same time he was preparing for the order that was now inevitable. The order that would send them into action. He had surveyed the lay of the land and the layout of the house, spoken to neighbours, and photographed the house from every angle. He now knew more about Rock Cottage than many of the people who lived in the area.

Butler opened the back doors of the blue Transit van he had parked beside the wall, and waited for his team by the gate. 'Good to see you, lads. Pile in, the farm's just a mile up the road.'

The men loaded their bags into the back of the van and climbed in. Butler got in the front and started the engine, pulling away just as a car full of reporters and photographers appeared around the bend. The car skidded to a halt at the gate and the photographers jumped out, cameras at the ready, but all they got was a view of the van driving off and the helicopter disappearing into the fog.

McGill stood at the front window. He had opened it slightly and had his ear to the two-inch gap. 'There was definitely a chopper out there, sounded like it landed for a few minutes then took off again. Can't hear it any more. If I was a bettin' man, I'd say the blades have just arrived.'

Sinclair sat in the kitchen cleaning her weapon. It didn't really need it, it was something she did, almost absent-mindedly, to pass the time and relax her mind – like popping bubble wrap. 'You really think they'll send them in?'

'As far as they're concerned, we're terrorists with a hostage and potentially some nerve agent. We've already repelled the police attempt to storm the building, special forces are the next step up. The SAS are the kind of people who would be brought here by helicopter.'

Hadley shifted nervously in his chair. 'Wouldn't now be a good time to negotiate your surrender?'

McGill looked at the radio in the centre of the table. It had been silent for more than two hours. 'I don't think they're interested in us giving up any more, we're a hopeless case. Let's face it, if we did walk out of here, Vadim would have us locked up and killed later, at his leisure.'

'How do you know that?'

'He tried to kill Ali enough times when she was in Mexico.

You could say he's got form.'

Hadley raised one hand towards the door. 'I could leave. I could go and talk to them, explain what happened, they'll listen to me.'

'I've told you already, you have no evidence. If we give up, we'll be arrested and put on remand to wait for our trial. Even if the evidence came to light in court, it still gives Vadim months to finish us off.'

Hadley held out both arms, pleading. 'At least let me go before they come in. I don't want to die in the crossfire.'

McGill shook his head. 'You're not going to die in any crossfire. They think you're a hostage, their job is to get you out of here unharmed, and they are very good at what they do.'

Sinclair finished cleaning her Glock and slid it into her shoulder holster. 'Maybe we could push him out of the door before the shooting starts?'

'Don't worry, I've seen those lads assault a building and kill all the terrorists without even messing up the hostages' hair. He'll be fine.'

Hadley wandered to the kitchen, shaking his head. 'You're both mad.'

Sinclair took a step towards McGill, lowering her voice. 'I know you, Frank. With all the defences you've put in, you must have planned a way out of here.'

McGill looked at the basement door. 'There's an old tunnel down there, been there for decades. I don't know what it was for, but it comes up in the barn. It won't help us, though, we wouldn't make it off the hill without being seen. Anyway, I'm not running. I'd rather go down swinging.'

Sinclair nodded. 'Me too. I'm not going back inside again.'

Hadley was listening: McGill and Sinclair weren't being as quiet as they thought. All he had to do was distract them, and he could be through the tunnel and away. He put his hand in his trousers and adjusted the phone he had tucked into the front of his boxers – the one he had pretended to throw out of the car window at the airfield. One phone call was all it would take, that was his way out.

* * *

The SAS team had taken over the police command and control vehicle and were now listening to the brief from their troop commander. Mick Butler took them through the likely scenarios for the assault. 'One team at the front entrance and one at the back. We'll blow the doors and go with CS and stun grenades. We know McGill has the place rigged with non-lethal booby traps so look out for them, and keep your heads down when we're waiting to breach.'

One of the men raised his hand. 'Do we have any plans for the place, Mick? Give us an idea of the layout?'

Butler shook his head. 'This place was built by hill farmers nearly two hundred years ago, they didn't use plans, they just built it. It's never had any planning permission submitted for the main house, so we don't have plans from there, either.'

'Could make things interestin'. We expectin' any surprises in the house?'

Butler pressed a button on a remote, turning on a screen behind him. He clicked through photo after photo of the house, covering every possible position for booby traps and ambushes. He took the team through the best places to launch the assault from, and how they would enter the house. 'I've

305

spoken to the locals and they've given me an idea of the basic layout inside.'

On a whiteboard next to the screen, Butler had drawn a plan of Rock Cottage. 'The footprint of the house is L-shaped. The main entrance leads into a kitchen or main living area. The back entrance opens onto a corridor that has rooms off it. We expect them to be in the main room. We have no idea how up to date these descriptions are, and McGill could have completely remodelled the inside of the house, but it's the best we've got.'

'Who are they, Mick? What do we know about them? Are they ideological, lookin' for a cause to die for, or are they likely to crumble under fire?'

Butler picked up the remote again. Various photographs of Sinclair and McGill appeared on the screen. 'These two are definitely professionals, be in no doubt about that. McGill is an ex-shaky, so he's had very similar training to our boat squadron. He's got a hell of a reputation in the SF community.'

Another man nodded. 'I worked with him once, seemed like a good bloke.'

Butler pointed at the screen. 'Sinclair is ex-intelligence and SRR. We trained her at Hereford. She shouldn't be underestimated.'

'They don't sound like the usual targets we come up against.'

Butler ensured the door was closed and no one could overhear them. 'To be honest, lads, I've checked up on them both, and I don't like it. There's somethin' not right about all this.'

'What do you mean, Mick?'

'I met Sinclair in a hanger in Rammstein, a short while back, before we went to Syria. She was definitely mixed up with spooks and didn't seem like the kind of person who'd suddenly go rogue.'

Some of the men exchanged glances. 'You think this is a set up?'

Butler paused. 'I need to make sure we've got the go-ahead from the COBRA Committee before we go in. I don't trust the copper that's running this thing at all.'

'What do we do?'

'We do what we're told, when we're told. We might not like it, but it's our job.'

DCS Thorpe stood outside the door of the command vehicle. He didn't like being told to leave; it was his operation and he should be in there. He dialled the Home Secretary's phone number. 'They're here, they kicked me out of the briefing room. I'm supposed to be in charge, I should—'

'Shut up and listen.' Enfield was in no mood to listen to Thorpe's shit. 'I'm leaving London and heading north. Do not tell anyone where I am, got it?'

'Yes, sir, of course. You can trust—'

Enfield cut him off again. 'What I want, is Sinclair and McGill dead and that folder in my hands. Do you understand?'

This time Thorpe didn't respond, he didn't want to be cut off again.

'THORPE.'

Thorpe almost dropped the phone. 'Yes, sir. I ... I understand. I'll do whatever ... Hello?'

The Home Secretary had hung up.

Thorpe was beginning to think he should walk away from all this. He should take the money he had saved and leave the country. If he wasn't such a bloody coward, that's exactly what he would do. 'Fuck.'

Inside the vehicle, Butler was wrapping up his briefing. 'Be ready for the unexpected, lads, there could be anything in there.'

The men filed out of the vehicle, past DCS Thorpe. The looks they gave him left Thorpe in no doubt that he had somehow made their shit list. He waited a few seconds before going up the steps to the door. 'I need a word.'

Butler had removed all his briefing material: the screen was blank and the whiteboard had been wiped. 'What is it, Superintendent?'

'It's detective chief superintendent. My job may not be as glamorous as yours, but I think I deserve some respect.'

Butler raised an eyebrow. 'You'll get my respect when you've earned it. Now, if you've got something to say, get on with it.'

Thorpe wanted to tell Butler what he thought of him, but his lack of spine stopped him. 'I wanted to tell you that the Home Secretary has given the initial go-ahead for you to go into the house and kill the terrorists.'

Butler stepped towards Thorpe, their faces inches apart. 'When the time comes, I'll decide whether we assault the house. I will only make that decision when I get the approval of the COBRA Committee, or the Home Secretary himself, directly. I won't be taking any messages through you.'

Thorpe puffed out his chest and stood straight. He was taller than Butler and for a fleeting moment was feeling brave. 'I'm the silver commander of this operation. You'll do what I say.'

Butler stared and said nothing until Thorpe had visibly shrunk back into his spineless shell. 'Back off, dickhead, you're out of your depth.'

Thorpe's heart was pounding. He had Enfield threatening to kill him on one side, and Butler, who looked like he was about to beat him to death, staring him down on the other. Thorpe knew he was beaten, he knew he didn't have the bottle for this. He looked at the floor and shuffled his feet, then turned around and left the vehicle.

Chapter 50

The Queen Victoria Veterans Hospital wasn't part of the National Health Service, but it wasn't a private hospital, either. It had been established after the Crimean War and was now run by a charity. The hospital provided care, treatment and support for members of the armed forces who were suffering from life-changing injuries, both physical and mental. After the terrorist attack on the hotel in Geneva, survivors who still needed care had been moved to the hospital's top floor. In the days and weeks following the attack, fortunately, they had all been sent home to convalesce. Only the Prime Minister remained.

Edward Lancaster and Simeon Carter approached the hospital in the back of a military ambulance, which had cost them a lot of favours. Carter, or General Carter as they were now passing him off as, was lying on the stretcher, covered with blankets and wearing an oxygen mask. The doctor with him, Colonel Lancaster, was wearing military uniform, rubber gloves, and a stethoscope. It probably wouldn't have passed intense scrutiny, but it was the best they could do at short notice.

At the wheel of the ambulance was one of Lancaster's most trusted officers. Victoria Thomson had a wealth of experience in the field. She started her career as an army nurse, but her intellect and talent for languages soon brought her to the attention of the intelligence corps. After her training she was pushed into some of the world's worst trouble spots, and was a natural. It was only a matter of time before MI6 came calling.

Thomson had worked for Lancaster since her first days in the service. He was the one who sent her on her missions and it would be him who looked after her when it all went wrong.

Deployed to Afghanistan to convince the tribal elders in Helmand Province that the British Army were there to help them, she was able to gather more intel than any other officer in the region. She was a rising star of the intelligence community and had begun to believe too much in her own invincibility. When she started taking risks, the Taliban were waiting.

Thomson was kidnapped and held for ransom, a ransom that the UK government refused to pay. She was held for months. Tortured and beaten, she was regularly paraded in front of cameras and threatened with beheading. She was broken: her mind, her body, her soul; she lost all hope.

Eight months after her abduction, a US Marine Corps unit, carrying out a raid on a Taliban stronghold, found a dishevelled, malnourished and dehydrated woman chained to the wall in a darkened room. It was only when they'd given her water and cleaned off some of the dried blood covering her face, they realised she was a westerner.

When she got home she was in pieces. Lancaster was there for her. He made sure she got the best of medical care. Her body still bore the scars of her ordeal, but she had recovered her health. Her mind, on the other hand, was a different matter. The psychiatrists did what they could and the medication helped, but she was still prone to bouts of depression and anxiety, which she sometimes treated with alcohol. Some in the service wanted her pensioned off – put out to pasture, a wounded hero, but Lancaster wouldn't have it. He kept her on, kept her working, kept her sane.

Thomson was fiercely loyal to Lancaster. When he had asked her to put on her old uniform and drive an ambulance, she hadn't even asked why. Now she was pulling into the car park of the Queen Victoria, preparing to break through the Prime Minister's security. It was good to be back in the game.

The ambulance stopped at the hospital's entrance and Thomson climbed through to the back. 'Okay, guys, remember, if you act like you belong somewhere, people will just assume that you do.'

Carter pulled the oxygen mask away from his mouth. 'I'll just keep my eyes closed, let you deal with the medical questions, Edward.'

Thomson put the mask back in place. 'I'll answer the medical questions, Simeon. Edward, you just look concerned about our patient.'

Lancaster nodded. 'Sounds like a plan.'

Thomson opened the back doors. 'Let's go.'

They pushed the stretcher out of the ambulance and up the ramp to the entrance. Thomson returned to close the ambulance doors then followed Lancaster into the hospital.

Thomson was right: no one questioned them at all. No one asked them who they were or even gave them a second glance. They walked straight past reception and into the lift. Lancaster pressed the button for the top floor and the doors closed.

The top floor of the Queen Victoria had eight rooms. Each one was fully equipped to care for patients with a variety of conditions; from recovery from minor operations, right up to full life-support, the necessary equipment could be wheeled in and hooked up. Each patient's status could be monitored from the nurses station, which was positioned halfway along the floor's main corridor, and any alarms reacted to quickly.

When the lift doors opened, Lancaster and Thomson pushed the stretcher to the right, along to the far end of the corridor, into the room farthest away from the Prime Minister's room.

The duty nurse came out from behind the nurses station and followed them. 'Excuse me?'

Carter was lying on the hospital bed and Lancaster was standing beside him with a clipboard in his hand, writing notes on the form clipped to its front. Thomson stood to one side of the door.

The duty nurse walked up to the bed. 'Excuse me, doctor, I wasn't expecting any admissions this evening.'

Lancaster took off his glasses. 'Good evening,' he looked at the nurse's name tag, 'Deborah. This is General Carter, he's an emergency case. We need to monitor his vitals and prep him for surgery tomorrow.'

The nurse hesitated. It wasn't unusual to get an unexpected admission, but something wasn't right about this doctor. She knew all the doctors who worked at the clinic and he wasn't one of them. She had to check on this, or at least let someone know what was happening. She turned towards the door.

Thomson raised her hand, the silenced pistol levelled at Deborah's head. 'Don't panic, Deborah, we aren't here to hurt anyone, especially not you. We just need you to stay calm and quiet, can you do that for me?'

Deborah nodded, scared out of her wits.

Carter removed the oxygen mask and got off the bed. 'I think you can lower the weapon now, Vicky. Deborah isn't going to give us any trouble.'

Thomson stepped back and checked along the corridor. No one was paying any attention to what they were doing. If any of the guards had noticed them, they were assuming everything was above board. 'Okay, we're looking good so far.'

Deborah was lying on the bed, Carter had tied her hands and feet. 'That's not too tight for you, is it?'

The nurse shook her head.

Carter took a length of bandage and used it to gag her. 'Can you breathe okay?'

She nodded.

'Good. We'll come back and let you go as soon as we can.' He smiled to reassure her. 'I'm sorry about this, but it's something we have to do. You'll understand when it's over.'

Lancaster and Thomson walked down the corridor and past the nurses station. Lancaster carried a clipboard and they appeared to be deep in conversation. As they neared the Prime Minister's room, the guard in the corridor stood up. 'Stop where you are, I'll need to see some ID.'

Lancaster stopped and took off his glasses. 'I'm Colonel Lancaster. I'm a consultant at another clinic and I'm covering for Doctor Standish. He's not well.'

Thomson walked straight past the guard towards the doorway. The guard took a step towards her. 'Stop right there, I need your ID, too.'

Thomson held up a photo ID that she had taken off Deborah.

The guard was too far away to make out the details and was about to tell her to bring it closer, but Thomson gave him a frustrated look. 'How many times do you want me to show you this?' She pointed towards the nurses station. 'I've been sitting there all night.' Her face broke into a smile. 'Or are you just trying to chat me up? If you want my number, love, just ask for it.'

The guard looked embarrassed. He was sure he would have remembered the nurse, though she did look kind of familiar. Hell, it was the middle of the night and he was tired, he'd probably just missed her. 'Okay, go ahead.' He looked back at Lancaster. 'I'll still need to see your ID.'

Thomson walked into the room. She smiled at the guard sitting in the corner and started to check the Prime Minister's pulse. The guard sat up and put down the book he was reading. 'I don't think I've seen you here before.'

Thomson smiled. 'I've been on holiday. First day back and I pull a night shift, lucky me.'

The guard relaxed. 'Me too. I've been fighting to stay awake.' He nodded at the sleeping Prime Minister. 'Do you think he'd notice if I put the TV on?'

Thomson was checking the PM's chart. 'They've got him sedated. I don't think he's going to be waking up until the morning.'

'Maybe just for a little while then.' The guard switched on the TV and turned down the volume.

Thomson was pulling at a lever at the foot of the bed. 'Could you give me a hand with this? I need to adjust the bed.'

'Sure, no problem.' The guard stepped over to stand beside Thomson. She looked past him into the corridor, where Lancaster was still looking for his ID. Lancaster nodded.

Thomson placed the barrel of her weapon on the side of the guard's head. 'Don't move, love. I wouldn't want to shoot you by accident.'

At the same time, Lancaster reached inside his white coat and pulled out his own pistol, pointing it at the other guard's forehead. 'Hands behind your head, don't even twitch.' He disarmed the guard and walked him into the room.

Thomson and Lancaster tied the guards to two chairs and switched on all the lights. Carter entered the room and looked at the Prime Minister. 'We've got to wake him up. We don't have much time.'

Chapter 51

Two of the Royal Navy's newest nuclear-powered submarines hovered a few metres below the surface of the eastern Mediterranean. The periscope of one of the Astute Class boats broke the surface and turned towards its target. The steel structure was barely visible above the waves as it scanned the horizon, gathering information and looking for potential threats.

Below the surface, in the A-Boat's control room, the captain and his XO watched the screen that showed the image from the periscope. The sun was setting and lights began to flicker along the horizon. They knew that, in a few hours, if the situation didn't change, they would receive the order from Whitehall to launch the first of the Tomahawk cruise missiles that would devastate the area they were looking at.

The implications weren't lost on the submarine's captain. Commander Graham Teal had been in command of the vessel since before it had come out of build in the shipyard in Barrow. He was due to move on in a few months – he was being promoted and moved up the food chain – a desk job beckoned. This was likely to be his last deployment, his first in an actual hot war.

His crew had trained for months to carry out this exact role.

They had taken part in exercises and practice missile firings, but this was different. By this time tomorrow, they would have unleashed the massive power of the submarine against people who wouldn't see it coming. People who had no way of stopping it, who had no influence on their government's decisions.

Teal looked at the screen again. He could make out vehicles, moving along the coastal road, probably locals going home after work. At dawn tomorrow, they wouldn't have to worry about work – their homes and offices would be reduced to piles of rubble. All they would have to worry about was surviving. The decision to launch wasn't his, that would be made back in London. He didn't envy those people, but he did trust them to make the right choice. He left the control room and went back to his cabin.

* * *

Mick Butler's team were back in the command and control vehicle, making final preparations for the assault. Various equipment was laid out on the tables: CS gas and stun grenades; sub-machine guns and sidearms, with spare magazines; respirators; radios and ear pieces. Everything they would need to make the operation a success.

The team members checked every piece of kit before stowing it in a particular pouch or pocket attached to their body armour. They checked their weapons last. Each one had a full magazine slotted in, but they weren't cocked, that wouldn't be done until the last minute. They would only arm their weapons when they were needed – when they were about to go in.

318

Butler was still uneasy about this job but he couldn't let that concern him. Once they were given the go-ahead, all he had to think about was the safety of the hostage and the safety of his men. Whatever was going to happen to Sinclair and McGill was in their own hands. The outcome depended on what they did.

* * *

The attendees of the COBRA Committee had begun to arrive at four o'clock. The deadline for Turkey to respond was at five o'clock, and they needed to be available to make the decision to begin military action. They also had to deal with the ongoing situation in Cumbria. The meeting had the feeling of a full war cabinet.

The Chief of the Defence Staff kicked off the meeting. 'Do we know if the Home Secretary is joining us?'

One of the junior ministers shook her head. 'I was asked to pass on his apologies. His doctor has told him to rest, but he will be phoning in around four thirty.'

'Thank you for that. Let's get started.'

The screens at the end of the room showed various twenty-four-hour news channels. Most of the attendees had laptops open and lines of communication had been set up in preparation to issue out the order to strike. Gold command were connected via video link and were currently giving an update.

'We've still had no communication from inside the house. If we are going to breach, I have been advised that the time to do it is now. They will be at a low ebb and easier to surprise.'

'Thank you, Commissioner. The Home Secretary is now on the line. Good morning, sir, were you able to hear gold command's briefing?'

'Yes. Thank you, General.'

'Sir, we have been advised by special forces that the optimum time to enter the house is just before dawn. Can you confirm your approval to deploy?'

There was a pause. 'It has become obvious that these people have no intention of negotiating. We cannot risk the release of more nerve agent. Therefore, I reluctantly confirm my authorisation to deploy special forces to bring this siege to an end.'

'Thank you, sir. Confirm authorisation to deploy special forces.'

The commissioner at gold command looked at the camera and nodded. 'Authorisation confirmed.' The video feed cut off.

Chapter 52

Thomson was looking at the PM's file. 'According to this, he is fully awake and aware during the day. They are sedating him at night as he is struggling to sleep.'

Carter shook his head. 'Just our luck. Normally you can't stop politicians from talking, we get the only one who won't even wake up.'

Thomson took out a hypodermic needle and injected its contents into the Prime Minister's drip. 'Should only take a few minutes.'

Carter looked at Lancaster and back to Thomson. 'What did you just give him?'

Thomson looked at the needle. 'You don't want to know, Simeon. An old trick, I thought it might come in handy.'

As they spoke, the PM opened his eyes. Thomson pressed a button on the bed and raised the end of it so he was sitting up. 'Good morning, sir.'

The PM looked out of the window. 'Are you sure it's morning?'

'There are a couple of men here who need to speak with you, it's urgent.'

Thomson stood back and Lancaster stepped up to the bed.

The PM was still a little drowsy and his eyes hadn't focused properly. He blinked and squinted at Lancaster. 'Edward? Is that you? I haven't seen you for ages.'

'It's good to see you again, sir. I'm glad you're recovering well.'

The PM looked at the two guards who were tied to their chairs. 'If I didn't know better, I'd think I was in trouble.'

Lancaster beckoned Carter to the bed. 'This is Simeon Carter, he's an old friend of mine. He was a spook in East Berlin during the Cold War. You can trust him, sir. You need to listen carefully to everything he says.'

* * *

Mick Butler's team gathered at the bottom of the track and readied their weapons. 'Right, lads. We've had the go-ahead. Everything just as we planned.'

They looked up the hill, only half of it was visible. The thick fog had descended to cover the whole area; the house was completely shrouded in mist and couldn't be seen from any vantage point.

Butler put in his radio earpiece and checked comms. 'We're being told that visibility up there is down to five metres. If we set off any of McGill's booby traps, we have to keep going. It'll tip him off that we're coming, but I imagine he knows already.' He looked at his watch. 'Time now is zero four thirty, we need to be in position at zero four forty-five, we go five minutes later. Ready?'

The men nodded.

The team split into two: four men climbed the hill from each side. They already knew the main track was rigged, and assumed the back was, too. The sides were the least likely to give them away.

DS Gardner watched the black-clad figures set off but soon lost sight of them. She looked around for her boss, DCS Thorpe should be there, but there was no sign of him. With special forces about to assault the building, the man who was supposed to be in charge was nowhere to be seen. She didn't like the way things were going, there had been something wrong with all of this from the start. She held up her phone and pressed the call button.

* * *

Carter told the Prime Minister everything. He went right back to the start: how he'd been recruited by Lancaster and how Sinclair and McGill were involved; he went through the events with Bazarov on the island and how they had stopped it.

The Prime Minister listened carefully, he had been told about Bazarov but had been led to believe it was the Americans who had brought him down. 'Let me get this straight; Sinclair and McGill basically saved all of us, and we let them take her back to prison?'

Lancaster stepped forward. 'We did everything we could but it wasn't enough. I'll always be ashamed of that, she didn't deserve the way she was treated.'

Carter nodded. 'We all owe both of them a lot.'

The Prime Minister sat forward and adjusted his pillows. He was obviously tired. 'These events are somehow linked to a conspiracy within my government.'

Carter carried on. He told the PM about Sinclair's unmasking of the Home Secretary as Vadim, and the extent of the conspiracy. He showed him some of the evidence from the folder, which Kinsella had sent to his phone. Lancaster would probably lose his job after this, but that didn't matter right now, they had to stop everything.

The PM was incredulous. He looked at Lancaster. 'This all sounds so implausible. How could something like this go on under the noses of our security services?'

Lancaster took over. 'There are a lot of people involved, Prime Minister, as Simeon has said, some are at the highest level. They've had people assassinated, and carried out the attack in Geneva and the shootings in Westminster. The security services are just following the orders that are coming down the line. They don't even suspect these people.'

'What do they want, Edward? Is this all about being in power?'

'Partly, sir. This organisation dates back to the Cold War. The people who set it up believed in the old Soviet Union, they want to see it resurrected as a global super power, that's why they're trying to destabilise NATO.'

The PM looked at Carter. 'But that's not all they want, is it?'

Carter shook his head. 'No, sir. If it was, it would be easier to predict, easier to deal with, just like it was back then.'

Lancaster turned up the volume on the TV. The BBC reporter was standing outside number 10 Downing Street. *'There has still been no confirmation that the Turkish have responded to the government's request for information on the terrorist attacks. If no response is forthcoming, by the deadline of five o'clock GMT, it is expected that UK troops will, once again, be sent into action. Back to the studio.'*

The PM watched the breaking news that scrolled along the bottom of the screen as the news anchor went through other stories. British troops had been mobilised, Russian troops had amassed on the Syrian-Turkish border, and US forces were preparing to respond to any Russian reaction.

Lancaster pointed at the screen. 'These people sit at the head of government organisations, as well as major corporations. In short, Prime Minister, war is good for their business.'

'I'm out of action for a few weeks and the whole world's gone mad. What time is it?'

Lancaster looked at his watch. 'It's four thirty.'

'Get me a phone, there's still time.'

* * *

Butler's half of the team had almost reached the barn when they triggered the flares. McGill had strung more fishing wire right around the approach to the building and rigged it to a chain of emergency flares. The bright white light destroyed Butler's night vision and meant that he and his team had to wait before carrying on. That was exactly what McGill had planned.

Inside the house, McGill saw the flares light up the image on one of his cameras. 'They're coming, Ali. Get ready.'

Sinclair opened the metal box and pulled out one of the assault rifles, she slotted in a magazine and chambered a round. 'Frank.'

McGill took the assault rifle and spare magazines that Sinclair passed to him, and went to the window to wait for the SAS teams to arrive. 'We won't have long. Once they're in position at the entrances, it'll be less than a minute until they blow the doors.'

Sinclair loaded the other assault rifle. 'I guess this means Simeon didn't succeed.'

'It was always a long shot, we're up against powerful people, they always seem to win.'

Sinclair joined him at the window, out of Hadley's earshot. 'This is it then. This is where we go out swingin''

McGill looked at the screen. 'There is a chance; there could be a way for us to get out and disappear.'

'Whatever you're planning, Frank, I'm in. If they won't believe us about Vadim, we'll just leave them to it. Leave them to their power games. What are you thinking?'

McGill looked out of the window. 'This fog is really thick, I can't even see the barn. If we wait until they appear at the door, we could leg it for the tunnel and make it out of here. They won't be able to see us.'

'What do you think our chances are?'

'If we're in here when they blow the doors, they'll kill us. If we get caught out in the open, they'll probably kill us. In this fog? Maybe we sneak away.'

Sinclair squeezed McGill's forearm. 'Sounds like a plan, let's do it. I'm not scared to die, but I'd rather not.'

Chapter 53

The COBRA committee members all stopped to look at the desk phone that was ringing at the far end of the room. People didn't usually dial in to meetings like this, and it definitely wasn't normal to receive a call from an unknown number.

The Chief of the Defence Staff pressed the answer button. 'Hello?'

The voice on the other end of the line sounded a little weak and was made tinny by the phone's loudspeaker. 'Good morning, General.'

The faces around the table looked shocked, they all recognised the voice. The general leaned forward towards the phone. 'Prime Minister?'

'Yes, General, how are you this morning?'

There was a buzz around the room. Everyone looked genuinely relieved to hear his voice. Not just relief that a man who most of them respected had recovered enough to call them, but relief that they would now get some actual leadership.

The junior ministers were keen but completely out of their depth. The military and senior police figures were uneasy at making such monumental decisions for the country. The

Home Secretary was leading them in name only. He was missing meetings, and, when he did turn up, his behaviour was worrying, bizarre, even. Although they had spoken to him for authorisation earlier, no one actually knew where he was. With the deadline approaching, and military action imminent, he should be sitting in that meeting.

The general reached out and turned up the volume on the phone. 'It's good to hear from you, sir. I'm glad you're well enough to join us. Are you aware of the situation we are currently facing?'

'I'm aware of the overall situation, General, but I am also in possession of some information that the committee and Parliament have not been party to.'

Everyone member of the committee was now leaning forward. 'Is it something you can share with us, sir?'

'Not on this line, General, not yet.'

'Understood, sir, what is it you want us to do?'

The line went quiet, they could hear low voices in the background, like a TV. 'In light of the information I have, we need to step back, General. We need to reassess our position. I want all military units to stand down immediately. We need to contact our allies and advise them of this change in our position.'

The general looked at the Royal Navy captain who sat opposite him, looking for some sign of agreement. 'Are you sure about this, sir? Militarily, the time to strike is now. The world is watching and expects us to act, our global reputation may depend on it.'

The Prime Minister cleared his throat. 'We are about to make a very dangerous mistake, General. There is more than our reputation on the line here. Delaying things for twenty-four hours won't affect the military outcome.'

The general looked down, staring at his hands. 'Understood, I'll issue the order to stand down for twenty-four hours. We need you here, sir. The committee will need to see the information you have.'

'I don't think the doctors will allow me out of here just yet. I want you to bring the committee to me. We'll continue the meeting at the hospital.'

The general looked around the room. Everyone was nodding their agreement. 'We'll reconvene in two hours. Is there anything else we need to do now, sir?'

'Yes, General. The operation in Cumbria must be stopped. The people in that house are not terrorists, they are the key to this whole thing.'

The general looked at his watch. 'It's four forty-five. I believe the assault to end the siege has already begun.'

* * *

Assistant Commissioner Robert Nicholson was watching the image on the screen at Counter Terrorist Control HQ. There was a degree of panic in the voice of the general and the COBRA committee. 'We need to stop it now, pull back immediately. Abort the operation.'

Nicholson was already on the phone, trying to contact DCS Thorpe at the scene, but the call wouldn't connect. He knew the mobile coverage in rural Cumbria could be flaky at the best of times, and most of the comms had been up and down for the last two days.

Thorpe looked at his mobile's screen, glowing as it rang. They had called him three times in two minutes, something was wrong. He had a feeling that everything was about to fold in on him, that he was going to be left holding the bag, but he couldn't just keep ignoring gold command, Vadim would be angry with him if he blew this. He pressed the green button and held the mobile to his ear. 'DCS Thorpe.'

'Thorpe, this is AC Nicholson. Abort the operation immediately.'

All the pressure, the stress and the fear weighed down on Thorpe like a sack of rocks. He knew he was finished. If they were aborting the assault, something big had happened. He hadn't heard from Enfield for hours, was he still in charge?

'THORPE.' Nicholson's voice boomed in Thorpe's ear. 'CAN YOU HEAR ME?'

Thorpe shook his head. 'I'm sorry, sir. I can't do this any more.'

'What? What are you talking about, man? Hello … HELLO?'

Thorpe ended the call and threw his phone into the field behind him. The screen lit up as it rang again, but he had already walked away.

Nicholson slammed down the phone. 'Get me the number of someone else on the ground. Contact the SAS troop commander.'

Mick Butler's night vision had recovered from the bright flash of the flares. He checked his watch, they were still on schedule. He knelt at the corner of the barn and peered into the fog. He could barely make out the silhouette of Rock Cottage. It was good that the targets in the house couldn't see his team, but they couldn't see the house, either. Sinclair and McGill could sneak out and he probably wouldn't see them. He pressed the push to talk button on his radio. 'Bravo two, this is Bravo one, confirm position, over.'

'Roger Bravo one, Bravo two confirmed at position one, over.'

Both teams were now just outside the area where they would be visible from the house, kneeling in the fog, waiting to advance. 'Bravo one to Command, confirm good to go, over.'

'Roger, Bravo one, confirm go, over.'

They had the final go-ahead. There was no turning back. 'All call signs, this is Bravo one, stand by.'

McGill closed the steel shutter at the window and went back to the screen. The CCTV camera was closer to the barn and gave them a view through the fog. 'There's someone kneeling at the corner of the barn. We've got minutes. As soon as they move, we get out.'

Hadley stood behind them, watching the screen. 'What are you doing?'

McGill didn't look up. 'We're leaving.'

'What about me?'

'They don't want you, just lie down and keep still. The blades are good at what they do. You can get back to your life and forget all about us. We can go and live on a beach somewhere and …' McGill stopped and stood up straight, he recognised the sound of a weapon being cocked. He looked behind him.

Hadley had taken one of the Glocks from the metal box and now had it pointed at Sinclair's head. 'That's not a plan I can work with. As much as I'd like to forget all about you, I can't risk you popping up in a few months and throwing a spanner in the works.'

On the screen there were four figures visible at the corner

of the barn. Butler looked at the other members of his team and gave them a thumbs-up.

'Stand by …'

Hadley took two steps back. 'Drop your weapons and move over there. He gestured with his head.

McGill lowered his assault rifle. 'What the fuck are you doing, Kelvin? You planning to take us in, be a hero?'

Hadley smiled. 'Not exactly what I had in mind. I was thinking more along the lines of: you both die during the assault and I'm the plucky survivor.'

Sinclair put down her weapons. 'Why would you do that? You've seen the evidence, you know what's going on.'

'What if I already knew?'

McGill backed up. He threw down his pistol and placed his assault rifle on the edge of the table. 'He's involved. The son of a bitch has been involved all along.'

Sinclair was stunned. Why hadn't they picked up on that earlier? 'But … at the airfield. Those men were trying to kill you.'

Hadley kept his nine-millimetre trained on them. 'No, Miss Sinclair. They were trying to kill you. They had no idea who I was. In the end, it's worked out quite well. People are saying I'm a hero. My political worth will be much higher after this.'

'Bastard. After all the shit we've gone through, we're gonna get taken out by this prick.'

The second SAS team edged forward to give themselves a clearer view of the rear door. They were all focussed on the operation. Nothing else mattered but this, the outside world may as well not exist.

'Stand by …'

DS Gardner stared into the darkness. She knew the special

forces teams were about to go in. Her phone vibrated in her pocket. 'Shit, not now.' She picked it up and looked at the screen. It was gold command. 'Shit, where is the chief super?'

Hadley grabbed the folder and put it into a backpack, hanging it from his shoulder.

McGill noticed movement on the screen. He could now see both teams ready to assault. 'Here they come, Kelvin. You need to think fast.'

Hadley's eyes flicked to the camera's image. It was all the opportunity McGill needed. His hand closed around the handle of a boning knife that was in the kitchen sink. He threw it across the room. It wasn't the most accurate throw, and it wasn't a balanced knife, but it struck Hadley in the face, slicing through his cheek. Hadley squeezed his trigger; the bullet was off target but accurate enough at close range. McGill went down.

Sinclair dropped to the floor and rolled to the table. She grabbed McGill's assault rifle and returned fire.

Hadley retreated to the basement door and fell down the stairs, landing in a heap at the bottom.

DS Gardner answered the call. 'Sir?'

The voice on the other end was rushed, urgent. 'Abort the operation now. Stand down, say again, stand down. Abort, abort.'

Gardner looked up the hill, heard the gunfire. It was too late.

Butler heard the shots inside Rock Cottage. He couldn't hear any incoming rounds, they weren't shooting at him. Whatever was happening in there gave them the perfect opportunity to breach.

'Go, go, go.'

The two teams moved in unison, closing the last few meters to the house. They crouched against the cold stone walls, two men attached explosive charges to both doors' locks and hinges then retreated two metres.

Sinclair went after Hadley, moving around the table and heading for the basement.

McGill got to his knees, blood pouring from the wound in his chest. He stretched out his hand. 'No, Ali.'

Butler whispered into his radio, 'Fire in the hole.'

DS Gardner sprinted to the command vehicle. 'Abort, abort. Direct orders from gold command.' She heard the explosion from the house. 'NOOO.'

The explosive charges detonated, shattering the doors. What was left of the frames fell outwards. Both teams threw CS gas and stun grenades through the jagged openings.

Sinclair spun around at the sound of the explosion. She saw the canisters fly through the doorway and into the room. Clouds of gas expanded to fill the space. Sinclair looked at McGill. He collapsed forward clutching his chest. As Sinclair looked back at the door, the blinding flash and concussive blast of the stun grenade overwhelmed her senses. She didn't even register the SAS troopers who were now flooding through the door and into the room; she didn't hear their warnings, their shouts to drop her weapon.

Chapter 54

DS Gardner walked down the steps and out of the command vehicle. She looked around at the chaos the assault had created. Police and paramedics gathered at the bottom of the track, waiting for the all clear from Butler before climbing up to the house. Some reporters had managed to get through the cordon and were trying to photograph the aftermath. At the back, away from everyone else's gaze, she could see DCS Thorpe throwing a bag into the back of his car. He was looking around, checking for anyone watching him.

DS Gardner had her orders from gold command: she had to stop Thorpe. If she was honest with herself, she was going to enjoy this, she had never really liked him anyway. She picked out two uniformed officers from the scrum at the bottom of the track, and approached the car. 'You goin' somewhere ... sir?'

DCS Thorpe was surprised by the sudden appearance of DS Gardner and the officers. He tried to look calm but the panic inside him made his voice crack. 'Out ... out of my way, Gardner, I've been summoned back to London. They need a debrief.'

Gardner smiled. 'That's strange, sir. I've just been speaking to AC Nicholson, and he didn't mention you going back to give him a debrief. What he actually said was that I should arrest you.'

'What? Don't be ridiculous, there's obviously been some mistake.' He waved the two uniformed officers away from the front of his car. 'Get out of my way, that's an order.'

Gardner nodded to the officers. They grabbed Thorpe by his arms and pushed him onto the bonnet of his car. Gardner handcuffed his hands behind his back and he was dragged, kicking and screaming, to a police van that was parked in the layby beside the wall.

Mick Butler came out of Rock Cottage through the tear gas that was still billowing out of the door and dissipating into the fog. He pulled off his respirator and threw it on the ground. Sinclair was draped over his shoulder like a broken mannequin, her arms and legs swung lifelessly and blood dripped from her head, leaving a trail behind them. Butler walked away from the tear gas and lowered Sinclair to the ground, laying her on her back.

Sinclair's clothes were covered in broken glass and splinters of wood from the assault, her hair and face soaked in blood from the wound on her forehead. Butler put down his weapon and took off his gloves. He pressed his fingers to her neck and checked for a pulse, he found one. Sinclair's eyes flickered open and she began to cough, her own blood and snot choking her. Butler rolled her into the recovery position, pulling her hair away from her face. He waved at the paramedics who stood close by. 'Get over here, now.'

The paramedics got to work. They cleared Sinclair's airways and checked her breathing. Her most serious injury was the long gash in her forehead: blood was pouring out and needed to be stopped. One of the medics shouted into her radio. 'We need an air ambulance ASAP.' She looked up at Butler. 'I need to get her back down the hill, she needs that wound closing up and she's losing a lot of blood. Her skull may be fractured.'

McGill was sitting up against the wall while more medics worked on him. His injury was less serious – the bullet that had struck him in the chest was a ricochet – it was nothing more than a flesh wound. The paramedics dressed the gash in his chest and helped him to stand up, just as Butler's men were lifting Sinclair onto a stretcher. 'Ali?'

Butler stopped McGill from getting any closer. 'Let us get her down the hill. You can stay with her in the ambulance after that.'

McGill tried to push Butler out of the way, but the SAS sergeant was too strong for him. McGill was in no fit state to fight anyone. Butler hooked his arm around McGill and they followed the stretcher down the track.

* * *

Enfield and Hadley sat in a beaten-up old Volvo, inside a dilapidated hanger back at the disused airfield. They had been on the run for more than two weeks. Hadley had managed to get away from Rock Cottage during all the chaos. At the bottom of the hill he'd heard the police officers talking of a conspiracy, heard them being told to look out for him. He'd spent the rest of that day hiding in an old sheep pen.

Once the sun had set, he'd walked up the fell then down into Ambleside, where Enfield picked him up before dawn the next day. Since then they had travelled at night, hidden in woods and slept rough. They both stank and hadn't eaten properly in days, but they hadn't been caught, yet.

Following the events that had taken place, the Prime Minister ordered a major security overhaul. Anyone mentioned in the folder of evidence was being rounded up and held for questioning. Many careers were being ended: MPs, police, military. The PM did everything to ensure they avoided a witch-hunt, but some people were too deeply involved to save.

The leader of the opposition was invited to become deputy prime minister, to ensure the government was being run in the best interests of the country. A general election would be needed in due course, but not yet.

Hadley lowered his window and looked out towards the runway. 'I've been at this airfield once already, and it didn't end well.'

Enfield was looking up through the windscreen. 'Where are they?' He checked his watch. 'They should have been here five minutes ago.'

'It's an illegal flight out of the country, I don't think they run to a schedule.'

Enfield drummed his fingers on the steering wheel. 'If anyone spots us here the police will surround the place. I can't go to prison, I wouldn't survive.'

'You won't go to prison, I can guarantee that.'

Enfield pointed out of the window. 'There they are.'

The unmarked helicopter was flying low, straight towards them. It flew a circuit around the hanger and came in to land. Enfield got out of the car and started to walk towards the waiting aircraft. 'Thank God for that. Let's go.' He gestured to hurry Hadley up.

Hadley had a nine-millimetre Sig Saur in his hand, pointed straight at Enfield. 'When I said you wouldn't be going to prison, I should have been a little more specific. I'm afraid you won't be going anywhere, ever again.'

Enfield backed up, trying to get away from the weapon. 'But I've done everything I was asked to do.'

'Yes, you have, Marcus, and you have been quite useful, but now you're just a drain on resources. You don't bring any skills to the organisation.'

Enfield was shaking and beginning to babble. 'I could learn new skills, I'm very loyal, I ...'

Hadley shook his head. 'No. I'm sorry, Marcus. I just don't need you any more.'

Enfield held his hands in front of him and tried to turn away from the shot. 'NO, Vadim, please.'

Hadley pulled the trigger, the bullet slammed into the centre of Enfield's chest and he collapsed, clutching the wound. Blood ran between his fingers and started to drip from his mouth. He looked up, his eyes pleading. Hadley shot him again, twice, then threw the Sig Saur down beside the Home Secretary's lifeless body.

The pilot of the helicopter was waving at Hadley, beckoning him over, trying to hurry him up. He knew that every second they spent on the ground increased their chances of being caught. Hadley ducked under the helicopter's rotor blades, opened the door and climbed in. The pilot twisted the throttle and they lifted into the air.

As they flew back over the hanger, Hadley looked down at Enfield's body lying on the runway. This wasn't the end, it was just a hiccup. The organisation was too big, too widespread for this to bring them down. For him, it was time for a new

339

identity, time to formulate a new plan. He settled back in his seat and smiled to himself.

Chapter 55

Sinclair was sitting up in her bed at the Queen Victoria Veterans Hospital. Doctors were happy with the way she was recovering and her head wound was healing well. They had decided she was now strong enough to have visitors and word had spread. A lot of people wanted to see Sinclair.

McGill sat on the edge of her bed. 'So, how's it going then?'

'The doctors have said I shouldn't be here long. I can finish my recovery at home, not sure where that is, though.'

'Rock Cottage won't be ready to live in for quite a while, they made a bit of a mess.'

Sinclair smiled. 'Will you be able to fix it up?'

McGill nodded. 'Yeah, Danny Kinsella is investing in the remodelling. Apparently, he wants to spend some time in the Lake District.'

'It'll be nice when it's all done.'

Lancaster stood up from the chair in the corner. 'We've got several apartments in London, you can live in one of those until you decide what you want to do next. They're quite luxurious, you should be comfortable enough.'

'I could do with a bit of luxury. Thanks, Edward.'

'It's the least I could do, Ali. You'll also be glad to know you're no longer an escaped convict.'

Sinclair tried to sit up. 'What? How?'

'Callum Porter's dad. He's got some heavy-duty contacts in his network. He's arranging for your sentence to be commuted to time served. In the meantime, the Mexican government are happy for you to be released into our care.'

Sinclair held her hand to her mouth, fighting back tears. 'It's over. My nightmare's finally over.'

Lancaster put his hand on Sinclair's leg. 'You've earned it, Ali. Now, relax, get well, I'll see you soon.'

As Lancaster left the room, Mick Butler appeared at the door. 'Mind if I come in?'

Sinclair waved for him to come over to the bed. 'All these visitors. Aren't I a lucky girl?'

Butler placed a bouquet of flowers and a small box of chocolates on the bedside locker. 'Just a little something, by way of an apology.'

'Apology for what?'

'Well, we did almost kill you both.'

McGill laughed. 'So where are my flowers then?'

Butler shrugged. 'I've never bought a marine flowers, and I ain't startin' now.'

McGill stood up and kissed Sinclair on the forehead. 'Don't overdo it, Ali. I'll see you this afternoon.' As he walked past Butler he patted him on the back. 'Don't worry, lover boy, I know I'm not as attractive as Ali. A bar of chocolate would've been nice though.' He winked at Sinclair. 'I'll leave you two alone for a while.'

Outside in the corridor, Callum Porter had just arrived. When he saw McGill he walked straight over and wrapped his arms around him. 'Thanks, Frank. Thanks for everything.

If you ever need anything at all, just let me know.'

Porter's father was standing behind him. He held out his hand. 'That goes for me, too.'

McGill shook Senator Porter's hand then turned back to Callum. 'You saved my life, Callum. I'll never forget that.'

Porter smiled. 'How's, Ali?'

'She's fine, just needs some more rest and relaxation. I'd give her a few minutes before you go in there, though. I think someone's trying to chat her up.'

Sinclair took a sip of water. 'What happened in the house? My memory's a bit hazy, the doctor said it's because of the head wound. No one else has explained it all, yet, probably don't want to stress me out.'

Butler perched at the end of the bed. 'It was a close-run thing. We received the abort message just as we were throwing in the stun grenades. A few seconds later and you might've been dead. We managed to check fire, seconds away from a major fuck-up. It was a shame you face-planted the concrete, though, you gave me quite a fright.'

Sinclair smiled. 'Remind me to thank whoever raised the alarm.'

'You've got DS Gardner to thank for that, or, Detective Inspector Gardner as she is now. She arrested her boss as well. She had quite a night.'

'I know the feeling.'

Butler checked behind him, making sure they were still alone. 'I'd like to make it up to you, over dinner sometime, somewhere posh, if you'd like that?'

Sinclair laughed. 'Bloody typical. The first time in years I've been invited to go somewhere nice, and I look like I've been in a car crash.'

Butler smiled. 'You look just fine to me.'

Chapter 56

Lancaster and Carter sat on the park bench beside the lake. A lot had happened since they'd last had a meeting there. The world was a very different place now, for both of them.

Carter picked up his cup and, as usual, took off the plastic lid and threw it in the bin. 'I still hate drinking through those things, gives it a funny taste. Next time, we meet in a nice café, use proper mugs, and have a piece of cake to go with it, or, better still, a full English.'

Lancaster nodded. 'It's a deal. It is nice to be able to meet as friends, though, Simeon. Not so much of the sneaking around, now the conspiracy has collapsed.'

'We still have to be careful, Edward. The world's a dangerous place. It's only the end of part of the organisation. We still can't be sure who to trust. Vadim is still out there, he still has backers.'

'Hadley was last spotted heading out to sea in a helicopter. We found wreckage, and the body of the pilot. There were no ships in the area that could have picked up a survivor. We have to accept that, in all probability, he's dead.'

Carter shook his head. 'I won't accept that until I see his body. I don't think Sinclair will either.'

'With everything else that's going on, the service isn't going to use up resources looking for a dead man. If any evidence comes to light to suggest he's still alive, I'll let you know.'

Carter knew that Lancaster would do everything he could to track down Vadim, but, in the current climate, his hands were tied. 'That's fair enough, Edward. I'll wait for you to contact me.'

Lancaster nodded. 'I've a feeling I'm going to need you and your team again. There's always room for an off-the-books resource, in today's messed up world.'

'I'm not sure the others will want to be seen as a resource for you to call on. I think they've had enough excitement.'

Lancaster sipped his coffee. 'If Sinclair gets the chance to go after Vadim again, or cause some problems for what's left of his organisation, I'm sure she'll be interested. Once you have Sinclair, you have McGill. They're inseparable.'

'At least give them time to rest, let all of us rest and get back to some kind of normality. There's going to be a shitstorm of political positioning until a new government's in place. We don't want to get mixed up in all that.'

Lancaster looked at his driver, who was tapping his watch. 'There are a lot of people who see this as an opportunity, a chance to climb the ladder – fill the holes left by the sackings and resignations. Typical politicians.'

Carter smiled. 'What about you, Edward? Head of MI6, who'd have thought that would happen?'

Lancaster finished his coffee and threw the cup into the bin. 'Not something I was looking for, Simeon, or particularly wanted. I'm not the kind of man who should be head of anything, I'm just the last man standing, who else would they choose to do it?'

'You underestimate yourself, Edward. You inspire confidence in your staff, they all look up to you. You'll make a great leader.'

They stood up and shook hands. Lancaster buttoned up his jacket. 'This new job means I'm going to be hard to get hold of from now on, Simeon. I'm going to be in a lot of meetings, locked away in rooms without windows, discussing things that the rest of the population are better off not knowing. If you, or any of the team need me, contact Vicky Thomson. She'll know where I am at all times.'

Carter nodded. 'I understand, Edward. Take care of yourself and I'll see you again soon.'

The two men separated and walked off in different directions. They didn't need to be so secretive about their meetings, Lancaster was the boss now and didn't have to explain himself, but it had become a habit, something they couldn't just stop doing. In the months and years to come, with Vadim's organisation looking to continue their quest under a new leader, and members of the conspiracy jockeying for power, it was a habit that would serve them well.

THE END

Acknowledgements

As always, this book wouldn't have been published without those behind the scenes who helped to make it happen. I'd like to say thank you to the following people.

Ali, the real life inspiration for my protagonist, and Vicky for joining her in the cast of characters. My wonderful editor, Jo Craven, who turns my inane scribbles into something readable. Mike Craven, Matt Hilton and Graham Smith for their unending and freely given advice on all aspects of writing.

All my friends at Crime & Publishment. Too numerous to mention here, but you know who you are and I couldn't have done it without you. Rosemary, Debbie, Chelsea, Keith, Andy, Graham, Jay, and Clive who've supported and encouraged me at every opportunity.

About the Author

L J Morris is an author with a lifelong love of books and storytelling that he developed as a child. He spent most of the 80s and 90s serving in the Royal Navy as a Weapons Engineer and now lives in Cumbria, with his family. He currently works within the defence industry and continues to write at every opportunity.

His short stories, 'Blood on Their Hands' and 'Cold Redemption' were published in Volumes 1 & 2 of Best-selling author Matt Hilton's anthology series 'ACTION: Pulse Pounding Tales'.

Other anthologies he has appeared in include 'Happily Never After', 'Wish You Weren't Here', and 'Liminal Time, Liminal Space' where one reader described his tale 'True Colours' as *"Riveting and powerful"*

His first novel 'Desperate Ground' was published in May 2018 by Bloodhound Books.

You can connect with me on:

- https://ljmorrisauthor.com
- https://twitter.com/LesJMorris
- https://www.facebook.com/LesJMorris

Also by L J Morris

L J Morris's first novel, *Desperate Ground* was published in 2018 and attracted good reviews.

'Morris is destined to be a big name thriller writer to watch for in the future.'
  – Matt Hilton

"Good solid thriller this. Morris knows his stuff and his writing is pacy and effortless."
  – M W Craven

"A taut, tense thriller..." – Crimesquad.com.

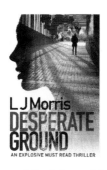

Desperate Ground

When the secrecy of a nuclear weapon agreement is thrown into doubt, a disgraced intelligence operative is recruited to find out if the deal is still safe...

Ali Sinclair, wrongly convicted and on the run from a Mexican prison, is enlisted to infiltrate her old friend's inner circle and find the evidence.

The only people on her side are an ex-Cold War spook and the former Royal Marine that was sent to find her. Together they discover that the stakes are much higher than anyone knew, and the fate of the world is at risk...

But when you've lived in the shadows, who can you trust?

Printed in Great Britain
by Amazon